KILL POINT

Kerry Michael Chater
Lynn Gillespie Chater

Kill Point

Kerry Michael Chater
Lynn Gillespie Chater

Published by Chater Books as *Fortune's Web* 2012
Published by Chater Books as *Kill Point* 2013

Cover photo of "Female Diver Over Pool" by Lawrence Sawyer
Crosshairs by Zsschreiner
Cover design by Christopher John Chater

The authors would like to thank the following friends whose valuable information helped fill the pages of this book: Erendira Alvarez, Patricia Aramayo, Eve Blackwood, Christopher John Chater, Elizabeth Chater, Major George Currey, Mike DuBose, Jess & Fritz Gillespie, Jesse Kirchhoff, Jessica Kneeland, Matt Little, Carolyn Maples, and Johnny Tipps.

To Bette, Mel, Jess and Fritz with love.

For more information about the authors, please visit
http://www.chatersongs.com

Callie —

Zumba Chica!!!

KILL POINT

Enjoy the book!

Lynn Gillespie Chater

PROLOGUE

Midnight scraped along the edge of the black horizon. The cold night wind chased the shimmery starlight over the rooftops of the sleeping town and brought a chilling blanket to the houses resting silently against the overshadowing forest. One house slept less silently than the others.

Tap. . . .

The sound softly bounced and rolled across the kitchen floor, like a tiny yellow-moon marble tossed onto a seldom-used floor mat, and drifted down the hall. It slipped past the aged plaster of the walls. It crept through the almost-closed door of the old bedroom.

Scratch. . . .

The woman turned uneasily in her bed and her earth-brown hair was crushed between the mature skin of her cheek and her pillow.

Snap. . . .

She turned again, putting her back to her still-sleeping mate. Her lips parted and her breathing became shallow and quick.

Tap. . . . Did she hear that or dream it?

Scratch. . . . Was that something she should wake for, or just the night wind playing its old tricks?

Snap. . . . Her eyes opened. There was definitely sound coming from the kitchen. Had she remembered to close the

1

kitchen window? She thought about waking Rolf, but he had worked hard all day and deserved his sleep. She could handle this alone. After all, it was an easy task to close a window. She yawned, pushed back the comforter, and put her sleepy feet into her slippers. As she moved across the room, she gathered up her robe from the old wooden rocker and put it on. She heard nothing as she went down the hall. When she stepped into the kitchen, she stopped to listen before turning on the light. No sound. Pale moonlight glowed through the closed kitchen window. Closed. Maybe it had been a dream. The chill of the night air touched her cheek and she knew that something must be open. But the only other possibility was the back door and, even in the dark, she could see that it was closed. She turned on the light. From behind her, a black-gloved hand reached out to cover her hand on the switch.

"Hello, Margreta." It was only a whisper in her ear.

She turned to see who it was. "Wolfgang?" she breathed.

"I'm here to make a withdrawal."

With a familiar click, the kitchen light went out.

His left hand smashed into her fleshy, aging throat before she could call for help. Under the padded glove, the tightly extended web of skin between his thumb and index finger shoved into her windpipe, destroying it. His thick fingers surrounded the muscles, veins, and cartilage of her neck. When her mouth opened reflexively, he brought the gloved fingertips of his right hand together and shoved them, like a leather-bound wedge, past her teeth and tongue, dampening any sound that could escape. Holding her by the jaw between his hands, he lifted her up until her eyes were level with his. She squirmed and twisted, puppet-like in front of him, her legs making a quiet kicking sound against his.

He jerked hard on her helpless throat. Her eyelids flared and her horrified eyes flashed into his possessed, night-shadowed face.

He squeezed her windpipe shut and pushed the fingers of his right hand farther down into the tunnel of her throat.

She jerked and bobbed and choked under him until there was no air left in her.

He watched, fascinated.

She snorted with panic and moaned with pain.

He observed, captivated.

In the last few seconds of her life, she thought of using her hands to defend herself. With awareness fading, she thrust those hands down onto his powerful arms and twisted her fingers into claws; but her nails did not penetrate the leather jacket.

He looked on, entranced.

She died.

He witnessed, obsessed.

He gently laid her body down on the kitchen floor, quietly stepped over her, and went down the hall to the bedroom.

Killing the man was easy: a simple blow to the temple of his sleeping head.

On his way back to the kitchen he noticed a picture of the couple taken not too long ago. He guessed they were on vacation. Their happy faces were smiling and they were waving at him from the glass-covered memory. He smiled back and quietly waved the fingers of his gloved hand at them.

The passenger door of the Mercedes was open and waiting for him as he stepped out of the house.

"That was rather . . . untidy, Mikki. I heard your entry all the way out here in the car. And the light, Mikki. You let them turn on the light?"

"It was that stupid lock-break."

"It's a poor workman who blames his tools."

"I put them down, Uncle. The job is done."

"The job has only begun. We've eliminated your secretary. Now, we kill you."

1

The tips of her slender fingers were like small white prunes shriveled by the warm pool water, the nails were bleached clean by chlorine.

She reached for the metal handrails of the diving platform ladder and, even though her hands were cool and damp, she felt the cold of the stainless steel in her grasp. Ascending to ten meters, she strode to the platform's edge. A thousand dives. A thousand times a thousand, and it was up to her to find the three basic necessities in each one: Elevation. Execution. Entry.

Elevation. The late morning sun rested on her smooth shoulders like a warm towel. A single bead of sweat started from the valley of her cleavage and wandered down into her red Lycra swimsuit, leaving a small stain above her navel.

Execution. The temperate Santa Ana wind brushed against her cheeks. She glanced down, then up, then closed her green eyes to block out any thought that might hinder her. She took a deep breath and held it. Her breasts pushed defiantly against her swimsuit.

Entry. The acrid smell of chlorine was far below her now. She shut the world out and all that filled her mind was body placement. She opened her eyes and raised her arms upward. Her toes gripped the edge of the platform. The muscles in her long legs drove the balls of her feet into the rubber matting, her body went up and out, and for a moment the sky held her. Then gravity began its inexorable task and she looked for the target spot on the water's surface created by the agitators.

Elevation— Suddenly, the water below her vanished and she saw sharp, jagged rocks, chiseled by ages of angry, slate-gray ocean waves. Fear struck her everywhere at once. Her heart gave one mighty pound against her ribs and echoes of terror ran through her veins. Shock filled her mind and there was an immediate ache in her stomach.

Execution— Instinctively, her arms collapsed into her chest and her knees came up to join them. Any attempt at perfection was lost as she braced herself against a fall onto hard granite ridges that fought their way up through a sea of turbulent foam.

Entry—

Jesse Fortune hit the water and the water hit back. It slapped her hard in the face and punched her thighs into her diaphragm, knocking the air out of her. In a dizzying haze under the water, the soft-white pool walls seemed bright enough to blind her and the parallel, black-tile lane markers seemed to bend and fade away. She fought to go up. When her head broke the surface, she gasped for air.

"What the hell was that?" Coach Matthew Braden yelled from the side of the pool. He was on his feet even before Jesse's body hit the water. Seeing her go in with arms and legs tucked in the fetal position, he barked the other swimmers out of the way and poised himself to go in after her if she didn't surface quickly.

Jesse twisted onto her back, closed her eyes, and floated for a moment, gratefully accepting each breath of air that painfully reached her aching lungs, and then she scissor-kicked once to propel herself toward the side of the pool.

Coach Braden relaxed when he saw her. When she was close enough that he didn't have to yell, he asked again,

"What the hell was that?" in a tone that was turning from concern to sarcasm.

Slowly, she put her arms out and rested her elbows on the warm pool decking. Her long legs hung limp in the water.

"Tell me you're okay, Jesse." Coach Braden hated babying his divers, but he hated the idea of one of them being hurt even more.

Without moving her head from where it rested on her arms, she opened her eyes and stared into the laces of his tennis shoes. She still had no strength to reply.

"You okay, Baby?" Worried again, he hunched down on his ankles.

She felt the gentle touch of his hand on the back of her head and she nodded.

"Well then, what the hell was that?" he repeated, coming to his feet.

Despite her discomfort, she joined him in a smile.

"It was so real," she whispered.

"Real? I'll tell you what's real! Elevation, execution, entry! That's what's real! Basics, basics, basics! Hell, you didn't do anything right! Unless, of course, you're inventing a new dive. What are you going to call it? The 'Jesse Special'? The judges are going to love that. A three-and-a-half inward pike-Jesse Special. You won't even get a zero point one from a blind judge!" And then he hunched down again and added quietly, "Are you sure you're okay?"

His attempts at humor were always awkward, but whenever his voice got this quiet, she knew he was serious. He rarely expressed this much concern. It made her feel better. He was more than her coach; he was her friend.

At twenty-two, Jesse Fortune was ready for the gold. Matthew Braden had seen to that. For fifteen years he had personally nurtured her, trained her, and driven her. He no longer remembered the scrawny little seven-year-old, holding her nose and jumping off the board feet first. But he would never forget having seen in her that innate light that shines forth from a real champion. Jesse had the "Gift." She also had tenacity and a wonderfully competitive spirit. She was a winner. With his guidance, she was fulfilling her destiny. He had watched her gather in the silver in 2008, and they had celebrated together in Beijing. Now, she was the best. Coach Braden was sure of it. In his mind, he was already planning the celebration in London.

She pushed herself up and out of the water and twisted to a sitting position on the deck. Her feet still hung submerged.

He didn't reach to help her. Caring for her was one thing, training her to be a champion was something else.

"I've had enough for today, Matt," she was finally able to say, but not without effort.

"What's that supposed to mean, 'I've had enough for today, Matt'?" he countered. "Do the words 'Stay Tough' mean anything to you? Are you forgetting why we're here? Hell, Monaco in two weeks!" He was strutting now and waving his right arm above his head. He was back to being "Coach" again. His short, well-toned and muscular body moved with a swiftness that seemed to ignore his fifty-odd years. A tuft of red hair swayed away from his forehead as it was caught by the mild breeze.

"I haven't forgotten," she said, wishing she had. The Monaco competition could wait. She was ready, she knew that. All she wanted to do now was take a shower and relax. Beyond the ivy covered, chain-link fence that separated the pool from the street, she could hear the traffic building up for the lunch stampede.

"Come on, Kid, let's hit it again."

Jesse hated his puns; she had made him promise he would never be a comedian.

"The same dive?" She laughed at herself for asking; she knew what he would say almost before he did.

"The Jesse Special? I hope not!"

She got to her feet, hunching over a bit, and started for the platform.

"Straighten up!" he yelled.

Taking a hard breath, she brought herself to her full height of five-foot-seven. She pushed her shoulders back and walked regally to the ladder.

"Jesse."

She looked back into his smile.

"Stay tough," he said.

She nodded.

From the platform's edge, she executed a $3\frac{1}{2}$ Inward Pike that made them both feel better about her chances in London.

On her way to the showers, she spotted her brother sitting on the bleachers.

"What happened to you?" he asked.

"You mean while you were over there hitting on Diana Linden? She just turned eighteen a couple of weeks ago, and you're twenty-one. You should be dating girls your own age."

"She's old enough to be busting out of that swimsuit she's wearing!" he quipped.

Chris was tall and his eyes were the same green color as hers. His hair was sandy blond and his well-muscled and tanned body was the result of years of Southern California surfing. He had teased and heckled her unmercifully as they were growing up, but now there wasn't anything he wouldn't do for her. They were as close as brother and sister could be. When she needed a confidant, she turned to him. She adored him.

"That last dive was the worst, Jess! What the hell happened?"

"My last dive was perfect, but you were too busy to see it!"

"You know the one I mean. So?"

"Take me to lunch and I'll tell you about it." She didn't know if she could explain it, but, if anyone would listen to her, Chris would. What had it been? A nightmare? A daydream? One of her visions? She wasn't sure what it was, but thinking about it again, she saw the last fading images of a jagged, rocky cliff, and felt that sickening, dull ache of fear throb in her stomach.

"That's why I'm here, Babe, to take you to lunch," Chris smiled, "I live for adventure."

"There are two kinds of women," Chris said smugly, looking across the table at Jesse.

"Only two?" she responded cautiously. "That's a good one, Chris. Now, maybe I know where the expression 'Oh, Brother!' comes from."

Although the allowance her father gave her didn't allow for much more than the rent on her small apartment, she had chosen Roby's restaurant on the Lake because it was more quiet than most of the other, less expensive places. They had missed the rush hour crowd and, at their request, had been seated at one of the outside tables that overlooked the serene, sun-varnished water.

"Yeah, just two," Chris continued, ignoring the view. "There's the kind that looks beautiful as a kid. You know, Momma's little darling. Looks cute at six or seven, but never looks that good when she gets older. Then there's the kind that's a tomboy as a kid. You know, the one who always has a dirty face and wants to play ball with the boys. Then one day you turn around and *bam*, she's *dyno*. She's in college and every guy in the world wants to date her. Two kinds of women . . . and Jess, you're neither," he finished, looking as though he'd found a lost equation.

"Thanks, Chris, that's comforting." She stared at him a bit stupefied.

"No, wait . . . that didn't come out right, did it?"

She continued to stare at him in silence.

"What I meant was, you were a beautiful kid and now you're a beautiful woman. Any guy in his right mind would want to date you. You're the exception to my rule . . . you know, my theory."

"Then how come I haven't had a date for months? I haven't had a real date since college."

"That's easy. When do you ever have time to go out? You're working out, diving twenty-four hours a day."

"It's more like eight," she corrected him.

"You know what I mean. You never have any time. You're never in a place where you can meet anyone new. You're always at the pool. Same people, same place. When do you ever give yourself a chance to meet someone worth meeting?"

"I went to a club with Cindy the other night."

"That was a month ago, Jess. A *month* ago! Come on, gimme a break. It was the same when you were in college. It was either diving or studying French. French or diving, that's all you ever did."

"Okay, wise-guy, I get the point. What do you want me to do? Should I go over to that table of men there and beg them to have pity on me? 'Listen, guys, I'm working to be an Olympic gold medalist and I don't have time to meet you. Would you please take me out? I can speak French.' Or, how about if I write my name and number on the wall? 'For a good time, call Jesse. She doesn't have time to call you.' "

"You're killing my theory, Babe," he said shaking his head. "Every great-looking girl should have a great-looking guy. And vice versa. Like me, I should have a great-looking girl. You were right. Girls like Diana are too young for me. I need a fantastic babe hanging on my arm—what's the matter, Jess? You look like you just saw a ghost." Absorbed in his favorite subject, girls, he had almost missed her abrupt change of mood.

"I'm sorry, Chris. When you said 'killing'. . . 'killing your theory' . . . I don't know, the word *killing* reminded me of something." Her stomach turned uneasily. The dull ache began again.

"What is it, Jess? You look strange. Are you okay?"

"I think something's going to happen. Something. . . ."

"Come on, Jess, everything's going great. You almost beat that Chinese chick at the FINA competition in Shanghai last month. And now, you're on your way to the big E. Europe! Monaco, Babe! You're going to win there, and then it's on to London. Think about it."

At the mention of Monaco, she stopped listening. She shivered hard; her shoulders trembled; her jaw clenched and her head lowered uncontrollably. "Something's going to happen. I can feel it. I've had these feelings before. You know that. And, most of the time, I'm right."

"Come on, Jess, you're scaring me." He wanted to comfort her, but he knew she was right. She had had these feelings before, and she had been right every time he could remember. He tried to talk her out of it. "You're having the best time of your life. What can go wrong? Of course, you don't have a great looking guy—"

"It's always been about someone else. Never me. But this time it's me. I think I'm scared." The tone of her voice was distant and dream-like, and she stared off into a world beyond Chris, a place he couldn't see or know.

"You're getting weird on me, Jess. You know, maybe you've just had a bad day. That one dive you took was the worst. Maybe you hurt yourself and don't know it. A delayed reaction kinda thing. Like when a person gets whiplash in a car accident, but doesn't feel it 'til the next day, and—"

"It wasn't the bad dive. It was . . . something else. A vision."

He tried to tease her out of it. "Wait a minute! Isn't that John Edward over there? Yes! Yes it is! John? Oh, Joohhnn!"

He paused to see if she would smile. When she didn't, he continued. "Come on, Jess. This isn't like you. I think you just need some rest. You've been working too hard."

She shook her head gently and rubbed her eyes lightly. "You're right, this is nuts. I guess I'm just worried about the competition in Monaco. Coach expects me to be the best. And I expect it of myself. It was easier three years ago in Beijing. I was younger and I didn't worry as much."

"You didn't win the gold either. This time you're gonna win, Babe. You want me to go with you?"

"No, that's silly. You can't afford it, and there wouldn't be anything for you to do over there."

"Nothing to do? With all those tan Monaco babes? Are you kidding? Think of it. Me kickin' back on the shores of Monte Carlo, a babe on either side, dressed in nothing but those dental floss bikinis. A Mai Tai on one of those little beach tables . . . and my surfboard waiting patiently under the hot Monte Carlo sun."

"Monte Carlo isn't a South Sea island, Chris," she said, finally smiling at his persistent attempts to make her do so.

"It isn't?" he smiled facetiously. "Oh well, forget Monaco. I can't afford it anyway."

When he said Monaco, she shivered again and stared off into space.

"I'm not coming back," she whispered, and wondered why she had said it.

2

HAUPTBOHNOF TRAIN STATION, ZURICH

Everything about Doctor Amir Hassasi suggested he had money: the full cut of the Givenchy overcoat with a black scarf resting carefully under its collar; the hint of a Benson & Clegg green silk tie and heavily-starched white shirt which occasionally exposed themselves as he moved; and the black Gucci shoes, polished to a glass-like shine. As he emerged from the cavernous entrails of Zürich's Hauptbahnof train station, his strut was confident and unhurried: the walk of the wealthy. When he turned onto Langstrasse and went toward Zürich's poorer streets, his gait did not change. He was unafraid, even in the part of town that poor men hurried through at night.

Once in the Langstrasse district, he pushed along the narrow streets, enjoying the futile struggle of the seventeenth century guild houses to gain a more honored place in antiquity. To any curious eyes peering through old worn curtains, or glancing out from sadly stained tavern windows, or staring down from the other end of these unwashed streets, he gave the impression that he was drifting slowly over the gritty, time burnished cobblestones.

Amir Hassasi felt no fear. That fact alone was the most likely reason why no one bothered him. Here, fear was something one man could smell on another. And here, as anywhere, fear was the aphrodisiac to the violent. There was a Walther PPK semi-automatic pistol in his coat pocket, but he did not carry it because he was afraid. He carried it because it was common sense to have a weapon in this part of town. His breast pocket held a scalpel with a one and a half inch, razor-sharp blade, in a polished leather sheath, but he did not consider this a weapon; it was a badge of honor earned from years of medical training.

In the thirty-five years he had lived in Switzerland, he had walked these Zürich streets thousands of times, going out of his way to walk through the worst parts of town. It was simply more interesting. The flagrant electricity of the prostitutes soliciting, the drunks begging and swearing, and the desperately solemn anger of the socially disjointed, was wonderful entertainment for him. The more belligerent and offensive it was, the more he enjoyed it.

The rest of the city held little interest for him. On his thirtieth birthday, he had purchased an estate at Rhine Falls near Schaffhausen, and converted its guest house to a state of the art facility for plastic surgery. He had moved his medical practice from his residence in downtown Zürich to the old chateau, more than forty kilometers to the north. He had developed and perfected his plastic surgeries, as well as other interests, in the sanctuary-like privacy of that forest setting. But, he had never given up his enjoyment of the decadent side of Zürich's night life.

This was the real city. The heart. The pulse. The lifeblood. He would take the underbelly day or night. Especially night.

He turned a corner and his eyes jumped ahead to confirm the presence of a man waiting for him on the street. As he closed the distance between them, he could read the nervousness of his South American friend. Amir was unmoved by the man's impatience. He pressed on, with the memory of their first meeting, nearly ten years ago, teasing his mind.

He had needed a large emerald of near perfect quality for his latest invention. In his search, he had found a highly strung, and somewhat ill-at-ease Colombian mine owner. In the privacy of a poorly lit back room, Amir had watched, fascinated, as the man unwrapped a black cloth on an old table and pushed its contents, three polished stones, around with his finger. Amir had been as interested in the way the man's eyes hovered and vibrated over the gems as in the gems themselves.

Rafael Santos had given him what he needed. In fact, Rafael had given him more than an emerald. Over the years, Rafael had given him friendship. Friends, he mused, the word almost escaping his understanding. With the exclusion of Rafael, Amir had never had, nor ever wanted, any friends.

Now, Rafael had been invited into the palm of a corporate hand whose fingers were digging into the fabric of many countries. But there was a price to pay; an initiation fee was required. Rafael needed something, and Amir was going to give it to him.

"Rafael, my friend, how are you?" Amir fashioned one of his rare smiles.

Every ounce of Rafael Santos was Andean: coffee colored eyes that were more black than brown, coarse black hair sloping toward thick eyebrows; and a stocky, barrel-chested miner's frame. A bushy mustache overtook the brown skin of his upper lip. At forty-one, Rafael was twenty years younger than Amir; but that meant nothing to either one of them.

"*Estoy muy bien, amigo.* It's good to see you." Rafael said, but his return smile held as much uneasiness as it did acknowledgement. He was uncomfortable in this part of the city, and an earlier glance into the untidy restaurant had only supported his opinion of Amir's choice of a meeting place. "When the taxi driver delivered me to this address, I thought he'd made a mistake."

"It's not that bad, my friend. Let's go inside," Amir coerced.

A cool evening breeze moved down the narrow street and the metal hinges of the overhead sign squeaked above the restaurant's name: *Das Goldenen Tier.*

Twelve round tables pushed a bar into one corner of the storefront restaurant. On a good night, the proprietor might count half of those tables being filled. If there had been better times for this place, they were long forgotten.

Amir took the seat nearest the front of the tavern and positioned himself in a way that gave him an unobstructed view through the large window.

Rafael sat down facing him. "Are we waiting for Mikel to join us?" His eyes jittered in a way Amir had become familiar with over the years.

"He is inexcusably late. We will start without him." But before he could start, he heard the rumble of the Porsche just beyond the atmosphere of the restaurant, and saw a flash of white through the streaked, plate glass window. "I see him now, Rafael. Shall we order some German beer . . . or is there a South American beer you would prefer."

Rafael's eyes turned to the bar, questioning the possibility of imported beers in a place like this. Was Amir joking? In all the years he had known him, Rafael couldn't remember any part of the man that held a sense of humor.

Mikel Rhen came through the tavern door like a downhill skier breaking from the starting gate, and easily navigated the slalom course around the tables. The sway of his stride was confident and fluid. His broad shoulders and narrow hips were accentuated by the soft texture of a black suede, waist-cut jacket. As he approached the other men, he smiled his apology: "Sorry I'm late, Uncle. That's a hell of a car and I couldn't resist a few more minutes behind the wheel."

"Sit down, Mikki. Rafael and I were just about to begin."

Mikel exchanged pleasantries with Rafael. They all ordered Löwenbräu.

When the beer had been served and the bartender was back behind the bar, Amir leaned slightly toward Rafael. "Tell me, my friend, how is Colombia?"

"The summer has been hot and dry in Bogotá. It makes us uh . . . lazy, *amigo*," Rafael smiled. Amir nodded his understanding and listened as Rafael went on. "But Enrico keeps me on my toes. He keeps all of us in the Corporation going at full speed. But how can I complain? Our success is amazing. Except for one little problem. And that, of course, is why I called you last week. I thought you might be able to help us with our latest uh . . . dilemma."

"I must admit, Rafael, that your telephone call surprised me. Pleasantly, of course. I was glad to have the week to study your problem. I believe I have the perfect solution."

"If it answers our needs, Amir, I'm sure you're right."

Mikel seemed bored with the conversation and played with his beer glass absentmindedly. Amir looked at him as he continued to address Rafael. "As I understand it, your competition in Medellin and Cali has closed you out of the Caymans. The Corporation needs a home for its assets and, more importantly . . . freedom, shall we say, to move its funds on a worldwide level."

"Freedom," Rafael repeated, his eyes coming to rest on Amir's thin lips. "Yes, freedom."

"Let me come right to the point," Amir brought his eyes back to Rafael, "I believe I can offer you and your associates the cooperation of a Swiss bank."

Rafael relaxed and took a sip of his beer. He was beginning to feel more comfortable with his surroundings. "That would certainly be convenient."

"A numbered account," Amir said, "buried and waiting for the funds from Colombia."

"I'm certainly intrigued, *amigo*. How do we get the services of this bank?"

"That is the most interesting part. My plan is to eliminate the bank president and put an impostor in his place."

"An impostor?" Rafael asked, honestly stunned, "What do you mean?"

"With some simple surgeries, I can change Mikel's face to that of the banker's. Think of it, Rafael. For one day, Mikel is the president of the bank. He can create your account, then disappear." Amir's eyes flared slightly with gathering excitement. "It's like a bank robbery in reverse." He sat back with a contented smile. "Timing is important; in fact, timing is everything."

"That's rather . . . wild. Is it even possible?" A slight sweat began to appear on Rafael's upper lip. "What about the bank president, and anyone who might know him? Can Mikel fool—"

"Possible? Of course it's possible! You of all people should not be surprised. You know what we do; we do the impossible. That's why you come to us." A glint of something beyond the large window caught Amir's eye, and then it was gone. "The mere fact that it *is* wild makes it easier for us. Most people don't believe things like this can happen."

"I don't know. . . ." Rafael said, leaning in and whispering nervously. "Do you forget who I'm negotiating for? Enrico Serva is building one of the most powerful corporations in Colombia. This sounds too wild, Amir. I'm not sure I want to suggest a plan like this to him."

Amir could except Rafael's nervousness. Rafael was nervous about everything and, over the years, Amir had learned to ignore it. Amir could also ignore Rafael's lack of vision. But his cowardice was something Amir would never ignore. He knew the plan was perfect. Rafael just needed a little push.

"Enrico Serva is a businessman," Amir said, matching Rafael's whisper. "His business may be cocaine, but he is still a businessman. He is powerful, yes; he is also smart. He has money to move, a lot of money. This will work, Rafael. Trust me."

"We've known each other a long time, Amir, but this is uh—"

"Trust me, my friend, it will work. Of course, an operation like this will be somewhat expensive."

"Expensive?" Rafael was still trying to recover.

"Fifty million dollars. I believe that will cover it. Cash, of course . . . I do not trust banks."

"Fifty million? That's a lot of dollars. Are you sure it would cost that much?"

"There is a larger profit margin on a contract like this. It is much more difficult for me, and much more dangerous for Mikki. Fifty million, my friend. Cash."

"If I'm going to tell Enrico of a plan like this, I'm going to need more information. You know, uh . . . details. I want to believe it can be done."

Over Rafael's left shoulder, another glint caught Amir's attention briefly. "All the details will be our concern. . . ." There it was again. A glint. Beyond the window, the street lamps had found an object across the street and illuminated it for a fraction of a second. The light had come from the darkened entrance to an alley. Amir's sharp eyes began to penetrate the shadows. After a few seconds, he was sure he could make out the top portion of a man's torso. The glint had come from the lens of a camera the man was holding. The camera was aimed directly at Rafael's back—and his face.

To Rafael and Mikel, Amir seemed to be lost in a distant thought. "Have you been followed, Rafael?" Amir looked curiously at his South American friend.

"*¿Que? No.*" Rafael's eyes began to undulate with concern.

Mikel leaned back slowly in his chair and began turning his half empty glass of beer in his hand. As he listened to the exchange of conversation, his focus was on the glass, but his attention was now on his uncle.

"Perhaps there was someone you saw more than once today? Think, my friend."

"No, Amir, I don't think—"

"I think someone is interested in you. Someone who wants a permanent record of this meeting. Listen carefully, Rafael. I'm going to tell you exactly what to do, and I want you to do it."

"But Amir, I'm quite sure—"

Amir leaned toward Rafael again. "We can both be 'quite sure' if you do exactly as I tell you."

Rafael left the tavern by the front door and turned right. He did not look into the shadows across the street. At the very next door, the entrance to an old hotel, he turned and went in. He walked slowly through the dingy, unkempt lobby and followed the sullied corridor to the back door. Without hesitation he opened the door, stepped into the alley, turned to his left, and hurried off into the night.

As Mikel started to leave, he felt a hand grab his wrist.

"Do not kill him, Mikki, unless it is unavoidable," Amir said.

Mikel smiled and walked away quickly. He moved quietly through the back door of the tavern and went down the alley to find a place to wait for Rafael's pursuer.

As he watched Rafael leave the restaurant, the man with the camera stepped back into the safety of his sheltering shadows. When Rafael entered the hotel, the man went across the street. After a glance through the hotel's window to avoid the possibility of running into his target, he entered the lobby. Not seeing Rafael, he hurried down the hall to the back door and stopped to listen. Hearing Rafael's footsteps echoing away, he stepped through the door. A flash of black lightning streaked out of the darkness and a fist as hard as steel smashed into his forehead, just above the bridge of his nose. The blow was paralyzing. He stumbled back into the hall and went down on his back. Dizzy, he reached out to put a hand on the wall and tried to get up.

Someone stepped into the doorway and stood looking down at him. It was one of the men who had been drinking with Rafael: the young one with the fancy car. He had watched him go into the tavern, and had gotten a profile photo, but this was the first time he had seen him up close. He was a soldier, trained and disciplined, committed and competent.

He got to his feet and assumed a practiced, defensive stance. The man moved around him easily and rocked him with another fist to the forehead. The pain was blurring and he went down on his knees. The walls began to close in on him and it seemed impossible to maneuver in what was left of the hallway. He went for his gun.

The man moved in on him and released a final, vicious blow to the side of his head. Then consciousness faded.

Amir helped Mikel drag the unconscious body out into the alley. "Well done, Mikki. Get the car. I will watch that he doesn't recover."

Mikel hurried off to get his Porsche.

The Porsche's headlights went dim and only the dull yellow glow of the parking lights remained to illuminate the small clearing in the dense forest.

"Get him out and put him against that tree," Amir ordered, motioning to a young pine directly in front of the car. He took the camera and got out.

Mikel went into the glove box for a plastic zip-tie. Then he tugged the cumbersome weight of the unconscious man from the inadequate space of the Porsche's rear seats. He dragged him to the tree and sat him down. Pulling the man's arms around the tree, he secured them with the tie. "Why don't we just kill him and get the hell out of here?"

"Patience, Mikki. We should find out what he knows first. A moan came from the man between them. "Empty his pockets. Put everything in his lap."

Once again Mikel did as he was told.

Before the last few items were removed from the man's pockets, he coughed, shook his head, and tried to move his arms. When his mind cleared enough to realize he was tied, he shook his head again. "What the hell are you doing?" he asked, watching his pockets being emptied.

"Let me see. . . ." Amir reached for one of the objects in the man's lap. "A Glock semi-auto. . . ." He tossed it back in the man's lap and reached for another item.

"Who the hell are you?"

"Identification . . ." Amir continued, ". . . John E. Balin, United States of America, Drug Enforcement Administration. Interesting. Keys, change, cigarettes . . . and what have we here?" Amir lifted a small white paper bag from Balin's lap. It had been rolled up for carrying. He unrolled it and withdrew a small box. He opened the box. "A Swiss Army Knife. . . ."

"Okay, boys, you've had your fun. Now let's get these hands untied and—"

"How American. Even when you are working, you still have time to be a tourist. Amusing." Amir unfolded the large blade. He examined the three inches of polished steel and briefly noticed the insignia on the bright red plastic handle. He handed the knife to Mikki.

"That's for my kid. Now untie me, asshole!"

"You were following *Señor* Santos, am I correct?" Amir asked as he opened the camera and removed the memory card.

John Balin struggled for a moment. He didn't think he could free himself, but he wanted to measure the resistance to his hands. Then he relaxed and leaned back against the tree. "Who are you guys, anyway?"

"Rafael Santos," Amir said, putting the memory card in the pocket of his jacket, and tossing the camera back into Balin's lap.

Mikel rested the blade of the knife under Balin's left eye. "Rafael Santos," he said, "works with Enrico Serva. Please don't make me do something as amateurish as cut your eye out. I'm really not interested in torturing you."

Balin glared back at his captors through eyes matured by military training and combat experience. In the army, he had faced death more than once and survived. As a field agent for the DEA, one official and personal rule remained: Give the enemy only name, rank and serial number. If he was standing at the edge of his last moment, he was prepared to carry his silence, like a flag, over the battle-drawn hill of mortality.

"We're getting nowhere," Mikel complained.

"How long have you been following *Señor* Santos?" Amir asked, ignoring his nephew's impatience. "Do you know who I am? Has your investigation of Rafael been thorough enough to tell you that? Or my companion . . ." Amir motioned to Mikel, ". . . do you know his name?"

Balin said nothing.

23

Amir took the knife from Mikel and squatted down next to Balin. "You bought this for your son? How touching."

"Fuck you."

"No, Mister Balin, fuck you. Your son is never going to receive this gift. The amount of time you have left in this life could be measured with a stopwatch. I can make it quick and painless, or slow and very painful. Do you know my name?"

Mikel put his hand in front of Balin's face and pretended to hold a stopwatch. He pushed his thumb down to start the timer.

Balin looked down at the Glock in his lap—so close, and so far away. He pulled one more time against the tie, and then he stopped the effort.

"I don't think we're going to get anymore from him."

"You may be right, Mikki."

Amir turned as if to rise and move away. Then he swung his body back around with the force of a prizefighter, and, with the precision of a surgeon, he slid the blade into the soft skin of Balin's throat, severing the carotid artery, and then flicked the blade back out quickly to avoid the immediate flow of blood that pulsed after his hand.

Balin's head leaned back against the tree, as his life-blood pumped from his neck and squirted into his lap and onto his legs.

From the safe position on the other side of Balin, Mikel moved the phantom stopwatch closer to Balin's face and a smile came into his eyes.

In less than a minute, the blood stopped pumping, Balin slumped forward, his jaw dropped open as if he were screaming, and a death moan pushed its way up from deep in his lungs. His last breath escaped without resistance. Even though he was dead, his eyes were open.

Mikel leaned in to study Balin's face for a moment. He put his hand up to show Balin's dead eyes the stopwatch. His thumb clicked it off.

"Get the tie, Mikki." Amir took a handkerchief from his pocket and wiped the blood and fingerprints from the blade and handle of the Swiss Army Knife. He retrieved the box, put the knife in it, wrapped it in his handkerchief, and put it in his pocket. He took the rest of Balin's belongings and put them in his pockets to be disposed of later. "Look around. Be sure we have left nothing beyond the body."

They did not speak to each other on the drive back to downtown Zürich. The power-filled hum of the Porsche's engine was the only sound either of them heard until Mikel pulled to the curb in front of the train station.

"I'm thinking Ferrari, Uncle," Mikel said with a smile.

"You can't afford it," Amir replied with a somber tone.

"Come on, Uncle. My share of fifty million? I can afford any car I want."

"You can't afford it," Amir repeated with more intensity.

"What do you mean, Uncle?"

"You're already drawing more attention to yourself than we need. Are we going to have a problem, Mikki?"

"No, Uncle."

"Where's Wolfgang now?" Amir asked.

"I believe he's in Monaco, attending a banking conference. He's staying on his yacht while he—"

"Go there immediately," Amir said, reaching for the door handle. "We need to stay current on Wolfgang's agenda. And you need to continue being his best friend."

"You mean tonight?"

"Of course I mean tonight," Amir said, opening the car door.

"But I had plans for tonight," Mikel whined. "Wolfgang will be there for two weeks. Can't this wait until tomorrow? I don't even know if I can get a flight this late."

With one foot on the sidewalk, Amir leaned back into the brown leather bucket seat and stared through the windshield. "Keep enjoying the automobile you have, Mikki. Drive. Tonight." He pushed himself up and out of the Porsche and slammed the door shut without turning back to see his nephew's frustrated expression.

3

NORTH HOLLYWOOD, CALIFORNIA

As fast as he was, Thomas Kelly was not going to beat his Doberman, RoboDobe, to the front door. His strong arms furiously fought the air in front of his broad chest, and his long, muscular legs turned power into momentum for his six-foot three-inch, one hundred ninety-five pound frame. His feet pounded the uneven cement sidewalk. For ten seconds, he applied everything he knew about running: he stretched his arms and legs as he had been taught by the soccer coach thirteen years earlier in high school; he pushed his muscles past the point of pain as he had learned in his R.O.T.C. endurance tests at UCLA; and he took his breaths short and fast, a leftover from his try for a Golden Gloves championship now eight years in his past. But it was useless. He couldn't win. The Doberman had the advantage of four legs and a lead it would never relinquish.

With Kelly only a few steps behind, RoboDobe jumped the three porch steps and landed without hitting the door—a feat that always amazed Kelly. Wagging a tail he refused to believe was gone, RoboDobe turned to collect the praise and admiration reserved for the winner of this morning marathon.

Kelly's athletic body fell to a sitting position on the porch like a receiver who'd just dropped a winning touchdown pass. He wore a dark blue cutoff sweatshirt, red shorts, thick grey sweat socks, and dirty white tennis shoes.

27

ɔDobe sat back on his haunches and turned to face
Panting, slack-jawed, his tongue hanging out of the
of his mouth, he seemed to smile at his master. The
.nner's smile.

"Okay, so you won again. So what? Tomorrow, I'm
gonna take your ass. You'll see."

RoboDobe slurped his tongue back into his mouth and
put his snout on Kelly's arm. His eyes gazed sympathetically
into Kelly's clear blue eyes as if he knew that tomorrow's
outcome would be the same as today's.

"Oh yeah? You don't think I can take you?"

The dog took his nose off Kelly's arm and bowed his
head as if he understood the question. Then, he returned his
gaze longingly to Kelly.

"You want pets! That's it, you want pets. You won, so
you want the reward."

Kelly grabbed the dog's head and rubbed it vigorously,
but his attention was drawn to a young woman exiting the
front door of the house across the street. She was carrying a
plate in one hand, and with the other, she waved to him.

Lorraine Harte was as beautiful as a woman could get.
Most of the time she kept her long black hair tied in a tight
bun on the top of her head, which only drew attention to her
unusually deep and hauntingly dark eyes. Her lips were a
seductive, pale pink color even without lipstick. She wore a
blue tank-top, and even from this distance he could see the
tautness of her stomach. She also wore white shorts, which
exposed almost all of her admirably long legs. She was a
ballet dancer; she loved to show her legs.

As she approached, he was struck, as he was every time
he saw her, by the graceful movements of her long and
slender body. He was also struck by the fact that he felt
nothing for her beyond the admiration for what God had
created, and the neighborly friendship they had developed.
No desire or lust or passion. Only friendship.

The first time he had realized that, it had surprised him. How could a red-blooded American boy like himself feel no passion for the most beautiful woman he had ever seen?

He had first seen her a year ago. He had been losing the race with RoboDobe, as usual, and when he had turned at the end of the street for the home stretch, he had noticed her car parked in the driveway of the vacant house across the street from his. She was moving in. A light rain was falling, so he had gone over, introduced himself, and offered to help her. One thing had led to another and he had finally asked her out.

They had both enjoyed the date and he had found her intelligent and informed, as well as incredibly gorgeous. But, when he had brought her home and walked her up to the front door, he had had no desire to kiss her or, for that matter, do anything else. He had blamed it on being tired and had gone home to bed. Since then, he had not pursued her. He didn't know why, exactly. There was no passion. That was enough why. They had become friendly neighbors. That was enough for him.

"Hi, Tom," Lorraine said as she crossed his small patch of front lawn. "I thought you might like some of these cookies. It's an old family recipe. We call them White Wine Cookies."

Beautiful, and she could cook, too. What the hell was wrong with him. Maybe he wasn't American . . . or red-blooded. . . . He stood as she offered him the plate.

He thanked her several times and mentioned how good the cookies looked. He thought about how she might look lying naked and willing on his bed, with her black hair falling all over his pillow. His blood flowed a little bit faster, but other than that, nothing. He was no virgin. And he was no fool either. He wasn't about to get involved with someone who lived right across the street unless he thought it might go somewhere. So far, he didn't think it would. In his life, he had felt a lot more for women who had a lot less. He didn't want to kid her, or himself.

RoboDobe sat patiently on the porch and stared at the unused portion of the lawn.

Kelly and Lorraine exchanged the usual pleasantries, and then fell into an awkward silence.

Kelly looked down at his dirty tennis shoes for a moment before he looked back at her.

She spoke first. "Well, gotta go. I'm trying out for a part in the ballet at the Music Center. It's a good part. Wish me luck."

"Thanks, Lorraine. Break a leg."

"Okay," she said, turning to walk back across the lawn.

"Lorraine," he called to her back.

She turned around.

"Thanks," he said, smiling.

She returned his smile, waved and went home.

He pushed the front door open and waited. RoboDobe turned and looked up at him. "Come!" he commanded. Even though his voice was stern and slightly raised, it still had a whispery quality to it.

The dog took one more longing look at the front lawn, wishing the playtime would continue, then turned quickly and trotted inside. Kelly followed him into the Spanish-style house. A glass-topped table, canvas couch, and matching canvas chair tried valiantly to squeeze themselves into the narrow living room. Two paintings and a medium sized mirror leaned against the wall where he had left them when he had moved in, three years ago. A telephone rested tentatively on a thin-legged table a neighbor had given him.

On the way to the shower, the cell phone in his runner's armband rang. He answered it.

The caller was already speaking. "Kelly?"

"Yes, Sir," he said quietly.

"It's a go for tonight."

"Yes, Sir," Kelly replied.

The caller did not identify himself, nor did he need to. Although it had never been stated, every agent knew that he or she was expected to recognize the voice of the SAC immediately. To the agents under his command, he was Hunt, and they called him that, or Sir. To the administrators above him, he was Evans Hunt: Special Agent in Charge of the Los Angeles Field Division for the Drug Enforcement Administration.

With the explosion of the Sinaloa cartel in Mexico, Evans Hunt's responsibilities had broadened, his attention was being divided between Mexico and Colombia, and his time was being absorbed with the need to be in Washington D.C., and in constant planning sessions for multiple offensive DEA strike operations.

"Good." Hunt began his instructions. "The New Man has put a shipment on the southern carrier. It should be arriving between twenty-two and twenty-four hundred hours. Stage 17. We'll stagger our arrivals. I've instructed Agent Fenny to be there at twenty hundred hours. I want you there at twenty-one hundred. I'll be there at twenty-two hundred. Understood?"

Kelly took his job seriously, but Hunt's manner made him want to chuckle privately. Hunt's military tone of voice—as if he were trying out for the part of Norman Schwarzkopf in a movie—and his perpetual use of code words and phrases made Kelly impatient. He wanted to say, "Right. Now let's go kick some ass." What he did say was, "Yes, Sir. Stage 17. Twenty-one hundred hours."

"Let me remind you, Agent Kelly, this is a reconnaissance operation only. No action is to be taken. We want to know the final destination of the shipment. We want to know just how powerful the New Man has become, and how strong his connection is to the L.A. family. Are we clear on that?"

"Yes, Sir." Kelly did not appreciate Hunt's tone. He had to remind himself that Hunt spoke to all the agents as if they were privates in his personal army.

"Fine," Hunt said.

Kelly heard the End Call click as Hunt terminated the conversation.

Wanting to make a difference in the outcome of his country's future, Thomas Kelly had chosen law enforcement in general, and the DEA as his career. He had come to the attention of his superiors because of his quick thinking and his physical abilities. He had appeared to be someone who could keep his head in a tense situation. The Administration had recruited him a few months after he had graduated from UCLA at the top of his class in Criminology. As far as the Administration was concerned, he was the "pick of the litter." If he chose to stay with it, he could go all the way to the top. They had told him as much.

He went to the refrigerator for some juice.

RoboDobe followed him.

Kelly took a swallow and then noticed that RoboDobe was staring at him. "You want treats?" he asked.

The dog's ears perked up and his head tilted to the side. He knew the word "treats."

Kelly went to the pantry shelf where he kept the dog biscuits and retrieved a handful. "Treats!" he said.

RoboDobe barked once.

Kelly dropped the biscuits onto the linoleum floor and left the kitchen.

In the shower, he translated Hunt's code. The New Man was Enrico Serva, the South American drug lord. He was relatively new on the scene. Although he had most likely been dealing for a decade or more, he had only recently achieved "Lord" status. Very little was known about him. The U.S. Government wanted to know more. Hunt had been assigned the project.

The shipment was cocaine, and the southern carrier was the Colombian freighter the *ALBARDA*. The time the freighter was expected to arrive was somewhere between ten pm and midnight. The place, The Stage, was actually Pier 17 at the Port of Los Angeles. Agent Jason Fenny was Kelly's partner on this assignment. Kelly liked and respected him.

The *ALBARDA* was early.

Very early, Kelly thought, as he parked his car a half a block away from the pier. He could see the enormous black and red striped stack pushing up like a man-made mountain above the two-story warehouse with the bold letters P-17 painted on it. The stack held the crested insignia of the Mutis Shipping Company.

On the pier, brilliant night lights lit the area between the warehouse and the South American freighter like a night game at Dodger Stadium. There were no long stretches of darkness to walk in. There were no gentle slaps of water against pylons to mask the footfalls of a man on his way to meet another man in a small, dark Ford sedan.

A crew of longshoremen had already offloaded the *ALBARDA's* cargo and gone on to another ship.

The customs officials had come and gone and it was obvious that they had dutifully played their part in Hunt's overall plan by missing the undeclared cargo Hunt had instructed them to miss.

Kelly stared down the long distance of the pier trying to find a secret path through the lights, containers, and machines. If the *ALBARDA* was this early, Fenny was probably feeling the dilemma of being alone. No back-up. No support. He couldn't see a way to get to Fenny without being seen.

As he hesitated, a dark blue Dodge van wound its way through the forklifts and cargo crates and approached the position he had taken at the end of the warehouse. It stopped at the stop sign. That act alone caused Kelly's attention to peak. A stop sign on the peer seemed perfunctory at best, and certainly most drivers would ignore it at this time of night, with little to no traffic in sight. Kelly got his cell phone and took a picture of the driver: a man with pock-marked skin and a scar just below his right eyebrow.

The driver studied the image in the van's side-view mirror.

Kelly's attention was drawn to the rear of the van.

From the dimness just behind the enormous warehouse loading doors, a Ford sedan emerged slowly, like a bloodhound, and took up the trail the van had left.

The van held its position at the stop sign, its solid front tires barely touching the double thickness of the white restricting line.

There was no mistaking Fenny's Ford. It was one of the covert cars used in surveillance operations.

The van wasn't moving.

The Ford was approaching from behind.

Kelly heard Hunt's words, "No action is to be taken," reverberate in his mind, but the muscles in his arms and legs began to tingle with impatience.

The van still wasn't moving. For Kelly, the moment seemed to be unwinding in slow-motion. If the van wasn't moving, there had to be a reason. In seconds, Fenny would be far too close; he didn't have a choice.

The muted rumble of the van's powerful V-8 RAM engine filled the silent space between the van and Kelly. Exhaust snorted from the tailpipe with the persistence of a boxer's gloved fists on a punching bag. The smell of the fumes reached his nostrils. He heard the soft mumblings of the driver through the open passenger's side window. He wasn't close enough to hear the words, but the intent was becoming all too clear.

Everything exploded at once. When the Ford was close to the Dodge's rear bumper, the van's driver gave a command, the double back doors sprang open, and two Uzis spit their deadly spray at the Ford with the precision of ice picks in the hands of sculptors. Nasty little holes stabbed into the glossy brown paint and ran viciously up the hood of the car, perforating the windshield into a gigantic, glassy spider web. Tiny shards and pieces of the sticky glass fell on the hood and into the Ford's interior.

Simultaneously, the massive sound of a pump shotgun rocked the night, covering the hissing snaps of the Uzis. The grill of the Ford erupted in a violent shattering of tin, metal, and plastic, and the hood bounced up and fell back to cover a dying engine. An immediate, second shotgun blast hit the windshield and it disappeared.

Kelly had never felt so helpless. His warning shout to Fenny was lost in the syncopated rhythm of the unrelenting gunfire and the squealing of the back tires as the van started to speed away, rear doors banging.

Kelly's Glock came up and out with practiced, automatic response and he fired six rounds into the vanishing messenger of death. Twice, he saw the sparks as the jacketed rounds slammed into the sheet metal of the van's back doors. He was sure that at least two more rounds had entered the van while the doors were swinging out. With three armed men in the back, he knew there'd be hell to pay to avoid his fire, but it was a small consolation for the damage they had done.

The gunmen in the van returned fire at this new target. A second later, the dark blue Dodge van seemed to evaporate into the black night beyond the peer.

As suddenly as it had exploded, everything around Kelly fell into a deeper silence than he could ever remember experiencing. He realized he was shaking. Every muscle in his body ached. Sweat trickled from every pore, and he could feel the fabric of his jacket through the sticky wetness of his cotton shirt. He had the tired feeling that comes in the wake of an adrenaline rush and he could still feel the adrenaline running in his blood.

He ran to what was left of the Ford, hoping against hope that somehow Fenny had survived the brutal attack.

What he saw made him sick.

"What the hell happened?" Hunt yelled, his face getting more red with each consonant. His right hand slapped the almost empty desktop to emphasize his anger. His other hand rested impassively on the hurriedly written, three-page transcript that constituted Kelly's report.

Kelly did not allow his eyes to wander around Hunt's Los Angeles office. He'd seen it before; he knew what it looked like. He also knew that the level of his attention was being measured, like a target, by Hunt's gunpoint-like stare.

"What the hell went wrong out there? Give me another breakdown on this thing, Agent Kelly, some kind of perspective I can deal with. What did you two think you were doing?" He rummaged through Kelly's report, not really seeing it.

"Our information was wrong. The ship was already—"

"The ship was already there! Somehow, that simple fact is supposed to make the death of one of our agents more palatable. What were you doing? Did we miss some valuable part of your training, like the procedure for maintaining surveillance of a motorized vehicle?"

"I wasn't in the car," Kelly said.

"No kidding! I can tell by the lack of bullet holes in you that you weren't in the car."

"He was caught. They stopped in the one place where he couldn't turn away. He had no choice but to continue on."

Still staring at Kelly, Hunt shook his head and issued a slow sigh for emphasis. Then he continued, "I thought you were better than this, Kelly. A real smart guy. An All-American, a hot-shot. What happened out there?"

"The ship was early." He knew he was repeating himself, but he couldn't come up with anything better. "There wasn't any time to get to Fenny—"

"The ship was early. The ship was early. The-Ship-Was-God-Damn-EARLY! Do I look stupid to you, Agent Kelly? Do you think I don't understand something when it's said the first time?" Hunt stared over his starched, bureaucratic white collar. The veins in his throat were apparent under his thick, command-worn skin. "This doesn't make us look good," he continued, waving an arm for emphasis. "Hell, we look like a bunch of God damn amateurs. The only thing that could've made this worse is if we'd given them the God damn *guns*!" he finished sarcastically.

Kelly was finding it hard to concentrate on Hunt's words. The SAC's seeming total lack of sympathy for a life lost, his thoughtless lack of concern for a fallen fellow agent, his soulless avoidance of the subject of Jason Fenny no longer being present among the living, was leaving Kelly in a mental haze of quiet confusion.

"Let's go over this one more time from fucking top to fucking clean-up. Let's see if there's any way we can come out of this without looking like a bunch of shit-faced monkeys to the boys in D.C.—damn, they're going to love this one!"

"I was thinking of how we must look to Fenny," Kelly said, his voice imbued with the whispery quality that was most evident when he was lost in thought. He wasn't sure if Hunt heard him. Either way, it didn't matter

"Whooa," Hunt said softly, dragging the word out for effect. He stared at Kelly for a moment, measuring the comment. Then he decided to ignore Kelly's philosophizing. Talking through clenched teeth, he began softly on his way to an explosive crescendo: "Have I got it right, *Agent* Kelly, when I start with the fact that when you arrived, the ship was already there, the cargo had already passed customs, the drugs were already being driven away, and you were in a gunfight that Agent Jason Fenny HAD ALREADY LOST!"

Kelly was stunned, but he let Hunt's officious sarcasm and condescending arrogance slide past his ears and away from his consciousness. As Hunt scrutinized every last detail of the operation—pouring over it with the resolve of an army statistician studying the results of a poorly executed battle plan—Kelly's thoughts, if not his eyes, drifted past the dirty tan walls and chipped, white enamel window frames of the grimly furnished downtown office.

"Clean-up! Let's go over it again." Hunt's voice brought him back to the under-lit, overly depressive atmosphere of his surroundings. "You didn't get the license plate."

"There were no plates on the van, front or rear."

"And as to descriptions?"

"In the report." Kelly said, motioning to the folder on the desk. "The same as I gave you at the scene."

"I know it's in the report. I already gave the descriptions to the LAPD. They're already looking for suspects who we both know will make bail before they're even arrested and will be noticeably absent at any arraignment . . . should they ever be found. But I want to know who they are and how they relate to the L.A. family . . . however minor that relationship is."

"I didn't recognize the driver. He must be new. I got a picture of him, but my phone was destroyed."

"Yeah, uh huh." As Hunt continued what sounded to Kelly more like a lecture than an evaluation, his mind

38

escaped again. Clean-up, he thought. The part the heroes of television and movies deftly avoid with a simple fade to black. But there had been no simple fade to black. There had only been the interminably slow ticking of the life-clock as he had waited for each LAPD officer and DEA professional to arrive and complete his or her task.

The dock workers had played their part by wandering out from wherever they had been after the sound of gunfire had died away—to stand around the chewed and twisted metal of what had been a Ford.

Weakened by the simple, but psychologically explosive task of opening the car door and placing two fingertips on Fenny's carotid artery to verify the all too obvious, Kelly had been racked by what he saw. Jason Fenny's blood had been emptied from his body and he had been washed with it. He had been blistered and broken, cut and raked, butchered and torn. Jason Fenny had been destroyed. Kelly had turned away, gone down to a sitting position, leaned his back against the car, and put his head between his knees.

One of the dock workers had offered to call 911.

Kelly had shaken his head, no. From his sitting position on the dock, he had reached into the breast pocket of his sport coat and found his I.D. He had held the badge up at arm's length and said, "DEA." Then he had gotten up and retrieved his cell phone from another jacket pocket. It hadn't worked. He had tried several more times, mostly out of frustration, to coerce the phone into duty, but it was useless. When he could focus more clearly, he realized that the phone had been hit by a bullet. He had examined his jacket pocket. There was a small black hole where the bullet had entered. And then another hole where it had exited after deflecting off the cell phone. He had taken incoming rounds from the shooters in the van. But he had not been hit. He had scanned himself quickly to confirm there was no blood visible. He had mumbled a prayer of thanks, and then had an immediate and overwhelming feeling of guilt that he had survived and his partner and friend had not. The dock workers had looked on in silence.

"Don't touch anything," he had cautioned the workers, feeling as if he were reading from a bad movie script. Then he had gone back into the Ford to get Fenny's phone. As he had searched his partner's pockets, pushing and pawing into the blood-soaked material of Fenny's clothes, he had wanted to scream and cry and throw up, all at the same time.

He had used the special Key Number to call the boss. "The Key," as it was called, was a speed dial number that connected the caller directly to Hunt, wherever he was. It also automatically scrambled the call. Kelly had no intention of letting Hunt arrive on this scene without proper warning of the conditions he would find.

The phone call had sped-up the process. From an unknown place in the vastness of the ponderous city, Hunt had gone to work. Within minutes, Kelly had heard the sirens. The flashing lights hadn't been far behind.

Clean-up. He had thought the words as he had watched the lab-boys and camera carriers, medics and coroners, trudge through their all too familiar investigative routine.

By the time Hunt had arrived, the clean-up was in full swing. He had approached the scene with the confident stride of the Commander-In-Chief. Placing himself just outside the perimeter of action, he had folded his immodest arms across his chest, cocked his head slightly, and begun an all-encompassing visual inspection. He, of course, expected Kelly to come to him with an account.

Kelly had gone to where Hunt was standing and, with his blood-stained hands stuck deep in the pockets of his Levi's, had given a verbal report.

As he had waited for Hunt's response, he thought about the fact that Hunt was wearing an expensive two-piece suit, a heavily starched white shirt, and a dark blue and red striped tie. He had wondered if Hunt had planned to come to the surveillance in those clothes. The idea seemed bizarre even for Evans Hunt.

"Put it in writing and meet me at my office in one hour," was all Hunt had said.

Following Hunt's orders, he had left the battle site and started out for the suite of musty offices they occupied in the Federal Building to write out his report.

On the road, it had occurred to him that he had not fed RoboDobe. In the anticipation of the operation, he had simply walked out and left the dog to guard the house. Figuring it wouldn't take that long, he had made the detour. He had found an impatient and hungry dog. He had filled the bowl, and then stood over the Doberman and stared into the food.

The picture of the outcome of the operation had filled his mind. Anger had filled the rest of him. It wasn't just the fact that Fenny was dead—it was the ease with which his life had been taken. Doors opened, shots fired, a man killed. Tragedy could strike at any time. That was something Kelly understood; that was the motivator that kept him physically fit. But the blatant disrespect for life left him disoriented. He wasn't naive, but there were times when he was definitely at a loss for answers. This was one of them.

He had never made the attempt to get close to Fenny; he couldn't say Fenny was his best friend. But Fenny was a good man. Fenny had been easy to work with and had a great sense of humor. Kelly was sure that, for a time at least, he would miss him.

Without hesitation, he had left the house—closing but not locking the door—and gone to the office.

An hour later Hunt had joined him and they had mulled over the disaster of the evening's event for more hours than Kelly wanted to count.

"Are you still with me, Kelly?" Hunt leaned forward and put his arms on the desk, "You look like you might be somewhere else."

"I'm here, Sir. But it's getting late, or should I say early. It's been—"

"There's something else you should know, Agent Kelly."

"Yes, Sir?" Kelly was immediately aware that the atmosphere in the room had changed. Even though he wouldn't have believed it was possible, the mood had instantly and certainly become more serious.

"We have discovered and identified the remains of Agent John Balin."

"Balin. . . ." Through this new and unsettling shock to his already overly tired system, Kelly remembered Johnny Balin. He hadn't known him well because Balin was a senior agent, and got his pick of assignments. Balin liked to travel and was gone to Europe most of the time. He had a wife and son.

Kelly debated expressing his sympathies. He decided that Hunt wouldn't think it was necessary or needed at this moment. Hunt did not want sympathy. This was work. "Where did they find him?"

"Just outside of Zürich. In the woods. He's been dead for at least three days, maybe four. He was observing Rafael Santos."

"I didn't think Santos was capable of taking out a trained agent by himself."

"He isn't." Hunt was always sure of his facts. "Obviously, the New Man's getting ahead of us. Now he's got dealings in Switzerland."

"Do you want me to go to Zürich and find out what's going on?"

"I've already got someone there. That's how I found Agent Balin."

"What would you like me to do, Sir?"

After a pause, Hunt responded, "What I want all of my agents to do. Get the bastard! Bring him down! Crush him!" Hunt allowed Kelly time to reply. When he didn't, Hunt got up. "That's enough for tonight. Get some sleep and we'll go over it again in the morning. Here, 0800." He stacked the three pages of Kelly's report on the desk and slid them into the top drawer. "Apparently, the New Man is playing for keeps and we're going to have to work a little harder to stay on top of this thing. What have we learned, Kelly?"

It was a well-known fact that Evans Hunt was one of the President's closest friends. The President had personally asked Hunt to take the appointment as the Special Agent in Charge of the Los Angeles division, and it was rumored that he hoped Hunt would inherit the top position when it became available. Still, Kelly did not appreciate being talked to like a child.

"We've learned more than we wanted to about Enrico Serva. Not only is he smart, but he's a snake . . . a very deadly snake."

"Let's make sure he doesn't catch us with our pants down next time." Hunt closed the desk drawer.

Kelly stood and turned for the door.

Hunt's voice was soft enough to be a prayer. "They were both good men. John was already an 'old soldier' when I recruited him after he left the army. I teased him that Janet was too good for him, and praised him when he married her. I was there at the hospital when Richard was born. I brought Jason in a few months after you. He was bright and honest and . . . righteous. I was with him when Amy was born. At the risk of sounding corny, I want to say that I recognize they paid the ultimate price for their country. I respect their bravery, I grieve their loss. We will honor their memory, and take care of their families. They will be deeply missed."

Kelly nodded, "Yes, Sir." Then he opened the door and walked out. Maybe, he thought, just maybe, Evans Hunt has a soul after all.

4

LA CONDAMINE, MONICO

Damn she's good!

Jesse watched as China's best diver cut the surface of the open-air Olympic-sized swimming pool and entered the heated sea water like a thread going through the eye of a needle.

"Damn she's good!" Coach Braden said under his breath. "Did you see the twisting action? And that kick-out . . . damn, she really went in clean. No splash. She's a damn diving machine."

"A diving machine," Jesse repeated, adjusting the straps of her swimsuit. She blotted her face with a small white towel, vaguely noticing that it was still damp with the saltwater she had wiped out of her eyes after each of the previous nine dives. She wasn't about to use another towel. This one was her lucky charm. She continued blotting. Her concentration went back to her next and final dive. Trivialities like towels and luck only got the smallest fraction of her attention.

"That's right, a diving machine." Braden returned his attention to Jesse. "And that's how we're gonna beat her. Listen, Kid, I want you to put every bit of yourself into this one. Make it human. Make it real. Put Jesse Fortune into every ounce of it. The judges have seen enough 'machine' today. I'm betting they want the real thing. So make it real.

Make it human. Make it super-human. Hell, Kid, show them art!"

Jesse Fortune—Y Lan Sung. Y Lan Sung—Jesse Fortune. It was as close a competition as the Stade Nautique Rainier III in Monaco had ever recorded in Women's 10 Meter Platform Diving. From the first moments of these Pan-European Games, the small but enthusiastic audience sitting in the bleachers had felt the rivalry building.

Y Lan Sung exited the pool smiling. She'd done well on her final attempt and she knew it. She had performed a Back 2½ Somersault Pike. The degree of difficulty was 2.9. As her score was displayed, the crowd erupted with admiration.

9.5, 9.5, 10, 9.5, 9.5, 9.0, 9.5

Total this dive: 82.6

It had been a sensational day for her, and her overall score was 348.5. Y Lan's coach hurried to intercept her prize pupil and offer congratulations. Y Lan turned away and allowed herself to be led to the shower.

That's it, Y Lan. Stick a fork in it, Babe, you're done. What am I saying? Concentrate! One more dive. Concentrate!

As many times as she had felt the cold steel of the handrail, it was always a surprise. Yet, as she climbed to the top of the platform, she used this sensation as a signal to start blocking out the world and focus on the dive she was about to perform.

Elevation, execution, entry. Get into the tuck sooner. Open sooner. Concentrate: perfect 10, perfect 10, perfect 10. . . .

Jesse had followed the young Chinese girl through the compulsory dives, her score never more than a point or two behind or ahead of her opponent. The Optionals had been even less decisive. It all came down to this, her final bid.

The dive: a 3½ Inward Pike. The degree of difficulty: 2.9. It was her favorite dive, and her best.

The moment Jesse's feet sprang from the tower, she knew she had it. In the take-off, she thanked herself for practicing this dive for so many hours. Her spring was strong and high, full of power. Her tuck in the hurdle was more than worthy of praise from Coach Braden, who never gave compliments. Every taut muscle in her body held its practiced position as she whirled and plunged through those milliseconds that held the difference between best and worst, winning and losing, glory and obscurity.

This is for us, Coach. You and me.

In the third turn, spotting the entry point on the water's surface was easier than it had ever been; it was right where it was supposed to be. Pulling out of the tuck, she grabbed her hands and stretched.

She stretched for the vertical entry; the goal of every dive, the aspiration of every diver.

She stretched to complete the flawless execution; to leave her mark as a champion; to finish with excellence.

She stretched for perfection.

With toes perfectly pointed, feet and legs tightly together, and body perfectly vertical to the entry point, Jesse punctured the glassy water and disappeared beneath its barely ruffled surface.

Under the water she breathed out, "YES!" She knew she had hit the entry perfectly. No matter what she scored, this was the best she could do. She swam triumphantly toward the surface. Her body broke the water with such force that her waist was nearly visible.

Braden was already at the edge of the pool. He wasn't waiting for the judges' scores. After twenty-five years of coaching, he knew a perfect dive when he saw one. She had done it. And this was more than just another step toward the gold in London. This was the first time she had beaten the Chinese girl, Y Lan Sung.

Braden had coached winners before, but this was different. He couldn't explain it, but he knew it was all a part of Jesse Fortune. She was, perhaps, the greatest diver he would ever coach. She was part of him now. The child he had never taken the time to have.

Jesse jumped out of the pool and hugged Coach Braden, soaking him. He didn't seem to notice. She regained her composure and went to the bench to wipe her face with her lucky towel. Looking over the towel, her eyes found the scoreboard:

10, 9.5, 10, 9.5, 10, 10, 9.5
Total this dive: 85.2

Total score for the day: 350.5. It was true. She had won.

A reporter for ESPN was already on his way to capture her for an interview for their coverage of the Games. She pulled Coach Braden into the interview with the sportscaster, and, while she answered questions, he stood like a proud papa, mumbling something that sounded to her like "Practice makes perfect."

Jesse stepped onto the first place position on the dais. Her friend Cindy stood to her left and took the bronze. Y Lan Sung accepted the silver medal and they all stood at attention as "The Star-Spangled Banner" was played. She struggled to fight back the tears of joy as she fantasized doing this same thing again at the Olympics. On an overwhelming high from the win, she promised herself she would train even harder for the ultimate contest in London.

As the anthem ended, Jesse congratulated Y Lan with a handshake, and Cindy with a hug. When she could, she pulled Cindy aside and said, "Tonight we're gonna celebrate. You and I are gonna find out what the Riviera is all about!"

"Mikel, Mikel . . . wait . . . I can't keep up the pace." Wolfgang Metter dragged his tired body in pursuit as Mikel

Rhen strutted into Cannes' prestigious Whiskey A Go Go. "I can't drink another drink, smoke another ah . . . joint, drive to another club, or 'observe' another beautiful woman."

"Sure you can," Mikel reassured his comrade confidently, without turning to face him. "Besides, you're already here. You don't have to—look at that!" Mikel motioned toward the bar area. Wolfgang's eyes followed Mikel's lead.

As she lifted her drink from the bar, a young brunette glanced at Mikel and, for a moment, they appraised each other.

"She's looking at you, Wolfgang. I think she likes you. This could be a lucky night for you."

"She's looking at you," Wolfgang whispered more than spoke, "and I don't need another lucky night. I'm tired."

They moved farther into the nightclub.

"Come on, Wolfgang. We'll just have one drink, then you can go to bed."

"I'm the one who has to get up in the morning, not you. You can sleep all day. I've got another conference—"

"Look at that," Mikel interrupted. Another beauty had found his attention. "I like this place. Don't you?"

"I wonder if we could sit down. My back is killing me from standing around all day."

"I thought bankers sat around all day. What's the matter, Wolfgang, won't your bank buy you a desk with a chair?"

"They won't buy me a portable one. I must have met a hundred other bankers today. And you've been keeping me out all night, every night."

"Poor baby. Don't expect any sympathy from me, *mon ami.* When you're done playing in the best nightclubs on the Riviera, you're going to go to sleep on one of the most beautiful thirty-five meter yachts on the Mediterranean. A yacht which you own; paid for by a bank which you own. Of course, you'll probably sleep alone if you don't wake-up!"

"I'm too tired to wake-up, Mikel. I'm going back to the *MARIE-CLAIRE* and get some sleep. You'll have to go on without me tonight."

The manager removed himself from a conversation with one of his waiters and presented himself to Mikel. *"Monsieur Rhen,* how are you tonight? May I show you and your friend to your usual booth?"

On his way to the booth, Mikel turned to watch his best friend leave the club. Before his eyes could be drawn away from the door, he noticed a young blonde woman pass Wolfgang on her way in. His eyes locked on her and held her. His masculine appetite was immediately aroused. Wolfgang may be satisfied with being alone tonight, he thought, but I am not.

He had seen this one before, somewhere. No, her picture had been in the afternoon newspaper. That was it, a sporting event. Yes, that was it.

Mikel Rhen had found what he was looking for . . . what he was always looking for. . . .

It was almost midnight when they converged on the Whiskey A Go Go. As they exited the taxi, they saw that the line to the club extended around the corner. There were at least three bouncers working the door.

Jesse had put on her cobalt blue velvet mini-dress: the only evening attire she had packed for this trip. Cindy wore a short red sheath dress that clung to every inch of her.

The amber glow from the street lamps cast a golden haze that filtered through their hair. The evening shadows highlighted the graceful strength of their bodies and the long smooth contours of their legs. Alone, either one of them would have collected her share of admiring glances.

Together, they were getting stares from all the men, and envious frowns from the women.

As they walked toward the end of the line, Jesse was intrigued by the chic neighborhood. The overflowing opulence spilled into, and effortlessly filled, the narrow street. Expensive apartments, each one boasting a wall of windows which overlooked the Mediterranean, stretched away from her in a broad sweep that followed the shoreline as far as she could see. Their balconies, laden with cascading, flowering vines, enclosed but did not hide the exquisite interiors of the rooms inside.

Mercedes, Porsches, Ferraris, and an occasional Rolls Royce were crammed—half on the street, half on the sidewalk—where their owners had carelessly parked them, in order to hurriedly secure a place in line.

The lighter, late night traffic wove its way slowly through the thin, compacted mosaic of people, parked cars, and luxurious dwellings, and Jesse wondered if "crowded and affluent" was a contradiction in terms.

"You know, if you went up to the door and showed some leg, you'd probably get us in a heck of a lot faster," Cindy teased.

"Really? Well if you're so brave, Lady Godiva, you do it. I'll hold your horse," Jesse teased back.

"Okay," Cindy said, smiling and spinning on her heels.

A bit stunned, Jesse watched Cindy's back sashay around the corner toward the entrance to the famed nightclub.

A few minutes later Cindy returned, still smiling, and grabbed Jesse's hand saying, "Okay, let's go."

"You got us in?"

"Come on. It's all arranged." Cindy began pulling Jesse toward the door, passing the other impatient hopefuls.

"How did you do it?"

"I told them that you're a celebrity; you just won a gold medal in the Pan European Games and you start training for

London tomorrow. At least, I think that's what I told them. Either that or I told them you were my anemic grandmother who's entering a monastery on Tuesday. Hey, my French may not be as good as yours, but it got us in!"

At the door, they were whisked into the lobby of the club by one of the enormous bouncers, who couldn't keep his eyes off Cindy.

"Is he a hunk or what?" she asked, winking at Jesse.

Lady Gaga's raspy voice, carried on waves of synthesized bass tones and oscillating guitar chords, rushed like a tide to surround them as they entered. They were immediately deluged with shafts of iridescent light flashing from all sides. A halo of silvery white lights was descending from the ceiling.

Jesse and Cindy delightedly accepted offers as every man in Cannes, or so it seemed, came forward to ask for the next dance . . . and the next . . . and the next. They were swept apart by their admirers, but finally drifted close enough to hear each other over the pulse of the music.

"I make it four in a row, but I may have missed one. Let's sit the next one out," Jesse yelled over Depeche Mode's, "World In My Eyes."

Cindy nodded agreement, and spotting a table, they politely brushed away the next two invitations in order to catch their breath.

Jesse took in the darkened nightclub. The walls were painted in deep and varied tones of marine blue. At the far end of the room, a painting filled the entire wall. Framed in bamboo, a naked Polynesian girl balanced on hands and knees, her breasts hanging at eye level. Her backside was provocatively arched as she pouted seductively at the clientele. Her skin had been done in varying shades of gray, and a dark gray lily adorned her black hair. She was surrounded by sand and rocks, and a metallic blue ocean added the color to her exotic island. A sleepy green palm tree completed the fresco. But it didn't end there. As Jesse looked more closely at the club's design, she noticed that the native girl had friends. Smaller paintings hung on the other walls, with other young island girls in equally suggestive positions. They were all outlined with fluorescent paint that caught the glow of the laser beams and black lights that bounced through the veil of smoky air on the crowded dance floor.

Cindy was also trying to absorb a bamboo framed illustration on the wall behind them. "I've never seen so many naked women in such blatant sexual positions in my life!" she finally coughed out. "I thought rich kids were supposed to have class."

"Are you kidding, Cindy, that's great art. We're in France, remember? What's wrong with you, Babe? Don't you know art?"

"I knew an Art once. He was a babe."

They were just getting started with the silly banter they enjoyed exchanging whenever they had a chance to go out together, when a waiter arrived with a champagne bucket, two stemmed crystal glasses, and a chilled bottle of Dom Perignon.

"*Qu'est-ce que c'est?*" Jesse asked, surprised.

In the frustrating way some French waiters have of elegantly ignoring their patrons, he began opening the champagne. As he filled their two glasses, his body movements reminded her of a magician she'd seen once. She did not acquiesce to his mildly contemptuous posture towards her by repeating her question. Nothing was going to spoil the best day, and night, she'd ever had.

"*C'est un cadeau de monsieur,*" he finally offered, motioning across the room. Then he turned away to wait on another table.

"What did he say, Jesse?" Cindy asked, unable to hear over the pulse of Rihanna's "Loud."

"I asked him what this was. He said it was a gift from the gentleman over there." Jesse gestured as nebulously as the waiter had.

"There are a hundred guys over there. Which one did he mean?"

"I'm not sure. He just kinda waved in that direction. But I've never had Dom Perignon before and I'm not going to let this opportunity go to waste. Want some?"

"Sure," Cindy laughed, reaching for the other glass.

The next gentleman to approach their table asked Jesse for a dance and admitted, after gentle questioning, that it was not he who had sent the wine. Neither was it the next man who asked Cindy to dance. They both politely refused the dances.

They sipped Champagne for the next half hour, and gave up on trying to identify the mystery man.

When the champagne was gone, the waiter materialized again, this time with a rose for each girl and a note for Jesse. As their pictures had been in all the papers, she didn't think it strange that someone might recognize them, but her curiosity was peaking as to whom it might be. She quickly scanned the club hoping that someone might be staring back at her waiting to be recognized. When that didn't happen, she opened the card, and over the blaring music, read it aloud to Cindy:

> *I would be most honored to be in your*
> *company. Please join me at my table.*
> *My waiter will accompany you.*
> *Mikel Rhen*

"*His* waiter? This guy must come here a *lot*!" Cindy chuckled. "What do you think? Should we go?"

"I don't know."

"What if he's a jerk?"

"Look around, Cindy girl. If he looks like ninety-five percent of the guys in this place, he's not a jerk."

"Yeah, you're right. I haven't seen one jerk in here tonight. All these guys are hot. I mean, this is great. So . . . are we going?"

"Okay, let's go for it! What have we got to lose?"

"Boy, that didn't take you long. You reached that decision in about the time it takes to fall from a ten meter platform."

"Am I going alone or are you coming with me?"

"Okay, but if he's a jerk, you're sitting with him, not me."

Jesse turned to the waiter, *"Allons-y, Monsieur!"*

Mikel Rhen's booth was among the best in the house, and his table was one of the few covered with a linen tablecloth. There was a candle flickering in the center. A bottle of Dom Perignon was chilling in a sterling silver champagne bucket to his left. He rose as the girls approached.

"Allow me to introduce myself. I am Mikel Rhen." He took each girl's hand and kissed it gently. He lingered on Jesse's hand and smiled.

She stared back into the light blue eyes peeking out from under his shoulder-length chestnut hair. His dark green Armani suit was impeccably matched with a powder-blue silk shirt, which, in the absence of a tie, was left with the first two buttons undone. His cologne was one she didn't recognize, but its essence emphasized his presence. His skin was the color of ivory, and he had that "little boy" quality about him. She was definitely impressed.

"Hello," was all she could get out. *Hello? Oh, brother. Why didn't I say enchanté . . . or at least, good evening? He probable thinks I'm a blonde bimbo.*

"Please sit down," Mikel offered, motioning to his table. "Please."

Jesse looked at Cindy. Cindy looked back at Jesse and glided into the middle of the crushed velvet, semi-circular booth. Jesse slid in next to Cindy.

As he sat down next to her, Mikel placed his left hand over Jesse's right, which was resting in her lap. Politely, he offered Cindy champagne and commented on her dress.

Jesse was surprised by his almost too familiar action, but she was curious enough about him to allow it. She left her hand resting passively under his as he poured champagne in her glass.

Then he filled his own glass.

She waited until he had placed the wine bottle back in its bucket, and then she said, "Great, three glasses with one hand and you didn't spill a drop!"

She immediately regretted having opened her mouth. Hearing the words ring in her head, she realized how inane they must have sounded. *Beautiful, Jesse. Just beautiful! Now he probably thinks I'm a dumb, blonde bimbo!*

Mikel laughed politely. He raised his glass, "*A votre santé.*"

"*Salut,*" she responded to his toast.

"*Ah, vous parlez français?*" he questioned hopefully.

"*Oui, je le parle un peu, et mon amie aussi,*" Jesse admitted humbly that she and Cindy could both speak French. She noticed his favorable reaction, and relaxed with the thought that she might have finally said something that didn't sound stupid. Maybe the tide was turning.

"*Formidable!*" he grinned, grateful for the opportunity to switch from English to French, with which he was more comfortable.

For the next few minutes, Mikel tried to make Cindy feel like she was the most important girl on earth. He asked her about her career, her schooling, and how she found Monaco, but he continued holding Jesse's hand.

The concepts of time and space seemed to evaporate as Mikel's sexy voice, mixed with that of Luciana and the prized French champagne, mesmerized her. In his corner of the club, the music was less intrusive and he spoke easily in French, occasionally slipping in an English word or phrase for emphasis.

"You know, Mikel, I don't understand half of what you're saying . . ." Cindy finally admitted, ". . . my French isn't as good as Jesse's. But, if it means something half as nice as the way it sounds . . . I'm impressed!" They all chuckled.

"I've noticed, Mikel, that when you speak French, you have a slight . . . and charming accent," Jesse said. Glancing down at his hand holding hers, she noticed he wore no jewelry.

"I'm Swiss. That's what you hear . . . I'm sure." His eyes took on a strange intensity that Jesse couldn't read.

Somewhere deep inside, she felt the echo of a chill. She took a deep breath and the feeling passed almost unnoticed. Swiss, she thought, that's it.

"Your French is very good, Jesse Fortune," he said, and his eyes returned to their sexy gentleness, "much better than most Americans."

The way he said "Americans" had a slight edge to it, and she thought of the waiter who had served them earlier.

"I've studied French most of my life. I have a degree in it. I'm hoping to teach it at one of the colleges in California after my diving career."

"Cindy noticed Mikel's interest start to hone in on Jesse, and although she was delighted for her best friend, she was beginning to feel like a third wheel. As she sat prominently in the middle of the booth, she realized that Mikel's table was just enough out of the way so that no one came over to ask her to dance. To make matters worse, Mikel's voice had softened and Cindy was lost to most of the conversation.

"*Tes cheveaux sont comme de l'or filé*," he said, smiling at Jesse.

"What did he say?" Cindy asked, almost interested.

"He said my hair is like spun gold." Jesse could do nothing but stare into Mikel's sexy eyes.

"Are you kidding me?" Cindy chirped, her interest renewed. "What a line—gees!"

Encouraged by the fact that Jesse's eyes had met and held his, Mikel continued. "*Je vous ai regardé dancer, et j'étais captivé par votre corps.*"

"Okay, I'm hooked, now what did he say?" Cindy was more than hooked. She was completely captured watching the exchange of electricity between Jesse and Mikel. He was obviously making his move on her, and Cindy wouldn't have missed this for anything. As far as she was concerned, this was better than Will and Kate. To hell with dancing!

Without taking her eyes from Mikel, Jesse spoke just loud enough so that Cindy could hear her over the music. "He said, 'I watched you dance and was enthralled with your body.'"

"Are you kidding?" All Cindy could do was stare at Jesse with her mouth open. "I'm outta here. Somebody ask me to dance," she yelled to the nightclub at large.

"*Je vous désire*, Jesse Fortune."

"Don't tell me!" Cindy cried, "I'm sure I don't want to know what *that* was." In fact, Cindy knew enough French to know exactly what Mikel had said. "Excuse me, kids, I've got to use the Ladies—sorry, the Mademoiselle's room."

Jesse had held Mikel's eyes through the entire exchange. She was proud of herself. This was definitely her day for challenges. And so far, she had met every one. She allowed her gaze to drift to Cindy and she smiled lazily at her friend.

"You're gone," Cindy said as a final comment on Jesse's condition. "And I'm gone too. I'll be back in a moment." She went off to find the restroom.

When Cindy returned, she was dragging with her the well-muscled bouncer who had admitted them. "I'm gonna dance, kids. Then, 'The Hulk' here, is gonna give me a lift back to the hotel. I'll see you there, Jesse."

The waiter brought another bottle of Dom Perignon, and Mikel sent him away with a request for the disk jockey to play a slow song. When the music started, he pulled Jesse out of the booth.

On the dance floor, he drew her to him and she felt the strength in his lean body.

She couldn't believe herself. She hadn't known this man for more than a couple of hours. How many hours was it? She couldn't think. She was light-headed. It must be the champagne, she thought. She relaxed into Mikel and let herself be swayed by the motion his body made to the rhythm of the music. He was doing everything right. He was polite and handsome and sexy . . . and she was falling for a guy she'd only met a few hours ago! She leaned her head back and looked at him. He smiled at her. She put her head back on his shoulder.

As the slow song faded away, and a new pulse was immediately picked up by a bass drum, she looked at her watch. Her Cinderella time was almost up. "Mikel . . ."

"What is it, Jesse Fortune? What can I do for you?"

She started to answer and he kissed her to silence her. His lips were warm. They pressed her words back into her mouth. She pulled back and looked at him.

"Mikel, this has been one of the most wonderful nights of my life. But, it's getting late. I should go. Coach will be worried."

"Your head is too beautiful to be filled with such worried thoughts, *Cherie.* You're safe with me."

"I've got to go." She wanted to stay, but she knew she couldn't. She wanted to stand right here in the middle of the dance floor, with all the other dancers bobbing and weaving around her, and slowly sway back and forth with Mikel. She wanted to put her hands on his chest, bury her face in that place between his shoulder and his jaw, and let his strong arms hold her. But it was just too late. "I've got to go," she repeated.

"Come, if you're so worried, we'll go." He sounded almost angry.

"Please, Mikel, don't be angry. It's late and I'm tired. It's been a wonderful evening."

He stiffened at her gentle appeal, and she realized he didn't like pursuing anyone's plans but his own.

"You know something?" she continued, "I don't think I've ever met anyone like you. You make me feel like a princess. And you haven't pushed me to do anything I don't want to do."

Her calm words and genuine smile seemed to soften him. She took his arm and moved him to the door.

Outside, Mikel guided Jesse toward his Alpine white Porsche Cabriolet. He opened the door and held it for her.

The conversation was light on the drive to the hotel. He offered to take her sightseeing each day for the duration of her stay. She told him that the team would be here for two more weeks training for the upcoming competition in Paris. He offered to fill every minute of the time she would have to herself.

At the hotel entrance he said, "I will kiss you goodnight." It sounded like a demand. Without waiting for a response, he pulled her to him and put his lips on hers.

After the kiss he whispered, "*À demain,* Jesse Fortune. "

"Until tomorrow," she repeated quietly.

She felt as if she were moving through clouds as she entered the hotel lobby.

Cindy was standing by the concierge desk, waiting for her. She had seen the goodnight kiss. "He's so hot!" Her voice was like a quiet explosion. "And a Porsche, too!"

"Tonight was great," Jesse offered to no one in particular.

"Yeah! Watching you guys was better than the movies on that German channel in my room," Cindy teased.

"Cindy, I've just had the best night of my life." Jesse smiled and started for the elevator.

"I mean it, Jesse. You guys are like Ken and Barbie or something. You look great together. Are you gonna see him again?"

"I don't know," was the only answer she ventured.

In her room and under crisp white sheets, Jesse thought about Mikel Rhen and the strange hold he already had on her. It must have been the champagne. Yes, it was definitely the Dom Perignon. She wondered why she hadn't met him sooner. Silly, she thought, where would I have met him before tonight? She realized she knew nothing about him. They had talked all night and she didn't even know what he did, or where he lived, or where he came from. Switzerland. Funny, she thought as she lazily wandered through the images of the evening, his accent was definitely Swiss, but there was a hint of something else. The Middle East? She fell asleep thinking of his baby blue eyes, his little-boy smile, and his sexy, "Swiss-accented" voice. . . .

5

PARIS, FRANCE

Paris . . . Electrifying . . . Mystical. Paris: flirting and intimate, brash and impulsive, reserved and reckless. Paris, fantastique!

They had entered the city shortly after dusk and Jesse's senses had come alive with the excitement of first impressions as she noticed, looming in the distance, the gigantic Arc de Triomphe sitting majestically in its circular throne. The trees on either side of the broad boulevard twinkled with thousands of tiny, starry lights, and an endless row of cars wove its way between the Place de la Concorde and the Place de l'Etoile, like a chain of comets passing through a satin-smooth, concrete galaxy.

She had felt a little strange telling Coach that she wouldn't be traveling with him, that Mikel was going to drive her. She had felt even more strange when he didn't reply, but simply walked away to round up Cindy for the ride to the train station. But the uncomfortable feelings were soon lost to the polished European highway and Mikel's clever conversation.

Mikel had promised her the grand tour: a long walk along the fashionable Avenue des Champs-Elysées, a look at the wealth of art in the Musée du Louvre, and a visit to the Cathédral Notre Dame. He had pledged they would sail toy boats in the pool in the Jardin des Tuileries. He had also vowed there were many boites where they could dance all night.

Deciding dinner could wait no longer, Mikel had parked the car and they had strolled arm in arm down the boulevard in search of the perfect café. Because of her childlike excitement, Mikel had allowed Jesse to pick the place, and she had pulled him playfully through the door of the first restaurant she discovered.

Inside, well-groomed tuxedo-clad waiters, with trays raised pompously high, flew about using bat-like radar to keep from colliding with each other. The air was thick with sizzling and sautéing and the polite clinking of seasoned silverware on oversized china plates. But their table, in the corner of the room, seemed cozy enough to concentrate on a lover's conversation.

"What? You're crazy!" Jesse's voice was louder than she meant it to be, but she ignored the glances her outburst collected from the otherwise contented clientele of the tiny restaurant.

"I want you to marry me," Mikel said for the second time.

Although he was smiling, his voice was stern and impatient. He was demanding again. It was the one thing she didn't appreciate about him.

He noticed her negative reaction and his smile broadened into his little boy grin.

She relaxed. It was difficult trying to remain serious when he got that grin. He could be like a small child at times, and she loved him that way. He seemed so carefree and charming. She just wanted to hug him and be carefree with him. She wanted to run away with him like the girl in Peter Pan. What was her name? Wendy, that's it . . . Wendy Darling.

"Please, Jesse, we should get married." He leaned across the table to emphasize his plea. His eyes caught the glow of the single candle on their table, and each eye reflected the flame. Jesse couldn't help but think of a Halloween pumpkin with burning candles inside. She tried not to laugh, knowing that Mikel wouldn't understand her silly thought, and his feelings might be hurt. She smiled brightly.

Mikel took her smile to be an acceptance of his proposal and he was encouraged. "We can get married tomorrow!"

"We can't get married tomorrow. I'm diving tomorrow, remember? Besides, shouldn't we know a little more about each other first?" She stared into his eyes, looking for the conviction to make what might be wrong into something she wanted to be right.

"What more do two people need to know than they're in love?" he asked.

She had to admit that the past two weeks had been the most memorable of her life. Her days had been filled with rigorous workouts, preparing her for the competition here in France, but he had occupied all of her free time.

He had arrived at the end of each workout with a gift for her; flowers or some other small item he had purchased at one of the street vendors in Monaco.

When she had confessed that her blue mini dress was the only fancy outfit she had brought along, he had parked the Porsche in front of an expensive boutique and had purchased four stunning evening dresses for her. She had hesitated wearing them, but soon acquiesced to his urging.

When she had mentioned that money seemed no object to him, he had told her simply that he had a rich uncle and she shouldn't worry about such trivial things. Still, she had felt guilty accepting all the gifts.

He had taken her to a gourmet restaurant each night, where his reservation would be waiting, along with a chilled bottle of Dom Perignon.

They had ended every night at a nightclub, dancing.

"You know I love you," he said.

She looked across the table and smiled, but said nothing.

"And besides, we haven't been alone the whole two weeks we've been together. I want to show you how much I love you. I want to touch you . . . and I want you to touch me. I want you, Jesse Fortune."

There it was again. His desire. His need. On one hand she was flattered, and because she wanted him as well, pleased. On the other hand, maybe some of what Coach had said was true.

"He only wants in your pants," Coach had mumbled in disgust.

"You don't mean that," she had responded, surprised that they were suddenly discussing her private life. But she knew he did mean it. Coach never said anything he didn't mean.

"Why are you saying that?" she had pressed. When he hadn't answered, she had followed him around the pool pushing him for a reason.

Then Coach Braden had erupted, "If he really cared about you, he wouldn't keep you out all night. Look at you. You're tired. You're tired and we're only halfway through the workout. This is your shot, Babe . . . your only shot. You're twenty-two, remember? There won't be a next time for you. It's now or never. He's letting you blow it. Hell, he's making you blow it. If he cared about you, he'd want you to win. Damn it, Jesse, he just wants in your pants. Can't you see that?"

Braden had regretted every word of his outpour. Unable to stop himself, he had continued to the bitter end. He had believed everything he had said, but he couldn't look her in the eyes. He had stared down at his shoes.

Jesse had been devastated. They had never argued before. Never. She had quickly walked away from the pool with an ache in her stomach. She had thrown-up in the locker room toilet.

"Marry me, Jesse." Mikel's plea pulled her back to the dinner they were sharing.

"Mikel, you could have any girl you want—"

"Except Jesse Fortune," he interrupted.

"I don't know. . . ."

"You know that I love you and will cherish you until the day you die?" He reached across the table and took her hand in his.

"I'm sorry, Mikel, I can't concentrate. This is too much to think about. With the competition and everything . . . I should be thinking about my diving—"

"Is there a rule that says married women can't compete?" he asked, kissing the ring finger of her hand. "Say you will, and stay with me tonight to seal our promise to each other." He turned her hand over and kissed her palm.

"If we're going to get married, we can wait until after the ceremony."

"Then we will marry tomorrow!"

"Wait a minute, Mikel," Jesse laughed. "I know this sounds old-fashioned, but I really think I owe it to my folks to include them. And I should do it in person."

"All right," he said, sounding frustrated. He recovered quickly. "That's what I love about you, *Cherie*, your old-fashioned ways. If you need to be with your parents, I'll send you. But only for a week. I can't do without you for more than that. I'll book you a round-trip ticket on Air France tomorrow. After the competition, you can go home."

"We could get married in Monaco, where we met . . ." Jesse's thoughts wondered into the candlelight between them.

"Of course, *Cherie*," Mikel filled himself with her agreement. "Now, shall we dance?"

"Not tonight," she insisted. "I wish we could stay here forever . . . it's so romantic. But I'm late again and I told Coach I'd be in early tonight."

Frustrated once more, Mikel's lips touched her hand. "As you wish, Jesse Fortune. I'll take you back to the hotel."

Outside the hotel, Jesse caught a glimpse of Coach through the large glass doors. He was sitting in the lobby, probably waiting for her.

"Oh boy, I'd better say goodnight here," she said turning towards Mikel.

He put his hand on the back of her head and pushed her lips to his. He held her there. He wasn't going to be rushed by some old American coach. He grabbed her breast.

She pushed back from him, gently removing his hand. "Patience, Mikel. I've still got a meet to concentrate on. After the wedding, remember?" She got out of the car.

At the hotel door, Jesse heard her fiancé call after her. "*À demain*, Jesse Fortune."

She didn't notice that as the Porsche engine idled, Mikel relaxed into the seat and smiled to himself. He enjoyed the fact that he had kept the coach waiting.

Belle De La Nuit.

She was very tall. And dressed only in her spike-heels, her legs seemed to stretch the full length of the bed.

"Keep your high heels on," he said, standing over her.

She's twenty-two, he thought, the same age as Jesse Fortune. But they are so different. This woman is pliable, controllable, and luxuriously easy. Why couldn't Jesse Fortune be like that?

Her shoulder-length, mahogany-colored hair was straight, shiny, and silky to the touch. Her tanned skin was baby-soft and incredibly smooth over the tight, exercised muscles of her ass. Her eyes were an intriguing crystalline blue. They sparkled when she came, he remembered.

She had painted the brightest pink colors on her eyelids and cheeks. She didn't look painted, he decided. She looked like a cover girl come to life.

Her lips were large and pouting, and she could deep throat, he reminisced.

She was round in all the right places, and flat in all the right places. But her lips were his favorite part. She always looked like she was giving someone a blow job.

"Did you know they call you *Belle De La Nuit?*" he asked, touching her thigh just above the knee.

"Beauty of the night," she repeated, amused. She stretched and took a breath, and the erect, deep brown nipples on her white breasts pointed to the ceiling.

The soft scent of Joy perfume filled his nostrils as he kissed her everywhere. Then he lay back to watch her.

"I didn't expect to see you tonight, Mikel," she said. Not waiting for a response, she put her lips against his almost hairless thigh and allowed the warm breath from her throat to touch his skin.

"She wants to wait," he said, leaning up to look at the space between her breasts. "She's not like you; she wants to wait."

"Wait for what, Mikel?" She took him into her mouth and began sucking gently and moaning softly.

The faint sound of her moan touched his ears and his erection stiffened and throbbed.

"Wait until after the wedding," he tried to say, but the words had to struggle through his gasps.

She released him. "You're going to marry her, Mikel?" she asked, then put him in her mouth again. Her head bobbed up and down as she established a slow rhythm.

Lost in pleasure, he couldn't answer.

She took him out of her mouth and caressed him with her hands. Then she slipped her mouth back over him. When he cried out excitely, she repeated the action several more times. Then she rubbed him between her breasts.

"I don't think I've ever seen you this hard, Mikel."

"She won't give in to my needs." He groaned with the ecstasy of what she was doing to him.

"Perhaps she's a virgin."

"I doubt it," he said, studying the firmness of her breasts again. "She's your age, *Ma Belle*. No, it's just a game she wants to play. 'Wait till *after* we're married.' I couldn't talk her out of it."

"I'm surprised, Mikel. You can be very persuasive." Once more, she put him in her mouth and then she slipped him down her throat.

"Oh, that's it! Yes . . . that's it. . . . I'm coming . . . I'm coming!"

Belle De La Nuit. It was said that she was the most expensive prostitute in France. He didn't mind; she was worth it.

"You do that so well, *Cherie*. I must remember to come to Paris after the honeymoon."

"I'll be here, Mikel . . . whenever you call."

SHIT! Jesse was in trouble from the moment her feet left the platform. *SHIT!* she thought again on the way down. It was a bad dive, lazy and tired. The discipline was gone. Her body wasn't doing what she told it to do.

Under the water, she closed her eyes and thought *SHIT!* one more time. She wanted to stay under the water.

I'll just have to do better on the next one. She began making promises to herself as an encouragement to surface.

Braden was waiting at the ladder when she arrived. He walked her to the bench, talking to her as she wiped her face with her lucky towel.

"Okay, Jesse, you've got to get more height from the spring. Reach higher before you go into the tuck. You came out too soon. You're overextending on your descent. Your legs are breaking a bit in the hurdle. Come on, Kid, concentrate."

"Okay, Coach," she said, more mad at herself than anything else. "I'll do better on the next one."

But she didn't do any better on the second dive, or the third. It wasn't until the fourth round that she even broke into the 9's.

With the exception of Coach Braden, no one paid more attention to Jesse's slow start than Y Lan Sung. She had been in top form from the moment she set foot on the diving platform. Her dives were tighter and more graceful than they had been in Monaco. She was on. And Jesse was off. Definitely off.

Braden noticed Jesse's eyes drift to the Chinese diver. "She's gonna be hard to beat this time. You're not only gonna have to have six perfect dives to beat Y Lan; you're gonna have to go some to even catch up to Cindy."

"I know," she agreed, frustrated. She covered her face with the towel.

"Where's your concentration? Even I can tell your mind's somewhere else. You gotta get it back, Kid. There's no time for daydreaming. If it's that two-bit playboy you've been going out with—he's gonna ruin your chance for a win."

"I'm just having a bad day, Coach. It's got nothing to do with him."

"I'll tell you why you're having a bad day. You've been knocking off practice early and staying out late. But this is neither the time nor the place to discuss it. Can we get back to diving, please?"

"Okay—okay!"

Her next dive was better, but not good enough to beat Y Lan Sung or even Cindy.

The competition seemed to drag on and on as she labored with every part of what she had been trained to do. There were no gifts. Nothing came easy. The edge eluded her and she fought for each small gain in her score. She watched Y Lan Sung's scores accelerate with the completion of each flawless dive.

The tournament seemed to wave and shimmer before her tired eyes, like a mirage melting into the warm Paris afternoon, and her performance improved only enough to give her a third place position. With the bronze medal around her neck, she stood on the dais while the Chinese National Anthem was played.

Before the anthem ended, she began making promises to herself.

After the wedding, she would practice twice as hard. She could get it back. She could still be the best.

After the wedding, Mikel would have to wait. He would have to understand. He would have to be patient.

After the wedding. . . .

6

RHINE FALLS, SWITZERLAND

"I have to kill you, Mikki. I am sorry, but your obsession with Jesse Fortune is ruining my plan. You have to die."

"What about her?"

"Yes, she has to die, too."

"But why, Uncle? She can't hurt you."

"When you told me that you were going to marry her, whether I liked it or not, I thought you had lost your mind . . . or at least, stopped caring about what we've created here and what we're doing with it. But I've come to understand that you can't help yourself. You need to have her, control her, dominate her. It's become an obsession with you, Mikki, and it has the potential to ruin all our hard work. That's when I realized you had to die. It's my fault really. I have spoiled you too much.

"And Jesse Fortune?"

"You definitely put me to the test, Mikki. But that's the best part. I realized we can use her death to our advantage."

"Can we kill her after the wedding?"

"I was going to change you back to yourself after we disposed of Wolfgang. Now I'll just have to kill you. You have chosen to make yourself a public spectacle by marrying a somewhat famous sports personality. You chose not to consult me on this. Tell me, Mikki, did you consider what a wife would do to our plan? A continual loose end. And how long could you stay married to her before she found out what you really do? That is something we cannot afford. We need an accident. Yes, a very tragic accident."

"I don't understand why we both can't die after the wedding night."

"Listen, Mikki, and learn. We have been contracted by our Colombian associates to do a job. We will not jeopardize our objectives with such trivial complications."

"But she's going back to America after the honeymoon. She has things to do. I could leave her there until we're finished. I could even shorten the honeymoon. She'd never know anything."

"What makes this one so different from all the other female companions you have enjoyed so foolishly during your lifetime?"

"I want her, Uncle. Jesse Fortune will never be a problem, I promise you."

"Well then take her, Mikki. But don't waste time."

"I can't have her that way."

"Regrettably, Mikki, you will be unable to have her at all. But she can be of considerable use to both of us. Her death would be of much greater interest to the international press than yours. Mikel Rhen will conveniently slip away under the shadows of Jesse Fortune's accidental demise. You will need a new face though, after Wolfgang's . . . yes, a new face. You can never be Mikel again."

"We could do it after the honeymoon. There's time. I could take her to the cabin at Rhine Falls. A hunting accident. What about a hunting accident, Uncle?"

"Mikki . . . Mikki . . . think. How are you both going to die in a hunting accident? Shoot each other by mistake? No. Leave the planning to me. It has always worked better that way. This is the job we have been waiting for, Mikki. This one contract will be more lucrative than anything we have done up to this point. And more challenging."

"Those damn South Americans. What do they know? They can wait. You can tell them to wait, Uncle. It would only be a short delay—"

"Timing is everything, Mikki. Obviously, you will have to decide. Do you want this American girl, or do you want the prosperity this contract offers? You have become very accustomed to the good life: your Porsche, your nice clothes, and your jet-set lifestyle. Are you prepared to give all that up? I do not think so. After this contract, you can have any woman you want. Every woman you want! Now, when are we going to execute this wedding? The day, Mikki, I want the day."

"The eleventh, Uncle. She's in America now—"

"Our little bride will have a wonderful send off. I will take care of all the arrangements. Do I make myself clear, Mikki? Mikki . . . ?"

"Yes, Uncle."

7

MONACO-VILLE, MONACO
Late Summer 2011

Jesse couldn't believe it was over. She had followed along in French, as the justice had spoken the words, and within a matter of minutes, her life had changed forever. She had married Mikel Rhen.

According to French custom, they had only completed half of the process. What remained, after the civil ceremony at the *Mairie* in the old section of the principality, was a short walk to the Cathedral, where a priest would perform the religious ceremony.

She looked down at her engagement ring. It was the most beautiful diamond she had ever seen. It was large, and yet, it wasn't gaudy. In fact, she thought, it looked like she felt at this moment, fragile. Mikel had given her the ring the day she had left for her week in California.

Jack Fortune had spent the entire week trying to make his daughter see the light. He had held on, mechanically at times, to the argument that she was throwing her career, and perhaps her entire life away, "for some joker in Europe who just wants to have sex with you."

"We're not doing that, Dad," she had countered in frustration, but the argument was on and she knew he had not won his legal cases by giving up easily. He still saw her as his little girl and would do his best to protect her.

"What does he do for a living?"

She had known he would ask that, but she had still hoped it would never come up.

"Does he *do* anything?"

"He doesn't have to do anything, his family is wealthy." She had known, even as the words escaped from her mouth, that he would never be appeased with that kind of statement. Jack Fortune believed strongly that it was what a man did, and not what he had, that made a man what he was.

"Family? What family? You said there was only an uncle that you haven't even met. He was not about to let her off the hook.

"It's gonna be all right, Dad, you'll see. You're gonna like Mikel," was Jesse's soft reply. How could her love for one man cause so much pain to the other? It was difficult to fight back the tears, so she had turned away, not wanting her father to see any weakness.

Ruth Fortune had come to her daughter's defense. "I'm sure your father and I will grow to love him as much as you do, Jesse. You know . . . if we only knew more about him—"

"Jesse, you're right in the middle of a European tour. At your first meet, you won the gold. Then you started going out with this 'Mr. Suave' character and your diving went to hell. You only got the bronze in Paris. Then you fly home with some harebrained idea that you want to get married. What does Coach Braden think?" Jack had continued unmercifully. "He's been right there with you. He's met this guy. He must have an opinion."

Jesse had shuddered remembering Coach Braden's reaction to Mikel. And another feeling had started to grow inside. Somewhere deep in her being, a voice had called to her—an alarm, warning her. If it was right about Mikel, then she was making an incredible mistake. She had tried to ignore the voice. These new thoughts only complicated the already strained atmosphere. On any other occasion, she would have listened to the two men she loved most in the world. But now, she had an argument to win.

The wedding procession dutifully made its way along the *Rue Sainte-Dévote* towards the Cathedral on *Avenue Saint-Martin*. Jesse tried to still her uncertainties by absorbing the ambience of the moment. The off-white buildings with their red tile roofs mounted the jagged slopes on their way to the Alps. The sunlight, reflecting off each stone-faceted structure, created the sparkling effect of precious gems.

A slight sea breeze delicately brushed the veil back from her face and gently rustled the ruffles of her dress, causing her to glance out onto the sea. It was a pool of liquid sapphires. The clean, sweet aroma of flowers, lightly sprayed with a salted mist, permeated the early afternoon air.

Mikel stopped abruptly and took her in his arms and kissed her. His stop was so sudden that the others almost bumped into them. Passersby on the street applauded the romantic couple, but Jesse could see that her father disapproved of the silly maneuver.

Now that Jack Fortune had met Mikel, he liked him even less. He found Mikel to be immature and spoiled, and not the kind of man he had hoped his only daughter would marry.

Embarrassed, Jesse wriggled free of her bridegroom's grasp and urged him to continue walking down the street.

The procession reached the ancient Cathedral and began to climb the worn, granite steps. When Jesse got to the top, she turned to greet each member of the incongruent group.

Her ever-supportive mother, immediately behind her, gave her a reassuring smile and a gentle hug.

Following closely on her heels, Jack Fortune kept climbing until he was face to face with his daughter. He took her hand in his and pulled her even closer, making sure Mikel would not be privileged to his words. As if giving her a kiss on the cheek, he whispered into her ear, "You don't have to go through with this, you know. Just say the word, Baby Doll, and we can all go home. It's not too late."

"Come on, Jack," Ruth Fortune tugged on her husband's arm, "this is a happy occasion, Dear."

Chris danced up the stairs. "When I told you to get a great looking guy, I didn't mean for life!"

Jesse's smile faded.

"Hey, it's a joke. Lighten up, Jess." He laughed as he followed his parents into the sanctuary.

Unimpressed by the ceremony, Coach Braden had wandered along with the procession. His opinion, that she was blowing her final chance for a gold medal at the Olympics, was obvious by his posture. She smiled brightly, although she knew he had not changed his mind about Mikel. As he passed, without looking at her, he spoke the single word, "Bronze," and shook his head.

She didn't need the reminder. Paris was behind her now. She would do better in London.

Cindy, with the customary bounce in her step, was next up the stairs. With her usual wide-eyed and bubbly demeanor, she grabbed Jesse's arm and said loudly, "Don't forget, I was the one who told you what a hunk he is!" She reached up and gave Mikel a kiss on the cheek, before scurrying into the sanctuary.

Wolfgang Metter was the best man. He took Jesse's hand in his and smiled at her. Not letting go of her hand, he said to his friend, "Mikel, you scoundrel, you don't deserve this beautiful lady."

Blushing slightly, Jesse smiled and looked to Mikel for his reaction. Mikel smiled, but said nothing.

Dr. Amir Hassasi was last. Mikel's uncle seemed gracious and polite, and also preoccupied with some distant thought. So far, Jesse had found him to be quite unemotional. It wasn't that he disliked her; it was as if he didn't feel anything for her at all.

"Come on, Uncle Amir," Jesse smiled, grabbing his arm to help him up the last step.

He stiffened. Then he relaxed and stared at her. His large eyes searched her face for a moment. His expression gave no indication of his thoughts. Finally, with the least amount of smile possible, "Thank you," was all he said.

Oh well, I'm marring the man, not his family. Jesse tried to reassure herself, but deep inside, she heard that voice again. She was making a mistake. She banished the unwanted thought from her mind as she watched the last of her party go inside.

In the narthex, the abrupt contrast between the brilliant daylight of the bright Monegasque afternoon and the reverent darkness of the massive stone church blinded Jesse for a moment, and she held tight to Mikel for guidance.

The musty odor of centuries of saints hung heavy in the air, and reminded her of the dust in her grandmother's attic, where long ago, she had explored a trunk of family treasures on a sleepy, summer afternoon.

When her eyes adjusted, she saw great beams of sunlight falling through the leaded, stained glass windows, composing colors throughout the fifteenth century Cathedral, and illuminating the sanctuary with the warm aura of glowing embers.

Mikel led her up the center isle as their guests filed into the old wooden pews at the front of the grand altar.

The priest had Mikel and Jesse kneel at the altar railing, and he performed the Holy Sacrament of Marriage.

Mikel pushed Jesse's veil aside and stared at her lips. Then he kissed her intensely.

Jesse felt her own warm tears on her cheeks. She wasn't sure if they were there to release the tension of the moment, or because she had truly done something wrong by marrying Mikel. She dispelled the latter from her mind and promised herself never to think of it again. She allowed her thoughts to be swept away by Mikel's kiss.

Cindy shrieked and clapped as the kiss ended. Unaware that she was the only one applauding, she grabbed Wolfgang Metter's upper arm and effervesced, "Oh, isn't this romantic? I just love weddings."

Metter smiled appropriately and adjusted his antique, wire-rimmed spectacles to a more comfortable position on his nose.

As he took in the happy couple, Chris unbuttoned the jacket of the only suit he owned. Jesse had told him that he looked older and more mature when he dressed up, but he still felt uncomfortable doing it.

Uncle Amir stood and addressed the intimate audience, "We will continue at the *Restaurant L'Orange.*" He had reserved, in total, the restaurant on the *Place de Carmes,* for their luncheon.

As the afternoon progressed, the wedding cake was brought in, and the final toast was made to the bride and groom. Mikel intertwined his arm with Jesse's, and they smiled at each other across the rims of their champagne glasses.

Claiming tradition, Mikel took his glass and threw it into the old stone fireplace. He smiled at her. She followed suit, throwing her glass after his. Uncle Amir was next, and each person, in turn, added his or her offering to the crystal fire.

Amir excused himself for a moment, but did not return to the reception.

Mikel seemed nervous around Jesse's family. To Cindy's chagrin, he garnered Metter for a private chat in one corner of the restaurant, but kept his eyes on his new bride.

Jesse moved easily from one guest to another, graciously accepting any salutary offerings in the quiet conversations. When she got to her mother, and was in the embrace of a goodbye hug, she began to feel a little dizzy.

Moving to support her, Mikel said, "It's only the champagne."

They began their goodbyes.

On the way to his Porsche, Jesse continued to feel light-headed and she stumbled.

Mikel caught her before she could fall and steadied her. He turned back to address the guests. "Too much champagne, I fear," he smiled.

After helping Jesse with her seat belt, Mikel got behind the wheel and they sped off down the road.

Darkness followed them.

Amir Hassasi had found the perfect curve in the road on the *Av. de la Liberté*. Three kilometers from where the wedding had taken place, he had taken a sledge hammer to a portion of the old stone wall that would have prevented the Porsche from going off the road. He had dressed in a stolen police uniform, and established a roadblock: telling the few motorists who were out that there had been an accident which had obstructed the provincial roadway.

By the time the newlyweds arrived at the scene, the drug in Jesse's champagne had done its work. Her eyes had closed and she had no wish to open them. She was awake but she was on the edge of unconsciousness, with no will to balance herself.

The car stopped.

Half in and half out of the dazed state, she thought she felt someone unbuckle her seat belt. She heard a voice, but couldn't remember whose voice it was.

"Get the ring, Mikki."

She felt a rough tug on her finger, but she couldn't open her eyes.

The car started moving again.

The Porsche convertible gathered speed as it headed for the turn it couldn't possibly make by itself. Then, as if it had finally found the wings Dr. Porsche might have envisioned when he designed his masterpiece, it flew into the Mediterranean night.

It was a wonderful feeling. *Flying car . . . magic . . . .* The ocean breeze had a salty smell . . . like the pool. *Magic pool . . . .* The wind rushed past her like it did when she was diving. *Diving.* She felt herself falling downward. Down toward the water. *Let's see now, eleva . . . execu . . . concentrate! Got to get this just right.*

She managed to open her eyes to focus on the target spot, but she couldn't find it.

She felt herself separate from what seemed like another, heavier body; a body that was propelling her faster toward the water.

She sprang up and out and reached, instinctively, to hit the surface head first, elbows straight, hands locked. Her mind screamed at her legs to straighten out, but they wouldn't obey. *This is bad . . . won't score much. . . .*

She smiled at the jagged rocks that were charging toward her. *Best day of my life . . . Mikel—*

Thunder slapped her ears. A cold wet chill smashed her head and scraped along her upper body. There was a dull, penetrating, sickening stab of pain at the base of her spine.

Then everything was quiet and calm and black.

8

BELOW AV. DE LA LIBERTE
CAP ROUX, FRANCE

"J'adore tes seins, ma petite," François mumbled, putting his lips where his hands had been on the soft, perfumed breasts he was admiring. He couldn't decide which shapely mound to caress first. As he leaned her against the only smooth rock of the cliff face he could find, he felt a tightness in his pants. He wasn't sure how much longer he could wait. The time was now. He had planned well. Everything was perfect.

The night was perfect, warm and balmy. The sea was calm and small waves, lapping up onto the pebbled shore, made a rhythmic sound to accompany the slow stroking of his body against hers.

The place was perfect. They had parked his *moto* off the road under some bushes by a little *piste*. With François carrying the blanket, they had tripped and slid down the narrow access path to a spot where he believed they would be undisturbed. His "private beach" was a thin sliver of pebbles that escaped below the cliffs of the French Riviera. It was invisible from the main road leading to Monaco, and in its time, had been missed by everyone from the Romans and Phoenicians as they stood on the decks of their lateen-rigged ships, to the few renegade tourists that ventured this far from their hotels on rented jet skis.

And the girl was perfect. Her body was warm and silky and she had great breasts . . . large and firm. François felt another wave of excitement surge through him. He pushed hard onto her. He knew she could feel him. He knew she wanted him. The time was now.

"Attends-moi, Cheri," Wait for me, Veronique whispered as she kissed the top of his head and stroked his dark hair with her nimble fingers. *"Quand je touche tes cheveaux, c'est comme la soie noire."* She tried to relax him with soothing words as he buried his face in her ample bosom. She felt the little love bites he inflicted upon her. She knew he wouldn't—couldn't—stop himself now. All she had to do was slow him down and it was hers. It. The grand pleasure. *La petite mort!* She felt it begin to simmer.

François' breathing deepened and Veronique feared he would come before he got inside her. No, no, not yet, she wanted to scream. Boys, men, they were all the same. She couldn't get them to slow down long enough for her to have her pleasure, before they were coming all over themselves and her. She hated when that happened.

It was her breasts, of course. They were her pride and her frustration. Her body was small, and her skin was smooth and blemish free. Her breasts were large, very large; they almost spoiled the line of her body . . . almost.

François fumbled with the button fly of her jeans, bothering to remove his head from her bosom only when his lungs needed a shot of the cool sea air.

"Doucement, Cheri, doucement." Slowly, she begged, slowly.

He struggled with her jeans. She wanted to help him, but she thought that he might want to do it by himself; to feel like he was taking her, conquering her.

"Doucement, doucement. . . ." There was a warm tightness between her legs and a tingle in the pit of her stomach.

François brought his head up for another gasp of air and she pushed herself into him. Finding his mouth, she probed deep and hard with her tongue. She felt the power start to flow inside her as he pushed her tongue back into her mouth with his own.

He pulled back from her, and bending down, he pulled, tugged, and coaxed her tight jeans over her slender hips and down to her ankles, and off. With one hand he undid his trousers to free himself and with the other, he brought her down to rest on the soft woolen blanket. Then François was on top of her.

Veronique felt she was on the verge of the best orgasm ever. Somewhere deep inside her, it was churning. It was taking over. *La Petite Mort!* She had successfully held François on that fine line between waiting and exploding. Now, she was ready. She stopped her gentle protests and slowly spread her legs. A moan of pleasure escaped each time she felt him move in her.

François heard Veronique moan and it excited him. He had used up every ounce of patience and was grateful he no longer had to wait. With her beautiful lips next to his ear, he was driven to new heights of stimulation each time a sound erupted from her delicate mouth. At first, a low moan. Then another, louder. Then a cry. Then another of pure pleasure. As she moved underneath him, her passion got louder and louder.

Her amorous wail was almost too loud. It was distracting. It was painful. It wasn't the cry of passion at all. She was screaming—screaming in his ear!

François pulled himself up and stared down into Veronique's fear struck eyes as 3,660 pounds of metal, in the last seconds of being an Alpine white Porsche Cabriolet, soared over them, not more than twenty meters above their heads.

9

AV. DE LA LIBERTE
CAP ROUX, FRANCE

"That was a great car," he said quietly as he stood watching that place on the horizon where the night sky met the curve in the road, and the Porsche had launched itself over the cliff.

"You'll have another car, Mikki. Now get in." Amir panted as he carried the barricades back and put them into the police sedan.

"She was a very special woman," Mikel said in an attempt to be profound. Pleased with his own seriousness, he got into the driver's seat.

"There are a thousand more like her," Amir counseled, slamming the passenger's side door of the car.

"Not like her, Uncle. She was different," he said with a sophomoric smugness. He turned the ignition key. "She was innocent." He paused for effect, and then continued, "I wanted our wedding night. I wanted to take that beautiful rose and deflower it petal by petal." The soft rumble of the engine drifted through the Citroën.

"Now, we go to Rhine Falls," Amir said as he unbuttoned his *Gendarme's* jacket, removed it, and threw it onto the back seat. He replaced it with a thick, black wool turtleneck and a dark brown, suede wind-breaker. "In a few months you will emerge as Wolfgang Metter, and our plan will be operational."

Ten kilometers down the road toward the Swiss Alps, they abandoned the police car in favor of Amir's Mercedes 550. The powerful automobile would navigate them safely over the winding roads, finally delivering them, like a veteran messenger, to the courtyard entrance of the large, remote hunting castle in Rhine Falls near Schaffhausen.

10

BELOW AV. DE LA LIBERTE
CAP ROUX, FRANCE

She fell through the air like a ghost, her long white gown dancing on the night wind. A few feet away, the Porsche hit like an albatross and began to sink into the ebony sea.

Within seconds, François and Veronique were both on their feet, scrambling to put on their pants. Looking out to where the car had hit the water, Veronique felt adrenaline start to pump through her veins.

"Do something!" She began to shape her concern into words. "Someone fell clear of the car. I saw it!"

"*Merde!*" François was slow to catch his wits. "Where?" He scanned the water's choppy surface intensely.

She hit the water on hands and knees, and the water hit back. An echo of torment reverberated down her spine. For a moment her head cleared and she fought to go up. Inside, she was filled with an agony of pain. Outside, she was surrounded by death.

Still churning and frothy, the sea digested its expensive metal nugget and seemed to belch with satisfaction.

"There," she yelled. She ran up behind François and pushed her arm past his shoulder so that his sights would be in line with hers. "There—more to the right—see?"

"Okay, yes, I see. I'm going in—you stay here." As François took off his sweater and pants again, he tried to keep his eyes on the gray phantom bobbing in the dark. "Guide me in," he yelled as he ran into the water. *"Ii-ee, MERDE!"* he yelped again as his feet hit the jagged rocks that hid below the surface of the small waves. He dove for deeper water.

"Plus à droit." More to the right, Veronique directed him, and he strained to swim faster.

"Too many *Gauloises*," he complained of his cigarette habit as each stroke became more of an effort and oxygen seemed as elusive as the unidentified object he was trying to find. And then he was there. Taking a large breath, he reached his hand forward to get a grip on the victim.

Something floated just beyond her. She tried a scissor kick but nothing happened. No movement. No pain. Nothing. She was starting to sink. There it was again, something floating above her. She reached for life.

He felt a hand grab him, and then an arm wrapped around his foot and pulled him down.

She was still sinking. Her lungs ached. There was an enormous pain behind her eyes. She couldn't think. She couldn't fight. The weight on her shoulders pulled her down toward the waiting arms of death.

François struggled under the water, writhing and contorting, kicking fiercely, trying anything to break free of the vice-like clutch of the phantom. His lungs were on the verge of bursting. He became tangled in what seemed like seaweed.

Like an octopus, with its sucker-bearing arms reaching out from the mysterious depths, something pulled and clawed and tugged and wrenched at her already hopelessly devastated wedding gown. She opened her mouth to scream. Water rushed past her tongue and down her throat. She couldn't stop it. It slammed into her windpipe and pumped into her stomach. It leaked into every crease and corner of her lungs. She gagged and coughed, but there was nothing but water. It seemed to fill her whole body.

Seeing the difficulty that her boyfriend was having with the rescue, Veronique ran into the water and swam rapidly to the spot where she had last seen him surface. She drew as much air as she felt her lungs would hold, and dove under. Her eyes stung with the salt and she had to force herself to keep them open. She saw François struggling to free himself and went to his aid. Probing her way deftly until she felt his arm, she pried the cold white hand, finger by finger, from his neck.

Death took its time. She could feel it cutting her loose finger by finger. She couldn't think . . . she couldn't breathe . . . she couldn't win. . . .

François propelled himself to the surface and broke the water with a loud gasp. He knew time was precious and didn't allow himself to dwell on the sweet taste of the oxygen. After three quick breaths, he prepared to dive again.

Veronique broke the surface with the unconscious wraith close behind. François swam to the other side and they each took an arm. Between the two of them, they managed to pull the girl onto the rocky sliver of shore.

Out of breath, Veronique whispered, "Put her . . . on . . . the blanket," as they dragged the cold, waterlogged figure across the rocks. "I . . . know . . . CPR, you go . . . get help."

François slipped his sweater over his head and pulled his pants on again. He put his shoes on as he ran up the steep path to the road. He found his *moto* in the brush.

Veronique heard the sputter of the motor and the sound of changing gears as the motorcycle sped away. She continued the CPR until the girl began to vomit. Turning the girl's head to the side, Veronique made sure that her patient did not choke. When she began to breathe on her own, Veronique wrapped the blanket around her and cradled the girl's head in her lap.

"Mikel . . . with me . . ." came an almost imperceptible mutter from the girl's barely parted lips.

"Don't try to talk. Help is on the way," Veronique shivered.

". . . no . . . help him . . ."

Veronique looked out onto the dark ocean. It seemed to stare back at her, expressionless. If there was someone else out there, the sea was not saying so. "Where are you, François? Oh God, please hurry!" she said to the void which was the night.

". . . can't move . . . need to help him. . . ."

She began rubbing the girl's clammy and cold limbs. A grayish white tint had replaced the usual flesh color, and she wanted to encourage circulation.

Far off in the distance, she thought she heard the siren of an ambulance, and then decided it was wishful thinking. It seemed an eternity was passing and she tried to stop shaking, but the shudders were becoming uncontrollable.

"I hear it. I hear the ambulance." Veronique looked down into the mask-like face of the young woman. "You're going to be okay. You're going to be okay. Hold on."

The girl didn't move or open her eyes, but Veronique saw her chest rise and fall with shallow, sporadic movements.

The two-toned siren of the medical unit grew louder, drowning out the deadly silence. The truck stopped directly above them.

As the paramedics jumped out of the back, François, wrapped in a blanket, exited the passenger's side of the vehicle, and began guiding the men down the narrow dirt path to his minute fragment of beach.

"Thank God you're here," Veronique said and began to cry. She watched the men put the girl on a stretcher and begin to carry her up the bluff. "I think her husband may still be out there somewhere."

She was given a blanket and escorted to the ambulance waiting on the road. As she climbed into the back, the medics made a place for her next to the girl she had pulled out of the sea.

11

RHINE FALLS, SWITZERLAND

Dr. Amir Hassasi's black Mercedes sped through the ancient gates of his estate at Rhine Falls, past the stone guest house that thirty-five years earlier he had transformed into a medical center for plastic surgery, and stopped at the entrance of the main residence.

The small staff was prepared for their arrival.

"Good evening, sirs. Welcome home," Ahmed greeted them, properly attired and standing with major-domo stiffness. He held the wooden-planked, iron-hinged door open as they entered. Ahmed had been in Amir's employ for nearly forty years. His face was rawboned and his eyes were dark and sunken, the perfect complement for his tall, skeletal body. His wife, Selena, whose ample form proved she did the cooking, and their daughter, Sheeza, who did the cleaning, rounded out the rest of Dr. Hassasi's personal proletariat.

"Will you need anything tonight, Sir?"

As Amir strutted by, he held out his coat for the servant to take. "Are there any messages for me?"

"The Brioni suit that you ordered from Bruno's in Zürich arrived this morning," Ahmed offered. "Selena will alter it tonight to the specifications that you gave her. Will there be anything else?"

"It is cold, Ahmed. Tonight we should have a fire. And then you may retire."

Ahmed went to light the wood in the massive living room fireplace. Seeing they weren't needed, Selena and Sheeza scurried away.

Looking back over his shoulder, Amir called to his protégé, "Get some rest, Mikki, and nothing to eat or drink after midnight. Be down in the operating room by five a.m., no breakfast."

"Are you sure you want to start tomorrow?" Mikel asked as he mounted the grand staircase on the way to his suite, "We haven't heard from the Colombians yet."

"Five a.m.!"

"Yes, Uncle."

Amir made no attempt to hide the modernization of his home. He was uninterested in the opinions of the few guests that might see, and make a comment on, the interior design of his domicile.

This fortress was the place Amir most enjoyed. If he could be anywhere in the world, it would be here at Rhine Falls. The old stone-walled castle still displayed most of its original décor: great hanging tapestries, paintings of former owners, and once used, but now ignored, wall torches. Dull-silver heating radiators, and pipes filled with electric wires, ran across and up and down the length and breadth of the inside, unavoidably changing it. There was the addition of the usual modern amenities.

Amir went to the library. Without scanning the titles on the bookshelf lining that room's hearth, he went directly to his copy of The Complete History of Medicine Vol. 1, and slowly pulled the book halfway out. The entire bookcase swung open on hinges, exposing a doorway. Amir replaced the book.

He opened the inner door, stepped through the archway, turned on the light, and descended the ancient stone steps. He heard the bookcase closing above and behind him.

At the end of a hidden ancient stairway were two large rooms that had been the cellars. The first room was now a state-of-the-art gymnasium where he kept himself exercised and stronger than most men his age. In this room, he had also taken a precocious boy and, over the years and with the help of highly trained martial arts instructors, he had developed him into a killing machine. But the second room was Amir's heaven on earth.

Amir hurried through the gymnasium, entered his paradise and switched on the lights. A barrage of white halogen bulbs ignited and for a moment he squinted.

This was the place where he performed those surgeries that couldn't be done in his regular office. The surgeries performed here were done for those patients who were willing to pay many times his usual rate to become anonymous.

Stretching out before him was a long operating table, its thin mattress exactly covering the top of the chrome and steel bed and its adjusting levers and controls balanced and waiting to manipulate the angles of the patient. One large operating lamp stood ready to illuminate the pillow-less head of the table, while another rested, unneeded. Sleek white cabinets covered the upper portions of the old stone walls, now veneered with Plexiglas for sterility; and bottles of liquids and pills, tubes of ointments and other medications pushed up against their glass-framed doors.

He began his preparations by turning on the main computer and going to the Wolfgang Metter file. He then got Mikel's file on a second monitor for comparison. Mikel was 2.54 centimeters taller than Wolfgang. There was nothing he could do about that, short of taking out that small amount in each of Mikel's shin bones. But, that would lengthen the amount of time Mikel would need to heal. Amir decided that was unnecessary. Wolfgang was 7 kilograms lighter than Mikel. He would be sure that Mikel lost that amount of weight in the time they had, and he would further guarantee their success by having the well-fitting Brioni suit, the exact match to most of the suits in Wolfgang's closet, let out 2.54 centimeters in the appropriate places, to make Mikel appear smaller.

He set up a cranium X-Ray of Metter, taken when Wolfgang had sustained a slight head injury during a hunting trip with Mikel near Rhine Falls. Amir had insisted on taking it, just to make sure there was no serious, unseen damage.

He brought up x-rays of Wolfgang and Mikel on the computer and projected them to the LED screens on the wall.

As he went to the drawers below the cabinets to collect and assemble the various instruments he would need to sterilize in the morning, he allowed himself the indulgence of a habit that he had only recently acquired: he began to talk to himself.

"When did we first meet Wolfgang, Mikki? Was it in that school I sent you to . . . *L'Ecole Supérieur?* I knew we'd need him someday."

He set three syringes in a stainless-steel tray. He placed the tray on a rolling stand and moved it to the operating table. He removed his badge of honor, his personal scalpel, his favorite, from its leather carrying case. "Remember when I taught you how to kill with a blade, Mikki?"

He went to Mikki's monitor and scrutinized the difference in facial measurements between the two men, in anticipation of the critically sensitive incisions he'd have to make. "But here, Mikki, your studies were very different. You learned the way of the kill."

He judged the position of the operating lamp, and placed it where he anticipated it would be the most beneficial. "You were such a bright child. You always gave me so much to work with."

He turned on the Gemini-A KTP Laser, and the Lux 1540, just to test them, and then shut them back down.

Another laser, his own invention, stood in a corner, patentless and quietly forgotten. Its heart, a pale-green Colombian emerald, no longer showed any signs of life. "Green eyes," he mused, as he studied Metter's monitored image. "How wonderful technology is. I wish I had invented contact lenses."

He unwound a rolled-up leather case and removed several scalpels for examination. "Mikki, I have prepared you well. You have all the tools you will ever need."

He took a breath and scanned the entire room to make sure everything was where he wanted it to be. He took one moment to realize how much this room mirrored his accomplishments: the highest quality, most expensive equipment money could buy. "I've spoiled myself, Mikki," he said, and smiled one of his rare smiles. "Perhaps you deserve a little spoiling too. You have worked so very hard and done so very well."

He reached out for his personal scalpel, held it up in front of his examining eyes, as if he were admiring the finest Samurai sword. "You have become a magnificent soldier . . . my soldier . . . an expert executioner. How many has it been, Mikki? Six? I have taught you well. But the American girl . . . that was a real challenge for me. Never mind, Mikki, she will soon be forgotten."

He went back to the computer and continued studying pictures of Wolfgang Metter. "Who will you become, Mikki? Who would you like to be next . . . after Wolfgang?"

Another photograph showed Wolfgang with his glasses. Amir went to a drawer to find the clone of Metter's glasses with the clear lenses. "The most difficult part will be remembering to put them on. It's always the small things that one forgets.

"A different nose . . ." he said absentmindedly as he studied the photo. "Higher cheekbones . . ." he whispered, rotating the picture in the computer its full 360 degrees, ". . . and brown, curly hair to complete the transformation."

"This is going to be one of our most interesting jobs, Mikki . . . and the most lucrative.

"Wolfgang Metter . . ." he whispered again, turning the picture to the left.

At 4:00 a.m. the following morning, Dr. Amir Hassasi began his preparations by sterilizing the scalpels, hemostats and forceps. He hung the IV bags on hooks, and brought the computer out of sleep mode. Finally, he activated the laser motors.

Mikel was right on time, and at 5:00 a.m., he entered the operating room wearing only black polyester gym shorts. "Good Morning, Uncle."

"Take off your shorts and put on that hospital gown. Have a seat on the table, Mikki." Amir reached for a medical chart. "Let's see . . . do you have any allergies to any medications?"

Mikel looked back at him, confused. "Is that a joke, Uncle?" he asked.

"It is. You don't find it amusing? I'm in a particularly jovial mood today . . . aren't you?" Amir threw the chart back on the computer desk behind him. "Lie down on your side and let's get that nasty little spinal injection out of the way."

"What's that for?"

"I'm going to give you an injection of lidocaine to numb you, and then I'm going to insert a catheter for ketamine into your spinal fluid to manage your pain."

"Can we talk about something else besides the medical shit?" Mikel relaxed onto the table and rolled over on his side.

"Well, of course. What would you like to talk about?"

"How about the next car you're going to buy me, now that you made me wreck my Porsche. I'm thinking Ferrari."

"Here we go." He took a syringe and injected Mikel right above his ass.

"Shit, that hurts!"

"You're a soldier, Mikki. You've had a lot more pain than this. Just relax; it's only for a minute."

"I'm usually the one who deals out the pain."

"Bring your knees up to your chest to open up your spine."

Amir inserted the long needle containing the catheter tube into Mikki's spine and waited fifteen seconds before withdrawing the metal needle through the tube, leaving the catheter in his spine. Then he taped the tube to Mikki's side. "Now, turn over on your back and rest comfortably."

"Damn, I thought I wasn't supposed to feel that!"

"I guess I could have waited a few more minutes for the lidocaine to kick in. Is it not working?"

"Shit, no! It's not working!"

"It's just cold that you're feeling, not pain."

"You get down here and let me stick a needle up your ass, and then we'll see if it's cold or pain!"

"What kind of car did you say you wanted?"

"A fucking Ferrari, Uncle. A 2013, F12 Berlinetta . . . Red!"

"A 2013? Does that mean the year?"

"Yeah. They're not out yet; but I should order it now."

"Ferraris are nice." He inserted an IV drip of phencyclidine into Mikki's right arm.

"What's that?"

"PCP, Mikki, isn't that ironic?" Amir said with a smile that held its own irony: the smile of a humorless personality. "The South Americans will pay us fifty million dollars to secure their profits from illegal drugs, and we're going to do that with the help of legal drugs that have been misused to the point where they're becoming illegal as well. But, I'm rambling, aren't I?"

"Yes, Uncle."

"Count backwards from one hundred."

"One hundred . . ."

"Just relax, let yourself go."

". . . ninety-nine . . ."

"Go to sleep, Mikki."

". . . ninety-eight . . ."

"Dream of Ferraris . . . beautiful red Ferraris."

". . . ninety-seven. . . ."

Amir stared down at the once beautiful face of his nephew, now broken and bruised.

It was the third day of their operations, and Mikel's body lay quietly anesthetized on the operating table. Although they had taken frequent breaks and long rest periods, neither one of them had left the cellar area in the seventy-two hours since the surgeries had begun. Ahmed had been instructed to set up a hospital bed in the gymnasium, and make it comfortable for Mikel's drug-induced hours of sleep. Amir had a bed set up in a small office off the operating room, but with the excitement of his work flowing through him, he had only used it once.

Over the three days, Amir had cut and cracked and lasered Mikel's face, working diligently to remodel one man into another. Without an assistant to help him, he had ignored the sweat on his own face until a drop of it had found its way past his surgical mask and dropped onto Mikel's cheek.

Amir wiped the drop of sweat from Mikel's unconscious face.

"What a shame it is that you have to lose your beautiful face, Mikki. You were always beautiful. Even as a child, peering into the door of your mother's room while I was fucking her.

"Your mother was beautiful too. She was a prostitute and she was a drug addict but that just meant she was easy to kill. I can't honestly tell you that your father was beautiful because I can't honestly tell you who he was. Your mother couldn't either.

"I never wanted a wife or family, not until I saw your curious little four-year-old face. I was just there to relieve my needs with a woman of the evening. I knew she had a child but I didn't care because she usually kept you out of sight. But, that one time, I was on the edge of a climax and I caught you staring at us from behind the door. Looking at you, Mikki, my climax was even greater. I remember slamming into your mother's body and staring at her beautiful little boy. That's when I knew, Mikki. That's when I knew I wanted a legacy. I wanted to create perfection, and you could be my canvas. I would make you strong and powerful, clever and quick. You were already beautiful, I wouldn't have to create or enhance that.

"Mikki. My beautiful, beautiful Mikki. You are everything I wasn't, and I am everything you will be.

"Now, sadly, I have to destroy you. Even with my skills, when I change you again, after Wolfgang, I know I'll never be able to make you as beautiful as you were."

Amir sat at the end of his long dining table. He had slept very little in seven days and although he was tired, he felt wonderful. The surgeries had gone better than planned. Mikel's strong face had taken the challenge exceedingly well, and he was recovering nicely. In a few months, he would be an un-bruised and scar-hidden, Wolfgang Metter.

Amir had ordered his breakfast: lamb and couscous; and nothing else. Selena had prepared it and Ahmed had ushered the plate in with the attention of a chaperone. Ahmed had also brought the newspapers of the last eight days with him. He laid them on the table next to the china plate.

Amir sorted through the folded stack of newspapers to find the earliest one. As he took his first bite, he unfolded the paper and read the headline. He stopped chewing; the lamb rested on the tongue of his open mouth as he skimmed the article:

Olympic Diver Survives Auto Accident
American Olympic hopeful, Jesse Fortune,
was pulled from the Mediterranean Sea
late last night by . . .
Fortune, who was just beginning her
honeymoon . . .
Fortune, accompanied by her parents and
her coach, former Olympian Matthew Braden,
will be returning to the United States
for further treatment of wounds suffered . . .
Fortune's husband, Mikel Rhen of Switzerland,
is believed to have drowned, his body has
not yet been recovered. . . .

Impossible! It could not be. He was sure it could not be. As he swallowed, he scrutinized his memory of the operation. He remembered gathering the hobby-horse barricades and putting them in the Citroën. What had he done next? He had gotten in the car and let Mikki drive him away.

He had not gone to the edge of the cliff to look over. He had not made sure. Unbelievable! She was alive! He had not even looked!

Amir threw the paper aside and reached for another one. He searched frantically for more information: another headline, another article, any update. There was nothing.

He put the newspapers down and stared into his couscous. She had survived. The one time he had not checked every detail, and this had to happen. She was alive.

He would never let this happen again. No matter how small a detail was, no matter how insignificant, he would check it. No matter how assumed an outcome, he would check it. If he could think of it, he could check it.

With that decided, there was only one more decision to make: what to do about Jesse Fortune. The answer came without debate: kill her. She was a loose end. He had never had a loose end. She would be his first, and his last. Yes, kill her. But how?

I will have the Colombians do it, he thought. Yes, I will tell Rafael to make it part of the deal . . . part of the payment. . . .

"Ahmed!" he yelled, his voice unusually high and shrill, "Bring me the satellite phone!"

12

NORTH HOLLYWOOD, CALIFORNIA
Fall, 2011

Thomas Kelly couldn't sleep. Even after a month, each time he closed his eyes, he still saw Jason Fenny's smashed and broken body leaking its lifeblood onto the bench seat of a bullet-torn Ford.

His eyelids came together in one more attempt to close his mind, shut off the vision, and end the review of the madness for the night.

He saw Fenny's head, without a face, jawbone exposed, teeth shattered.

His eyes opened again. He drew a breath slowly over his lips, shook his head, and gave up trying to sleep.

As Kelly threw the covers off and put his feet on the floor, RoboDobe came awake and watched him curiously. If Kelly didn't want to sleep, RoboDobe wouldn't either. If Kelly wanted to go out, RoboDobe would go with him. If Kelly moved to another part of the house, they both moved. RoboDobe was ready for whatever Kelly decided to do. It was his sovereign duty to accompany his master at all times.

"What the hell are you lookin' at?" Kelly whispered across the darkened room.

RoboDobe continued to lay against the wall closest to the bed and stare at his mentor.

"I'm lookin' at you, Jerk Face," Kelly spoke for the dog. "How come you ain't brought this guy Serva down yet?"

RoboDobe turned his head slightly, as he sorted through the words he was hearing to find one he might recognize.

"You mean bring him to justice?" Kelly asked, taking his part again.

RoboDobe gave up trying to understand either side of the conversation and laid his head back down on the floor with a deep canine sigh.

Kelly went to the kitchen for a beer. Before he could open the refrigerator, RoboDobe was in the kitchen with him.

"You're following too close, Agent Dobe. They're gonna spot you every time. You're gonna get your ass kicked following too close."

RoboDobe looked at his food dish. Seeing that it was empty, he turned his attention back to Kelly.

"Following too close. . . ." Kelly repeated as he wandered the three steps to his glass-top kitchen table and sat down in one of the three wicker chairs that tried to surround it.

As soon as Kelly was seated, RoboDobe circled twice and lay down on the kitchen floor.

Kelly stared at the heap of paper that rested uneasily on the table. To everyone else who had seen the stack, it appeared to be an unmanageable mess of newspapers and paid and unpaid bills. But, to Kelly, it was just another desk top.

On top of everything, a thick, off-white folder stared back at him. The red, stenciled letters on its cover read:

Enrico Serva

Current as of 11/01/2011

Top Secret

E. Hunt was handwritten in the bottom of the left corner. TK was initialed on the right.

He flicked at the bottom of the folder, but didn't open it. It was heavy and thick, but there was nothing in it he needed to see again.

The CIA, the FBI, and the DEA all had different investigations going on Enrico Serva. The CIA was busy analyzing the political implications of his international dealings. The FBI wanted to know about his covert and illegal trade inside the national borders. And the DEA was concerned with everything about Enrico Serva that had to do with drugs, which was almost everything that had to do with Enrico Serva.

What made it difficult was that Enrico Serva had done a great deal for the native Colombians. They loved him. They were not about to give out information about him.

He had paid for Professor Eduardo Rodriguez Elementary School, which had been built in a small town south of Bogotá. A few pictures had been taken of him shaking hands and politicking his way through the ground-breaking of a development he had financed for the poor. He had jaunted casually through a crowd celebrating the opening of a hospital he had built. He was becoming a national hero to the Colombian natives. But, for the most part, he continued to deal his business from his compound on the rural outskirts of Bogotá. Deal being the operative word.

The cell phone rang.

Although Kelly wore a watch, he ignored it and looked at the clock on the front panel of the stove: 12:05 a.m.

RoboDobe brought his head up off the floor to observe how Kelly would handle this intrusion into their privacy.

The phone rang again.

"What do you think, Agent Dobe? Do we answer after midnight?"

RoboDobe put his head back down on the floor.

"Call me when it's time to eat," Kelly scripted for his constant companion. He answered it in the middle of the third ring.

"Agent Kelly?" Hunt's greeting was purely rhetorical.

"Yes, Sir."

"I know it's late, but I thought you should have this information immediately."

"Yes, Sir."

"My Colombian sources have informed me that there is going to be a meeting at the Serva estate. All the generals will be there: Mutis, Mendez, Perez, and of course, Rafael Santos."

"Yes, Sir."

"Something's going on, Kelly. The New Man hasn't been making his usual shipments. As far as we can tell, he's not moving to make up for the loss. He's holding back for some reason we can't determine. I've talked it over with my boys in the city division, and they tell me that the streets of Los Angeles are drying up. It's not critical yet, but there's a definite trend here. I think he may be planning something big. Have you gone over the file?"

"Yes, Sir. I have it right here."

"Good. I don't want to be caught with my pants down again. Go over it thoroughly. See me in the morning in my office." He hung up before Kelly could confirm the order.

Kelly held the phone against his ear for another few seconds. Then he put it down.

RoboDobe got up and stretched, eyed his food dish to be sure no one had filled it behind his back, circled two more times and went back down on the floor.

"Okay, Agent Dobe, let's go over this again." Kelly opened the file. As his eyes wondered through the familiar facts, he started to wonder what *wasn't* in it.

13

A light rain had fallen steadily through the early morning hours, and by noon Bogotá was saturated. Heavy, rolling white clouds tinted with neon grey covered the city.

In the wake of the shower, the smell of wet stone filled the air. Tiny streams wandered down each aged street. In the center of the city, the trees and shrubs, terraces and telephone lines dripped and dribbled the overflow onto the more recently poured pavement.

Enrico turned onto the downtown street faster than he had intended and lost his balance. He had chased Bernardo through two alleys and did not want to lose him now. Coming out of the second alley, he was only two or three steps behind Bernardo, and had he kept his balance, Enrico would have caught him. As he turned, he slipped on the wet sidewalk, his feet came out from under him, and he went down on his side. He slid several feet and his body jammed up against the leg of a tall man standing in front of a café.

"Hey, *Muchacho,* where are you going so fast?" The man bent down and lifted Enrico to his feet. He did not release the boy's arm.

Enrico looked up into the man's face and said nothing. He tried to pull away, but the man held him.

"I asked you a question, little one. You owe me an answer," the man said with the hint of a smile.

"I owe you nothing," Enrico responded, "and don't call me little."

"You see this leg?" Still holding Enrico, the man pointed with his free hand to his calf. "You bumped me right there. You didn't say 'excuse me' or anything. So, maybe you owe me an answer to my question."

Enrico considered struggling until he got away, but the grip the man had was far too strong. It didn't hurt, but it held him. He thought about arguing, or even kicking the man to make him let go, but decided against that for the moment. "I was after Bernardo," he said and looked in the direction the other boy had gone. "If these stupid shoes weren't so big, I would've caught him."

"So . . ." the man said as if everything was suddenly clear, ". . . and what would you do when you caught this Bernardo?"

"Kill him. Now lemme go!"

"Kill him?" the man laughed, "You are one tough *hombre*. But look at you. Your face is dirty, your pants are torn . . . and look here, your arm is bleeding." He gently twisted Enrico's arm to expose a scrape on the skin that the street had left. "I haven't seen this Bernardo, but it looks to me like he's winning the fight. Where is your mother to mend your wounds?"

"I got no mother," he said quietly, as if it were a secret. He felt the man's grip loosen slightly. "Lemme go!" Enrico started struggling.

"Why do you want to kill Bernardo?" The man did not let go.

Enrico stopped struggling. "Because he said there was no God."

"You would kill Bernardo for his lack of faith. Even in this city of Catholics, that seems a rather strong remedy. Where is your father to teach you the Christian ways?"

"I don't know what you're talking about. Lemme go, mister!" Although he wouldn't have admitted it, there was something about this man that Enrico liked. His voice was kind.

"Where is your papa?"

"I got no papa." Enrico was tired of this game. He stared off in the direction Bernardo had gone.

"So . . . no papa, no mama, and maybe no God. I'll bet you're hungry too. All that running and fighting makes a boy . . . ah . . . a man hungry. So, maybe you're hungry." The man's grip began to loosen again.

"Maybe," Enrico said bringing his eyes back to the man's face.

"My name is Professor Rodriguez. I teach at the university. I come to this café every day to have my lunch. I come here at twelve noon . . . every day. My back is getting tired from bending over to hold onto you. If you'll apologize for bumping into me, I'll let you go. If you're hungry, you can join me for lunch." The man let go of Enrico's arm. "What do you say?"

Enrico darted away in the direction of the lost Bernardo. As he rounded the corner at the end of the street, he heard the man's gentle voice call after him. "Every day . . . noon . . . if you're hungry."

The cracked and broken street had no name. Like an old man without hope, it turned its back on the great terraces with their elaborate gardens, and the well placed plazas with their perfunctory statues of the heroes of Santa Fe de Bogotá, and followed the streams as they ran down the sloping plain into the old section of the capital city. On each side of the street small houses, with decaying thatched roofs, huddled against each other as if they feared the monstrous city might devour them.

The third house from the end on the west side of the street had no permanent residents. An Indian woman had raised two children in its one room and had watched them leave from the single, blanket-covered doorway. They had gone to seek a better life in the city, promising to come back for her. She had died three months later. Since then, the house had only been occupied on an occasional basis.

Enrico huddled in the only corner of the dirt floor that was not mud from the morning's rain. He thought about Bernardo and the night seemed colder. *Wait till I find you. I'm going to kill you, fucker.* No matter how many times he used that swear word, it always sounded strange to him. He had never been sure of what it meant, but it made him feel better to use it. It helped him stay angry, and anger kept his mind from other problems, like hunger. His stomach growled and he thought of the man, the professor. Professor something. *Professor Rodriguez.* His stomach growled again. *Damn you, Bernardo. There is a God. I'm gonna kick your butt.* But, he couldn't stay angry. He couldn't keep his mind on Bernardo. Somewhere inside him, the memory of the kind voice of the professor mixed with his hunger to produce a painful curiosity.

A distant thunder rolled across the night sky.

"Don't rain!" he said, looking up toward the deteriorating ceiling. As if to answer him the sky rumbled again.

Enrico had many places throughout the city where he could spend the night. This one was his latest find and his least favorite. It was farther out of town than he liked to be, and he had not taken time to leave the necessities hidden nearby. He lacked even the simple things like matches and a candle. His favorite place, his "home," was an empty storage room in a little used warehouse near the city hospital. He and Bernardo had shared that spot for almost a year, and most of his few belongings were there. There was food there also.

I'm gonna kick you till you bleed, Bernardo! Enrico knew his threats against Bernardo were as empty as his stomach. Bernardo was older, maybe a year, maybe more, and stronger. He had only run from Enrico because it was a game to him. Enrico was the only family he had.

From the street in front of the café, Enrico had gone directly home, expecting Bernardo to have done the same thing. He had waited for several hours, but Bernardo had not returned. Finally, in frustration and anger, Enrico had set out to find him. Sometime past midnight, he had ended up here, too tired to go on and too hungry to sleep. "Damn you, Bernardo," he whispered into the dark shadows of the empty room. The dank walls absorbed his words like bread in soup.

What did the man say? The professor. *Every day . . . noon . . . if you're hungry.* Well, he was hungry. And he sure knew how to take a sucker. One thing he had learned was how to survive. The man had a nice voice; maybe he'd be good for some food. The thunder rolled again. *God, don't let it rain. God, don't let it rain.* He fell asleep repeating his simple prayer.

It didn't rain.

"Is there a God?" Enrico had pushed his way through the crowd of city laborers that pressed and squeezed their way into and out of the small café. At several points in his journey from the old house, he had considered the cut and run tactic. He wasn't sure why. Now, as he watched the surprised look on the professor's face turn to a warm smile—and he took in the thick smell of cooking food that filled the room—he was glad he had pursued his goal.

"So . . . the warrior returns," the professor said. "And with a mighty question. Join us, warrior. Perhaps we can solve this mystery together."

The professor sat at a scratched and dulled rectangular hardwood table, pushed up against the window. He was sharing his lunch hour with two other men. A fourth chair, diagonal to him and next to the window, was vacant.

Confused as to what to do next, Enrico blurted out, "I'm not a warrior." Then he stared into the professor's eyes and waited. The crowd behind him was busy but not overly loud.

The professor leaned his arms on the table and stared back at Enrico without expression. Then he smiled. "What is your name?"

"My name's Enrico," he said with a thread of pride.

"Good!" the professor responded. He thrust his hand toward Enrico. "Join us, *Señor* Enrico. Take that empty chair."

Surprised by the professor's hand, all Enrico could think to do was shake it. He almost smiled. The man across the table from the professor slid his chair in, and Enrico squeezed past him and sat down.

"What would you like to eat, Enrico?" the professor asked, and when Enrico appeared lost he added, "We are sharing vegetable soup and *tortillas*, cheese and fruit. Help yourself." He passed what was left of the cheese and the bread to Enrico and located the waitress: *"Una sopa, mas, por favor."*

When the soup arrived, Enrico accepted it eagerly.

"He may not be a warrior," the man sitting next to Enrico said, "but he sure eats like one."

The others chuckled briefly and then returned to their conversation. They spoke in quiet and hushed tones, sometimes straining to keep their voices low and still be heard over the café noises. Whatever they were discussing was important to them.

It was not important to Enrico. He ignored them and continued eating. Before he realized it, the other men had gone and only he and the professor remained. He had been so busy eating, he hadn't noticed that the café was almost empty. It was much quieter. He felt the stare of the professor as he scraped the remaining crumbs of food from his plate. When he felt brave enough, he looked over to the professor.

"Is there a God?" He still had no answer to his question.

The professor slid down one seat so he was directly across from Enrico. He looked out the window for a moment. Then he returned his attention to the boy.

"There are many clouds today," the professor said quietly.

Enrico turned his eyes to the window and said nothing.

"They come over those big mountains," he continued. "You can see them reflected in the streams that run through the city."

Enrico waited with an impatient silence. His stomach was full and he was ready to be released. He wanted to run away again.

"Did you make the clouds?" the professor asked.

"What?"

"Did you make the clouds?"

Enrico turned his attention back to the professor. "No," he said simply.

"Did you make the mountains?"

The professor's next question was just as easy to answer. Enrico said, "No."

"What about the water in the streams?"

"Why are you asking me these silly questions? You know I didn't."

"And I know I didn't. So maybe someone bigger than both of us did. You come back tomorrow and we'll talk again. But now, I have others to teach."

The professor went to the counter, paid for their meals, and left the café.

Enrico looked back at the mountains. He couldn't explain it, but they looked different to him now.

In the weeks that followed, Enrico found himself showing up at the café almost every day.

The professor never questioned him about where he came from or where he went after each hour they spent together, but he did make sure that Enrico ate lunch before they began any new lesson. For both of these things, Enrico was grateful. His home was his secret, to be shared only with Bernardo. Since the day of the chase, Bernardo had not returned. But, when he thought about it, Enrico was sure that he would, eventually. Although he wanted to trust the professor, he had never trusted anyone but Bernardo before and he found it difficult. Lunch, of course, was a welcomed event. Most of the time, it was the only food he would get in a day.

By the third week, they had fallen into a routine of lunch at the café and a half hour at the university library. When his time was up, Enrico would follow him with a borrowed book, as the professor strolled toward the building where he taught his classes. Enrico would watch as the professor entered the building, and he would wait until the professor was out of sight before going home.

After each session, Enrico would lie on the cot he had made in one corner of the storeroom. His mind would whirl with the new information he was learning. He was given books, most of which were intended to help him learn how to read. He studied them hard, pouring over them for hours at a time.

Never having known his parents, or any family, he had been leery, and at times afraid of the professor. But as the weeks went on, his fears and defenses fell like small coins from a hole in his pocket.

Enrico was late. Even though he had run all the way, he had almost missed the lunchtime. When he arrived at the café, he found the professor seemingly surrounded by the presence of two angry men. Enrico had not seen these men before, and hearing their raised voices, he stopped a few meters away and waited.

The professor glanced briefly at Enrico but gave no acknowledgement and then his attention returned to the strangers. They were young and strong and dark, and dressed in an identical manner: a white, short-sleeved shirt with thin black tie, black pants, and black shoes.

Enrico felt the hurt of being ignored. On every occasion he could remember, the professor had stopped whatever he was doing when he saw him. He had always greeted him— sometimes interrupting himself or others to do so—and he had come to expect this greeting.

One of the men looked down angrily, and for a moment, Enrico thought the man was going to strike the professor. The other man restrained his companion and they both started for the door. As they passed Enrico, they pushed him out of their way; and then they were gone.

Enrico watched as the professor stared into his coffee cup. He said nothing and waited. A minute passed before the professor looked up and smiled.

"So, *Señor* Enrico, today you will join me at my *hacienda*."

The professor's home was the most wonderful place Enrico had ever seen. It was filled with the smells of musty books, friendly meals, and ash from morning fires in the fireplace. The furniture had definitely been used, but that only meant it was comfortable. By city standards it was a small house, but it was the largest home he had ever been in. And it was warm.

As he followed the professor into the living room, he noticed something else, something that took his breath away, something that almost made him forget where he was. . . .

From the living room window, sunlight moved through particles of dust to surround an over-stuffed chair. In that chair, Enrico saw the Madonna. Her long brown hair fell gently over her slender shoulders, her brown eyes stared down into her lap, and her divine countenance reached into his soul. He had never seen a woman as beautiful as this. He wanted to worship her. He wanted to adore her. He wanted to pray to her.

"Papa," the Madonna spoke, "you're home early. Is everything all right?" She took the book she had been reading from her lap and placed it, still open, on a small table next to her chair.

"*Si, mi pequeña flor*. But, the military is everywhere. The soldiers seem to enjoy tormenting old men who don't agree with them."

"You mean Ortega? You saw him again today?"

"Sergeant Ortega . . . an ugly little man," the professor continued, removing his jacket and hanging it on a dark oak coat tree in the entryway. "I think he is owned by the FARC."

"Please Papa, you must be more careful. Who is that hiding behind you there? Have you found another supporter for the new government?"

With one eye peering past the professor's arm, Enrico stood transfixed by the beautiful face of the woman in the chair. As she rose to welcome her father and his guest, he saw, for the first time, that her stomach was swollen. Madonna was with child.

"So . . . ?" Reminded of his companion, the professor turned to find Enrico. "No, no. This is not a new recruit. Enrico is not a warrior; he is a friend. Come in, Enrico. Let me introduce you to my daughter."

The professor turned back to receive a welcoming hug from his daughter. The extent of her pregnancy was emphasized by the awkward posture they had to take to hug one another. The radiant beauty of her face, however, was not diminished by her maternal state.

The Madonna kissed her father lightly on the cheek and looked beyond him to where Enrico was waiting. She smiled angelically as the professor continued.

"*Señor* Enrico, this is my little flower, and the light of my life . . . since her mother has gone to rest in the arms of the Benevolent One." He crossed himself. "May I present to you, my daughter, Ana. Ana, my dear, allow me to introduce my most earnest and diligent new student. His name is *Señor* Enrico . . ." The professor stalled in his intentionally formal and grandiose introduction, realizing he did not know Enrico's last name. He had never asked.

Ana immediately understood what the pause meant. Her smile broadened and she curtsied as if she were meeting royalty. To help fill the small gap of silence, she said, "It is an honor to meet you, *Señor.*"

Enrico didn't notice the professor's hesitation. He was struggling with a hesitation of his own. He was so taken by the Madonna's beauty; he didn't know what to do. Should he shake her hand? As he started to, he saw her curtsy. Should he bow? He tried, but it was a feeble attempt. He was paralyzed. He was relieved when she continued.

"Please come in, *Señor,* and sit down with us. It is a pleasure to have you here."

They moved farther into the living room and Enrico took a place next to the professor on the couch. The Madonna went back to the chair where she had been reading earlier.

"Ana's husband was a good man," the professor said quietly, leaning back into the comfort of the sofa. He stared into Enrico's eyes as if looking for confirmation of his statement.

Not knowing what to say, Enrico tried to let his undivided attention be his response, but he remained mesmerized by the Madonna's aura.

"His name was Carlos Cepeda," the professor went on, "and he was a brave soldier for the new government. He fought the FARC. But you know those criminals," the professor continued in stride, "they wage war—" He stopped himself. "What am I saying? You know nothing of these things. You are not a soldier. You are my little friend, Enrico."

For the first and only time in his life, Enrico allowed himself to be referred to as "little" without protest.

"We'll have an early dinner, Papa. I'll go now and prepare it. With that, she rose, somewhat awkwardly, and went to the kitchen. The sounds of pans and plates echoed through the small rooms of the house.

The professor spoke to Enrico for a few more minutes, and then fell silent. He seemed to drift away into thoughts of his own. Enrico stayed where he was and waited patiently, moving as little as possible. His mind was filled with visions of the Madonna come to life.

Ana's call from the kitchen, that dinner was almost ready, startled both of them. The professor smiled at Enrico, "It's time to wash-up, *Señor.*"

Enrico had seen very few bathrooms, and even fewer with cloth towels. Everything was immaculate. Clean white tiles gleamed up from a floor stained only by time. A porcelain sink rested on a pedestal against one wall, and a mirror was framed above it. A bathtub stood on four clawed feet against the opposite wall.

The professor washed his hands and reached for a white towel which hung on a hook. As he polished each finger, he spoke quietly to Enrico. "Be sure to get your hands good and clean. Ana notices when I forget and she lets me know. With a woman, Enrico, it's always better to remember these things."

Enrico doubted that the professor had ever forgotten to wash his hands, but he appreciated what he realized was another lesson. He certainly didn't want to make a mistake in front of the Madonna.

"Please make use of the toilet in the next room if you need to, and wash your hands." The professor turned away and closed the door.

Alone in the small bathroom, Enrico studied himself in the mirror. He decided that his face, although pleasant, was not worthy of being in the same room with the Madonna.

The faint sound of glass breaking reached him through the closed door. He stopped thinking for a second and listened.

In the next second, the door to the bathroom exploded in on him and pieces of it splintered over his body. A power like the hand of God knocked him against the wall and ripped the breath from his lungs. A sound hit his ears so hard he thought they would break. He sank to the floor and was covered immediately in debris.

He lay in stunned silence for a moment as dust settled into his nose and mouth. There was an angry pain in his right arm where a large sliver of door frame had penetrated his skin and muscle. Barely missing the bone, it had lodged itself in the tissue and stood up like an arrow. There was an intense ringing in his ears, and beyond that, he could hear nothing. His head was spinning.

His entire body was tingling painfully and he began to shake uncontrollably. He felt something wet on his legs and realized he was urinating on himself. *Oh God, no! I'm pissing in my pants! No! Not in front of the Madonna . . . Oh God. . . .* His world slipped away into blackness.

"Can you hear me, *Muchacho*?" a strange voice called from somewhere just beyond the darkness.

Enrico opened his eyes to the face of a stranger leaning over him, dressed in white. He felt the presence of others around him. They seemed to be moving him gently.

"Don't call me little," he said. His voice was raspy and there was a bad taste in his mouth. He looked around, trying to remember where he was. He heard the sound of running water and his eyes went to a broken pipe hanging from a torn and charred wall. It looked as if it were bleeding. Everything was in ruin. He was sure he was inside, but he could see the night sky.

He decided he was hungry. Slowly, his memory returned. The Professor. Early dinner. The Madonna. The Madonna, he thought, where was she? He looked back to the stranger. "Don't let the Madonna see my pants."

Thinking that Enrico was having delirious visions of Heaven, the stranger looked back at him and said, "You'll be fine. The Madonna won't see any part of you today, *Muchacho*." He raised his voice to one of the others, "Let's get them out of here!"

"Don't call m-m. . . ." He went to the blackness again.

He felt a jolt and opened his eyes. He was inside a medical truck. He turned his head. There was someone else in the truck with him. On the other side, mostly hidden under a white sheet, he could see a body move with the bouncing and swaying of the truck. He heard a soft moan. It was her. It was the Madonna!

As the truck turned again, her head rolled toward him and he could see her more clearly. Her face was a mask of burns, bruises, and dried blood. The hair on the left side of her head had been burned away, leaving an exposed area of cracked and puckered skin.

An attendant appeared from out of the shadows behind her and began bandaging her wounds. The motion of the truck made it too difficult for him and he sat back down in the shadows.

She moaned again, more softly than before, and then she was quiet.

Enrico didn't want to believe it was her, his precious Madonna, so badly broken and scarred. But it *was* her. He felt a tear roll down his cheek, and then the blackness once more.

"Can you hear me?" A new voice woke him from his nothingness. "You're going to be fine, just fine." It was a woman's voice. Soft. Kind. Interested. He opened his eyes.

"Can you hear me?" she repeated.

He nodded slowly. He felt the tight hindrance of a thick bandage on his arm. Most of his shoulder was included in the wrapping.

"Oh, that's a good boy. You've been sleeping for several hours. We were worried about you."

Confused, he looked around the room to try to place himself. His eyes froze on a man standing by the door. It was one of the strange men from the café.

"Where is the professor?" Enrico asked, looking back to the nurse. He wished the man by the door would go away.

"You've been in a terrible accident," she replied as she straightened the sheet that lay across his chest and under his arm, "We're here to help you—"

"El profesor esta muerto," the man said confidently.

"Was that your father," the nurse continued, concerned. "I'm so very sorry—"

"The professor had no son," the man interrupted. "But I've seen this one before." He had been leaning against the wall with his hands behind him. His eyes had not focused on anything in particular, and his words seemed to be given to the room at large. He pushed himself off the wall. His vision grabbed and held Enrico's bandaged arm as if he were afraid to look Enrico in the eye. His broad brown face smiled mildly, but his voice did not fulfill the promise of friendship that his smile was promoting. "What is your name, *amigo?* How do you know the professor?"

Enrico didn't answer. He turned his head toward the wall. His hatred of this man was clearing his mind. He felt awake. He wanted to curse the man. He wanted to hurt the man. He would tell him nothing.

Before the man could continue, the door opened and another nurse stepped in quickly.

"We're losing her, Sergeant Ortega. You should come right away."

Without further exchange, they both turned and left the room, with the first nurse following them down the hall.

Her. Enrico knew who they meant. They meant the Madonna. She was in trouble.

He threw off the sheet and got out of bed. He felt a little dizzy, but he stood still for a moment and it passed.

He saw his pants on the only chair in the room. His shoes had been left under the chair, but he didn't see his shirt anywhere. Maybe he didn't have a shirt anymore. He wasn't going to worry about that now. There was an old sweater at home he could get later. The Madonna needed him. He would help her if he could.

He pulled his pants on and slipped into his shoes, then opened the door quietly. He glanced in the direction the others had gone. Seeing that the corridor was empty, he left the room.

As he made his way down the hall, he heard faint noises but he couldn't determine exactly where they came from. The hallway was empty. Some of the doors to the other rooms were open and he looked into them briefly as he passed. Most were empty. In one, he saw a man with a bandage covering most of his head.

At the end of the corridor, he could go right or left. To the right, another empty corridor stretched away into the sterile silence. To the left, a small indent ended with an entrance to the stairway. He took the stairs and went down one flight. Opening the door carefully, he stepped into the shadow of another small passageway.

On the wall to his left, he saw two doors with round windows in them. He could hear voices behind the doors. He was about to go and look through those windows when one of the doors swung open and a nurse exited the room. She stopped to remove her mask.

Enrico recognized her as the one who had been kind to him moments earlier. He moved slightly.

Catching the movement in the corner of her eye, she turned her head and looked into the shadows. "Who's there?"

Enrico took one step out of the darkness.

"Mother of light!" she exclaimed, her full voice narrowing to a whisper, "It's you. What are you doing out of bed?" As she spoke, she moved to where he was and pushed him back into the shadows.

"Where is the Madonna" he asked quietly, but firmly.

Confused, she looked back over her shoulder to make sure no one had followed her out of the operating room.

"What?" she asked as she turned to face him again. Not waiting for an answer, she bent down slightly so she could get closer to him. "I think you may be in trouble. The man who was in your room is a very bad man. He might try to hurt you. How do you—"

"I'll kill him," he said with confidence.

"Gracious Mother!" she crossed herself, "No, no. You must go. How do you feel?" She bent closer to him. "Do you feel well enough to leave?" She put her hand on the shoulder that wasn't bandaged. "Are you all right? Can you run away? You must leave as soon as you can. Now, if possible. Right away—"

"Where is the Madonna?" He searched her troubled eyes for an answer.

"The Madonna? What do you mean, the Madonna?"

"The professor's daughter."

"Mother of God," she said, finally understanding. She looked back to the operating room doors again, and then she pushed Enrico through the door behind him. She stopped him on the stairwell and bent down. "We took the baby an hour ago. He's fine. The nurses are calling him Juan. But the mother is . . . how do I say this? The one you call the Madonna is. . . . She has gone to Heav—God has called her to Him."

"You mean she's dead," he said without emotion.

She straightened up. "Yes," she said, a little surprised.

"And the professor?"

"The bomb killed him instantly. They didn't bring him . . . his body here to the hospit—"

"A bomb? That's what happened?"

"I thought you. . . . They are saying that the gas stove exploded accidentally. But, I overheard one of the doctors say that from the look of the wounds—" Surprised by the calm way he was asking her questions, and the mature way he seemed to be accepting the answers, she had been lulled into talking to him as she might an adult. She shook her head gently to clear it. "Mother of Mothers. Listen, you must go! You are in danger. Can you leave now?"

"I want the baby."

"What? What do you mean?"

"Can I take the baby with me?"

"You mean the baby Juan? Is that who you mean?"

"Yes. He is like my little brother. I'll take good care of him."

"No, of course not!" She heard the sounds of people moving and talking on the other side of the door. "You must go now. You are well enough. Do you know the way out? This is the ground floor. You must leave from this floor, but you can't go out there now. I hear someone out there. Go up the stairs. Go down the corridor, past the room you were in. There is another stairway at the other end. Go down those stairs. You can find the way from there." She pushed him gently to hurry him.

As he started up the stairs, he paused and looked back at her. "I know his name. It's Ortega! I'll kill him. Someday, I'll kill him. You'll see." He almost smiled at her.

"Mother of God," she said, and crossed herself.

Three blocks from the hospital, Enrico rounded the corner to the alley and stopped. Two workmen stood at the door he used to enter the warehouse. As he waited and watched, a third man came from the inside of the building. This man was carrying most of Enrico's belongings. He threw them into a battered trash can that was pushed up against the fading brick wall. Enrico listened as the man told his companions to come and help clear the mess left by the bums.

When they had all gone inside, Enrico went to the trash can. It only took him a minute to find his sweater. He pulled it over his head. Then, he walked toward the morning sunlight at the other end of the alley.

Something in the smell of the worn and weary threads around his neck reminded him of Bernardo. He wondered where Bernardo had gone. Where had he been all this time? There was so much he wanted to tell his best friend. So much he wanted Bernardo to know.

By the time he reached the end of the second alley, where it had all started, he knew there was only one thing Bernardo needed to know.

You were right, Bernardo, he thought. There is no God.

14

BOGOTA, COLOMBIA
Fall, 2011

The limousine skimmed through the night, its occupants ignoring the great terraces with their elaborate fountained gardens, and the well-lit plazas with their new statues of carefully chosen, old heroes of Santa Fe De Bogotá. It slipped easily through the old section, protecting its passengers from the bath of dull, yellow neon that covered the unwashed downtown streets.

"You should let me do this, Enrico. Killing a captain of the Secret Service could start a war. If they think it's you, it could get . . . unpleasant." Bernardo was anxious for answers. "And what's the point? This guy can't hurt us. He's nothing. We buy and sell guys like him every day."

"It's already a war, you know that." Enrico was calm. "It has always been a war. But Captain Ortega is my business. And tonight he's going to die. Turn here," he said to the back of Juan's head, "into that alley."

Juan turned the limousine into the alley, and they cruised along the worn, uneven blacktop running parallel to the major arteries of the capital city.

"I don't get it." Bernardo couldn't let it go. "You called this guy yourself. You told him you wanted to turn yourself in. You suckered him into meeting you here—"

"Slow down, Juan, we're almost there." Enrico was not in the mood for explanations.

The limousine pushed its way slowly down the industrial passageway and stopped in the shadows of an abandoned warehouse. The engine was turned off, the lights turned out. The rear window went down with a smooth, soft hum.

It had rained earlier in the day and the smell of wet stone edged its way over the black paint and polished chrome of the door frame and touched Enrico Serva's face.

"Is this where you told him to meet you?" Bernardo asked as he looked at the old warehouse. He knew this place.

"Yes."

"You shouldn't bother with shit like this. Just leave me here and go home. I'll cut that old bastard's throat. What about it?" Bernardo's voice was moving toward the border of impatience.

"No," Enrico replied softly. His thoughts were clearly not on his lieutenant's debate. As his eyes continued to examine the details of the fragmenting warehouse, his mind saw two small boys chasing each other through this same alley, many years ago. "We've come a long way, Bernardo."

"When is he supposed to get here?" Bernardo was not in the mood for memories.

"Midnight. Remember this warehouse?"

"Fuck the warehouse. That was a long time ago."

"Don't ever forget where you came from, Bernardo. That's the only way to enjoy where you are."

"I like it just fine where I am. I don't need to remember anything to enjoy myself. I would just like to know what the fuck's going on. You want to off this son of a bitch—I don't know why—some kind of secret kill. We never had secrets before." Bernardo's patience had passed the borderline, and he knew it. He softened his tone as he repeated his plea. "Let me take care of this. That's my job."

"This man has a debt to pay. He's going to pay it to me."

"Fuck." Bernardo shook his head.

"You're a little impatient tonight. Is there a problem?"

"We've got the world by the balls, and that's because of you. You're the smart one, I know that. But I think it's kind of risky for you to be here. If you want someone dead, let me do it. I've always come through for you before. You can trust me."

"I trust you, Bernardo. And I need your help. You're right, we should be ready. Let's go inside and wait for Captain Ortega."

Their footsteps crunched over the debris and dirt as they went down the cluttered corridor toward the old storeroom.

"You don't really think he'll come alone, do you, Bernardo?" Enrico asked. He didn't try to look back over his shoulder.

"He'll bring as many as he can get into one car. Four, maybe five. Anymore and he'd need two cars. He won't make that mistake," Bernardo answered, stepping over a large, fallen board.

"And you can handle that, can't you?"

"I can handle it. As soon as I see where you're going to be, I'll go and take care of it."

"Good. Take Juan with you. He can help."

"Let Juan drive the car. I can take these assholes out myself."

Bernardo had Juan open the trunk of the limo while he checked his Browning Hi-Power, semi-automatic. Then he put the pistol in his belt and reached into the trunk for two Uzis. He checked each magazine.

"What do you want me to do?" Juan asked.

"Nothing," Bernardo said flatly. Then he looked at Juan and reconsidered. He went back into the trunk for another

Uzi. Throwing it to Juan he instructed: "There's going to be four or five of them. They'll come in one car. They'll drop Ortega off here." He stopped to study the alley. "There's not enough room for them to get around the limo, so they'll back out," Bernardo continued, the exasperation of having to deal with an explanation clearly showing on his face. "Then they'll drive around the corner as if they're going away. But they'll come back on foot. They'll come in fast and quiet. As soon as you see them, you take them out." He paused to look at Enrico's adopted son. "Just be fucking careful where you point that thing. Don't take me out! Got it?"

A dark green sedan, with no special government markings or insignia, drifted down the alley and stopped by the back entrance to the warehouse. The passenger-side door opened and Captain Manuel Ortega stepped out carefully. He studied the backside of the warehouse and looked at the empty limousine parked a few feet away. Then he turned back and nodded to his driver. As his car backed toward the end of the alley, he stepped apprehensively through the warehouse door.

Enrico looked into Ortega's eyes. The small naked light bulb, hanging from the ceiling, cast a yellowish glow on the dirty storeroom walls and on their faces.

"Did you come alone?" he asked, knowing Ortega would lie.

"You said on the phone that you would give yourself up to me—if I came alone. Here I am." Ortega did his best to hold Enrico's gaze. But there was something about this man, this drug lord, that scared him. He could feel the fear moving through his bones. What was it? What was there about this man, Enrico Serva, that terrified him so much? And then he knew. Enrico Serva was not scared. He was not afraid. He did not fear being captured—or killed. He wasn't nervous or even worried. His eyes were calm and confident. Thank God for my soldiers, Ortega thought. It will all be over soon.

"You don't remember me do you?" Enrico allowed himself a small smile.

"Remember you?" Ortega probed. Seeing Enrico smile sent a chill through him. "I know who you are. You're Enrico Serva. Should I remember you?" He tried to return Enrico's smile and his lips trembled with the effort. His mind began to race. *Where are my men? They should be here by now. What the hell is keeping them?*

"You've been bouncing back and forth all your life. You've worked for the government, and taken money from the FARC. You're a Captain in the military and you take bribes from Medellin and Cali. But that's not your greatest sin." Enrico hesitated to enjoy Ortega's confusion. "You killed the Madonna."

"I what?" *He's crazy. Enrico Serva is crazy. Too much cocaine or something. Where the hell are my men?*

"Twenty years ago you threw a bomb through the window of an old man's house. He died instantly. His daughter died in the hospital later that night. The doctors saved the baby inside her. The nurses bandaged a little boy who was in that house."

"That was you? That was—"

The sound of gunfire ripped through the warehouse. It seemed to come from every direction—and no direction. It snapped and hissed and smacked around them. They stood face to face—neither one moving—and waited for the sound to end. It cracked and bounced and reverberated away from them and into the night air. They remained motionless—waiting, searching each other's eyes. More gunfire burst up from the darkness beyond the open storeroom door. Then quiet.

There was another sound. A muted, ragged groan. A moaning cry of pain. Then one final gunshot—a pistol this time—and the whisper of breath exiting the lungs—of life leaving the body. Enrico and Ortega stared at each other, unmoving. The sounds were silent.

Enrico smiled, and his eyes said, *I thought you came alone.*

"You couldn't believe I'd come alone?" Ortega asked—almost apologetically.

Enrico did not respond, but his eyes continued to speak for him. *Shame on you. Shame on you for lying. Shame on you for deceiving. Shame on you for living.*

They both turned as a large man appeared in the doorway.

"There were only four of them, Enrico. It's all clear now. If you need me, I'll be outside." Bernardo smiled at Captain Ortega and closed the door as he left.

Even though Ortega saw it coming, there was nothing he could do to stop the blade from ripping into the flesh under his earlobe. His half-scream, cut off at its apex, echoed through the warehouse and out onto the city streets.

"¡Permisso! ¡Permisso!" The young medical technicians yelled their way down the sterile corridor of the *Clinica Del Country,* as they ran the rattling, squeaking gurney toward the main operating room.

The few late-shift interns, on-duty nurses, and exercising patients who had chosen this hallway—with the emergency entrance at the end—stepped aside quickly. Their gaze was also quick; their eyes did not linger on the mutilated shape being rushed past them.

The man on the gurney did not hear the alerting calls of the medics, or the complaining outcry of the wheeled stretcher under him, or the hushed whispers of the onlookers. He was beyond the sounds of the living.

The front of the gurney smashed into the porthole-windowed swinging doors, bursting them open; and the technicians delivered their charge to the middle of the large, emergency operating room.

Before the last squeak of the gurney's wheels had echoed into the ether, two circulating nurses, who had been waiting in a shadowed corner for this arrival, came forward to help direct the placement of the patient under the massive, round operating lights.

Another set of double doors exploded open at the opposite end of the room, and a surgeon entered, followed by two assisting physicians.

The nurses went to prepare the surgeon: dressing him in his pale-blue surgical gown, putting on his mask and hat, and holding the gloves as he slipped his hands into them.

When the surgeon was ready, he moved toward the operating area with the practiced stride of authority.

The technicians moved away from the gurney as he approached.

"Wait," he said, and they stopped where they were.

Standing a few inches from the gurney, the surgeon stared down at the blood-smeared form lying with cadaver-like stillness on the table before him. Without taking his eyes from the carcass, he shook his head and sighed heavily. Then he continued to stare.

The double doors swung again and a man entered slowly and quietly. He was dressed in the overly-unobvious uniform of the secret police: a plain black suit, white dress shirt, and thin black tie.

Everyone but the surgeon looked over to where the man stood. They were immediately unnerved by his presence.

The surgeon did not bend to examine the body; he did not reach to touch the candlewax-like, graying, lifeless skin;

he did not lift the flap of the eyelid with his latex-covered thumb. He remained motionless, staring.

One of the nurses went for a surgical sheet. She brought it to the table and started to spread it over the patient.

"Take that away!" the surgeon ordered sternly.

The deep incision started with a bruise-rimmed puncture two centimeters below the left earlobe. The laceration continued across the full width of the throat, exposing the severed thyroid cartilage and partially destroyed Adam's apple. The wound widened slightly before it terminated at the right ear. In the widest part of the recalcitrant trench, a tiny piece of the jugular vein rested in a glob of jellied, dark-red blood.

"This man is dead," the surgeon said, his voice carrying the tone of a complaint. He looked at the technicians. "Why did you bring him here? This man belongs in the morgue!"

Nervously, all eyes but the surgeon's went to the man by the door.

"Captain Ortega is a prominent member of the military staff," the man said. "He is of great importance to our government."

"Captain Ortega is dead," the surgeon replied, finally looking at the man. "He's not important to anyone anymore." He turned to leave the room.

"You should have more respect," the man said to the surgeon's back.

"Take him out of here!" the surgeon called back over his shoulder.

The man approached the operating table, took a last confirming view of the body, then left the operating room.

When the room was empty of all but one nurse, she approached the gurney and looked at the dead man's face.

She remembered a child, a small boy with a bandaged shoulder, standing in the stairwell just beyond the swinging doors. How long ago was that? It didn't matter how many years had passed. This was a child she would never forget. His defiant little voice echoed across the distance of her memory.

"I know his name. It's Ortega! I'll kill him. Someday, I'll kill him. You'll see."

"Mother of God," she whispered as she crossed herself.

15

LOS ANGELES, CALIFORNIA

It was easy for Thomas Kelly to get to the office by 7:00 a.m. Wanting to cheat his mind of more nightmare images of Jason Fenny, he had kept himself awake reviewing the Enrico Serva folder until the sunlight had pushed him out of the kitchen and into his morning shower.

In the underground parking garage of the Federal building, he noticed the limousine that was permanently assigned to Hunt stationed near the elevator. Hunt was ahead of him.

But, as he pushed his tired frame down the corridor, he saw that Hunt's door was closed, the signal that he didn't want to be disturbed. Kelly continued past the door without a second glance.

He threw the Serva file down on his desk, dropped into his aged imitation-leather swivel chair and fought the urge to get back up and go for a cup of coffee. His muscles stitched a pins and needles complaint at having been kept up all night. He stretched and shook his head, but it didn't help. He thought about closing his eyes for just a moment's rest, but decided against it. His eyes closed anyway.

"Yo, Kellyboy, are you asleep or just antisocial?" Larry Anderson's voice called to him through ears that were filled with clouds.

"What?" Kelly opened his eyes and looked at his new partner. "No, I'm not asleep," he said gruffly. He glanced at the clock. 8:05. He had dozed for almost an hour.

"Right." Anderson smiled as he sat down easily on the hard pad of the armless, chrome-legged chair that was reserved for Kelly's guests.

Hunt had brought Larry Anderson in to fill the spot left vacant by Jason Fenny. Anderson was a tall man with a heavy bone structure and long dense muscles. When he spoke, it was usually in quick, short sentences.

Kelly didn't know much about his new partner. Up till now, Anderson had been a soldier on the streets. He had kicked in doors and made his share of dynamic entries and arrests. It seemed to Kelly that Anderson was excited to have this promotion. Kelly wondered how long that excitement would last when he found out that this was more of a desk job than anything else.

"Been studying the new stuff?" Anderson indicated the folder with his light-blue eyes.

"You know what's missing?" Kelly leaned back in his chair.

"What?"

"A girlfriend. Hell, the guy's thirty-one. Has he ever had a serious relationship? What have we got on Serva's girlfriends?"

"Serva likes women," Anderson advised. "As far as I've heard, it's always been in the plural form. Lots of broads. Never just one. Never anything serious. But, what the hell, let's go ask Mama." Mama was Anderson's pet name for the agency's new computer.

As they walked down the hall to the control room, Anderson amused himself by mumbling, "Broads in the plural form. What a concept. Some guys have all the fun."

Kelly held the door open as Anderson moved past him and into the brain center of the Los Angeles headquarters.

Mama's residence stood as a testament to Evans Hunt's ability to secure a large budget, and a showcase for high-tech equipment. Three spacious, adjoining offices had been broken down to make one considerable expanse. In a closet designed for protection, Mama's brain, the size of a refrigerator, sat in matronly silence, her vital life signs indicated only by the intermittent flickering of a few small red, green and yellow lights. One wall was filled with a hundred inch, LCD Monitor. In the center of the room was a clear, rectangular console desk, where images could be swept up to that monitor with the wave of a hand. There were various stations where computer technicians or agents could connect to Mama from their personal laptops, monitors and smart phones. Because it was never empty of agents and programmers, it had a busy atmosphere.

All the terminals were occupied. Anderson nudged one of the programmers on the shoulder and gave him the "get out of the way" thumb movement. After saving his current data to memory, the programmer acquiesced without complaint. The programmers were only there to input the information gathered by the agents; the agents had priority in the control room.

Anderson sat down and rubbed his hands together. "Let's see, how do you spell 'Serva's girlfriends'?" he joked as his trained fingers began to tick and tack with a speed that amazed Kelly.

"How do you do that?" Kelly asked enviously. "Mama never cooperates when I'm sitting there."

"It's all in the wrist, Kellyboy. Of course, Mama always liked me best." The monitor blinked twice and letters began to chase each other across the screen, lining up like soldiers late for reveille. "Here it comes . . . quite a list . . . lots of names . . . mostly hookers . . . and a lot of them . . . an occasional Colombian socialite. . . ." The screen jumped once, the top name disappeared, and a new one appeared at the bottom. "Like I said, broads in the Plur-L; some guys have all the fun."

16

BOGOTA, COLOMBIA
Spring, 2012

Lying on his back, his eyes still closed from sleep, Enrico Serva felt the soft warmth of a woman's arm across his chest. The arm, he remembered immediately, belonged to one of the two whores Bernardo had sent to his room the night before. He could also feel other, more prominent parts of the woman's body as it paralleled his own.

He opened his eyes and stared into the beautiful young Indian face. That's one, he smiled to himself, but where is the other one? Turning his head, he found her on the other half of the king-sized bed. Lying almost on her stomach, her black hair fanned out over the nakedness of her back. She looked like an Incan princess.

Both whores were asleep. They had devoured the cocaine Bernardo had provided for them, and then, after giving Enrico everything he had wanted, they had fallen hard into dreams of their own . . . cocaine dreams.

The black-haired beauty stirred, stretched like a cat, and rolled onto her back. Her legs tangled in the blue satin sheet, pulling it halfway down her perfumed body. Unconsciously, she ran her hand over her large, burgundy-colored nipple.

Enrico sat up, admiring the tease the Incan's delicate fingers made on her perfectly-shaped breast. Then he turned his gaze back to the first whore.

This girl was clearly Andean. Her gorgeous face was more sculptured than formed. Her brown hair hung straight except where it curved slightly to follow the line set by her high cheekbones. Her shoulders were broad and her breasts were firm. Her skin was smooth and there was no extra fat on her anywhere.

As his eyes absorbed her flat stomach and the tight skin of her hips, he felt an erection come into full hardness. He gently rolled the Andean beauty onto her back and carefully put her arms above her head. Then he straddled her chest. He felt the warm softness of her skin on the inside of his thighs as his knees dug into the satin covered mattress. He hung, throbbing, above her slender throat.

"Ummmm . . ." she moaned, as her eyelids lifted to reveal the startling depth of her brown eyes.

Without a word, Enrico leaned forward and put one arm out to the carved teak headboard to balance himself. He reached his free hand under her head, and taking a fistful of her hair, he drew her sleepy face toward his now aching groin. He leaned back from the headboard so he could hold her head with both of his hands. He tilted her face up to look at his. "Wake up, *gata,* I have something for you."

Her lips parted slowly and he guided himself into her soft wet mouth.

As he rocked himself in and out of the Andean girl's mouth, he began a low guttural groaning. Watching what he did to her excited him even more, and his groan grew louder and higher. The sound of her lips smacking and sucking only added to his feverish passion.

With the noise and movement on the bed, the other prostitute began to stir. "Join the party," he managed to grunt through his near breathless lust.

She twisted on her side, with her legs still tangled in the sheet, and slid across the bed until her lips touched the top of his kneecap. Her tongue licked his thigh as she pushed herself up to join the Andean girl.

"Not there," he said as she came in range of his grasp. "We'll have to find you another place." He gripped the back of her head, as he still had the first girl's, and started to maneuver her toward his back. Tangled as she was in the sheet, she almost fell over his calves. But somehow, she kept her balance and adjusted to her new position behind him on the bed. She knew what he wanted. She also knew better than to refuse him. She had heard rumors of what had happened to women who denied Enrico Serva. It was nothing she wanted to think about, now or ever. The money was good. Better than good. She would give him anything he wanted without hesitation. She pushed her face into his ass and her tongue began searching the hidden part of his skin.

His domination of the two whores was now complete. Each of his fists held one of them by the hair at the back of her head. He strained to see the girl at his back, but all he could see was the side of her head and the lower part of her legs lost in the sheet. He turned his visual attention back to the Andean.

He felt the warm wetness of the girl in front of him as she applied a soft pressure, and the delicate penetration of the tongue of the girl behind him, and he lost himself in pleasure. And then the tongue found its mark.

A spike of electricity shot through every vein in Enrico's body, and he spilled himself into the soft willingness of the brown-skinned Andean whore.

She did everything she could to keep control as Enrico's cum hit her like waves in the throat. His last thrust was too deep. With his unrelenting grip still on the back of her head, he pushed himself hard into her. He stayed down too long. She choked. Her body jerked as her esophagus muscles reacted to the foreign object pressing on them. Gagging, she pushed both hands into his abdomen in an instinctive effort to free herself, and threw her head back, gasping for air.

Enrico sat back on her legs and his ankles, and the other girl twisted and fell off the bed, taking the sheet with her.

Coughing, the Andean lost some of what Enrico had left in her. It spit out over her lip and lay in a thin, clammy line on her chin.

Enrico only looked at her for a second. And then he exploded. Grabbing her by the throat with his left hand, he raised her up and smashed his right fist into her cheek. She felt and heard the crack of the blow all the way down her spine. Her head snapped out of his grasp and she fell back on the bed. The left side of her face began to swell immediately. Incredibly, she did not lose consciousness.

Enrico grabbed her by the throat again, and pulling her up to face him, he whispered, "I've killed women for less than that, bitch." Still straddling her, he pushed her back down on the bed. She turned her head away from him and tried, with everything she had, to stifle the coughs that still remained in her.

As he debated the idea of finishing the beating he had started on the Andean girl, a strange, soft sound reached him. It took him a moment to realize that it was the other whore praying.

From somewhere off the end of the bed, her whispered appeals—imploring her maker to extricate her from this *valle de la sombra del muerto*—came to Enrico like the sound of an ancient song. The silky tone and gently rhythmic melody of her voice lifted his mood immediately. He realized it was the first time he had heard her speak. She had said nothing either the night before or at any time during the morning's escapade. There had been no reason for her to talk. He certainly liked the sound of her voice. He felt good again.

"Where are you?" he called out as he took himself off the Andean and stood on the floor.

There was no reply, but he merely had to lean a little to see her huddled on the floor at the foot of the bed.

"Come over here," he said. When she looked up, he added, "On your hands and knees."

The tone of his voice was not threatening and she obeyed. She crawled over to him, and sat back on her heels with her hands still on the floor. Her beautiful breasts hung like teardrops, close to his strong legs.

He noticed again, the deep burgundy color of her nipples. "Kiss me," he said.

She reached her hands to his legs, and leaning in, she began licking his thigh as she had before.

"Now sing to me." He smiled down at her.

"¿Que?" She looked up, confused.

"Pray, bitch. I want to hear your voice. Say something!" He was angry again.

"No entiendo," she said, moving her head back and forth very slowly.

The sound of the telephone took his attention away from her, quite possibly saving her life.

Deciding to take the call on the more private line in his study, he called back over his shoulder, "Don't be here when I get back."

When she was sure he was out of the room and couldn't hear her, the Inca leaned up on the end of the bed and whispered to the Andean, "We're lucky we're not dead."

The Andean said nothing.

They both began gathering their clothes swiftly in the silence.

17

NORTH HOLLYWOOD, CALIFORNIA

At first he thought it was the rain that had awakened him, the undemanding rhythm on the windows and roof.

Then RoboDobe came up off the kitchen floor, barked once, and stood at attention.

Kelly lifted his head from the folder on the kitchen table and leaned back into his chair to listen. Beyond the persistence of the mild shower, he heard the sound again: a timid tapping on the old wood of his front door.

RoboDobe's eyes went to Kelly with the look of a battle-ready soldier awaiting orders.

Kelly looked at the stove clock: 9:47. He gave the "Stay" command to RoboDobe, went to the front door, opened the small security window, and looked through.

"Hi, Tom . . . it's me." Lorraine's dark eyes searched for him through the 3"x5" opening.

He opened the door immediately.

Lorraine Harte stood on his porch holding two foil-covered plates of food, one in each hand. She had buttoned herself into a slick, yellow raincoat and matching, full-brimmed hat. She also wore large, yellow-rubber rain boots with thick, black soles. Any other woman would have looked like a crossing guard for an elementary school, and he would have chuckled at the outfit. But Lorraine made it look like high fashion.

"Something told me you didn't make yourself any dinner," she said, smiling softly, "and I thought you might be hungry." Her soft, sultry voice was the perfect extension to her beautiful face. "Just a hunch, I guess. Am I right?" She held out the plates for Kelly to take. "Lasagna, tossed salad, and there's some cookies here, too."

"Are you kidding? You must be psychic, Lorraine. Dinner. Thanks a lot. Hey, come on in."

"No, I don't want to bother you; I know you're busy. I just thought you might like to have this. By the way, I got that part in the ballet—you know, the one at the Music Center? The other girl broke her leg. Can you believe it? Everyone always tells you to 'break a leg' for luck, and she really did it."

"That's great, Lorraine—that you got the part, I mean. I guess I better not say 'break a leg,' right?"

"Right. Well, see ya." She hesitated and he thought she might change her mind about coming in.

He almost wanted her to, but he was not in love with her, and he didn't want to fool either one of them. And, she was a neighbor. And. . . .

"Oh, by the way," she reached inside her raincoat and brought out a large, manila envelope. "Here's my new headshot . . . thought you might like one. I don't need as many copies since I got the part. Well . . . bye." She turned away.

"Bye Lorraine." The echo of his whispery voice trailed after her as she crossed the rain-dampened street.

He watched her go home. When she was safely through her own door, he turned back into the house and confronted RoboDobe.

"She got all the way up on the porch, and knocked before you woke up. Good thing we don't have a lot of enemies, cause you're worthless!" Kelly continued his admonishment as he strolled back into the kitchen. "Man, I'll tell you, Agent

Dobe, Enrico Serva would eat you for lunch . . . and spit out the *bones!"*

Agent Dobe's head jerked when he heard the familiar word.

18

BOGOTA, COLOMBIA

Enrico sat in his study, naked. When he moved, his skin stuck to the oxblood leather of the antique, wing-backed chair. As he answered Bernardo's call, he surveyed his surroundings.

He had chosen everything in this room carefully and had enjoyed arranging it himself. From the original Picasso hanging on one wall, to the pre-Columbian ceremonial gold flask, which had been purchased on the black market and now held a privileged position on the third tier of his fifteenth century bookshelf, the atmosphere of his study hung heavy with the reflection of his wealth.

"They're at the gate," Bernardo said and waited for instructions.

"Bring them to the conference room," Enrico said with a reflective tone. "I want to take a shower. I'll be down in a moment." He paused, then continued, "Make them comfortable, Bernardo."

Bernardo waved the three Mercedes limousines through the massive, black iron gates of the Serva estate. Before he got into the golf cart he used to negotiate the grounds, he called the housekeeper, "Anita, four at the front door."

As if it had been rehearsed, the front door opened slowly as the three limos arrived.

If my timing was always this good, I'd never need rubbers, Bernardo thought as he joined the guests entering the Enrico Serva residence.

When Enrico entered the conference room, he smiled at his guests. He had kept them waiting. "Gentlemen," he said with absolutely no apology in his voice, "it's much too beautiful a day to be stuck inside. I've arranged for luncheon to be served on the east terrace."

Enrico enjoyed being a host. His slim, strong body was the perfect showcase for his internationally elegant taste in clothes. His skin was a light shade of brown and gave the impression of a perpetual, jetsetter's tan. His shiny black hair was combed back off his forehead like soft, malleable steel. Under his thick black eyebrows, tiny red flecks swam in a pool of brown, as his eyes glowed with the promise of ample wit and intelligence. Immaculate white teeth basked in a smile that any politician would gladly pay to own.

His charm easily captured his guests' attention. They relaxed as he led them through the luxury of his home and into the bright Bogotá sunlight.

As the four Colombian businessmen seated themselves under the soft white and yellow umbrella of the patio table, Enrico indulged himself with a deep breath of the thin fresh air that migrated down from the mountains.

Standing off from the others, he looked across the manicured lawn which gently sloped upward, and was lost in a stand of cashew nut trees that walled this part of the estate. Over the trees he could see the two mountains, Guadalupe and Monserrate, and the churches resting placidly on their crests. The view from this terrace never failed to inspire him. Somewhere in his mind, he hypothesized that his domain did not end at the trees, but included the mountains as well, and everything beyond.

"*¿No va a sentarse con nosotros?*" With a slight hint of impatience, one of the guests encouraged him to join them.

Enrico's meditation left him as if it had been cut off with a knife. He went to the table where the others were waiting and smiled at them reassuringly as he took his place. Lifting his glass of champagne, he said, "*¡Viva México!*"

For a moment, the stunned group stared at him not knowing if he was toasting or joking. And then, slowly, they raised their glasses and mumbled a confused, "*¡Viva México!*"

Rafael Santos was the first to question. "Why are we toasting them?"

"Because, my friend, those violent, low-life, drug-dealing assholes are taking all the press and the heat away from us." His eyes drifted back to the mountains. "Wonderful, isn't it?" His gaze returned to his guests. "When was the last time you heard anything about the Colombian drug cartels in the international press?" He nodded to Anita to begin serving. "Gentlemen, enjoy your lunch."

The sun hung like a sailboat anchored in a cobalt ocean as the help, supervised by Anita, slipped quietly in and out of the current of conversation with carefully practiced indifference.

Enrico had collected and congealed these four Colombian businessmen into a powerful group. As their power grew, so did his control over them. He smiled and nodded and joked as he considered his guests.

Alberto Mendez was the current head of a family that had raised sheep—for more years than anyone could remember—on the sloping hills that spilled down out of the Andes and into the city of Paz Del Rio.

Leon Perez was Alberto's brother-in-law and had his own ranch farther to the north near Cucuta, where he raised cattle.

Both men shared more than a rancher's life. Together, they controlled, farmed, and guarded a vast stretch of land in a quietly remote section of the Eastern Cordillera. Their

Valle, as they referred to it, had been cleared and replanted with the best Peruvian and Bolivian coca plants, and was continually cultivated by the youngest and strongest Chibcha Indian subsistence farmers they could hire.

Next around the table was Antonio Mutis. The Mutis Shipping Company had ships at port in Buenaventura for commerce to the west coast of the United States and the Far East, and Santa Marta to transport freight to the east coast of the United States and across the Atlantic. Their legitimate enterprise had become the perfect cover for Enrico's not so legitimate cargo. Under Enrico's direction, Antonio had shipped Alberto's and Leon's "crop" to most of the major ports of the world. Antonio lived in Medellin because he had been born there and because he didn't care much for the coastal cities.

Enrico knew the least about the fourth man.

Rafael Santos was a thick, dark man who had chipped and strained an existence, if not a profit, from a small emerald mine in Muzo. He was less wealthy and quieter than the others. But Rafael seemed to have connections everywhere in the world: strange, nameless friends who would do things no one else would do. Instinctively, Enrico had known that those connections would be important to the group.

The luncheon menu, prepared by Anita, centered on seafood. The meal started with baby shrimp lying on a bed of shredded lettuce, delicately enhanced with a rich cocktail sauce.

Enrico noticed that Rafael was filling his salad fork with a large bite. He decided this would be an interesting time to challenge the man with a question. "Would you think it impolite of me, Rafael, to offer you a cabernet wine with your fish? He had timed his question so that he spoke the man's name as the fork was nearing his lips.

The fork stopped in mid-air and Rafael stared at Enrico for a second. Then, with the shrimp still dangling, Rafael's eyes darted to the other guests around the table. Enrico could see that Rafael was definitely confused as to whether he should put the fork back down and answer, or wait and eat the food as the others watched him.

"You know . . ." Enrico turned his attention to the others, but kept a peripheral view of Rafael. ". . . I have this wonderful cabernet from Chile called *Concha Y Toro* . . . but I don't want to appear ignorant by offering the wrong wine with this meal."

The two brothers-in-law and Antonio, having been raised in the strict social atmosphere of Colombia's old rich, poured forth with flattering comments on the beautifully designed lunch. They hastened to add that they would be more than willing to try the Chilean wine.

Rafael put the fork down and waited. As the others took up the conversation, he took his bite.

Like small waves sliding on the beach, the entrées were slipped before the men by the almost invisible hands of two white-jacketed waiters: swordfish, thickly sliced and broiled, and brown rice.

Rafael's moderately laden fork started for his waiting mouth.

"Will you have some *tortillas*, Rafael?" Enrico finessed a wicker bread basket toward his associate.

Rafael paused again. His lips pursed then curled into a thin smile. His flickering eyes squinted at Enrico as he put his fork back down on his plate. He accepted the basket.

"You know," Enrico continued to the others, "Anita makes such delicious *tortillas* . . . I prefer them to any other kind of bread."

Leon tore a portion of the bread over his plate. "We should all be as fortunate as you, Enrico, to have someone like Anita."

Enrico smiled and nodded his acceptance of the compliment. He could never forget where he had come from.

He had worked many hours to gain the ability to be a good host.

At the proper time, the entrée dishes were gently swept away like pieces of driftwood from a summer shore. Coffee was poured from a silver urn.

Rafael lifted his cup.

"There's nothing like Colombian coffee is there, Rafael?" Without taking his eyes off Rafael, Enrico sat back in his chair, crossed his legs, and put his cup in his lap.

"Something you don't control, eh, Enrico? Rafael held his coffee cup at chest level and smiled over it.

"No. I'm afraid Juan Valdez sold out to the Americans before I could get to him," he joked. "Maybe some of your emeralds would persuade him to sell to us?"

"I have better things to buy than coffee." Rafael did not attempt to drink from the cup. It remained at his chest.

"Tell me, Rafael, what's more important than Colombian coffee?" Enrico smiled and casually put his cup to his lips.

Alberto couldn't stop himself from interjecting, "A bank is more important. Wouldn't you say a bank is more important, Enrico?"

"I think he's playing with us, Alberto," Leon apprised his brother-in-law.

"Gentlemen, please." Enrico enjoyed the attention.

"The warehouses are full, Leon," Alberto leaned forward in his seat and put his elbows on the now cleared table, "Full of money we can't use. The rats are eating it, for Christ's sake."

"No more games, Enrico. What can we do?" asked Leon.

Enrico shrugged and slid his empty cup back onto the table. "You're right, Leon. The other corporations have successfully kept us out of the Caymans. And you know, it's not just as simple as typing account numbers into a computer. At some point, you actually have to deliver the cash." He looked at Rafael. "I believe Rafael is going to help us with that. Rafael?"

Rafael still held his full and cooling coffee cup in front of him. Realizing that all the attention had shifted to him, he put the cup down carefully with a slightly shaking hand. His eyes oscillated from one business associate to another. He cleared his throat. "We need the . . . ah . . . support of a friendly bank," he started tentatively, "but there's so much attention these days on money laundering. It hasn't been an easy search. However, some European associates of mine have come up with a plan that may be of interest to us. It's rather ah . . . tricky."

"Get to the point," Leon belched.

"It sounds a little ah . . . wild when you first hear it," Rafael continued, trying to ignore Leon's impatience. "However, most of the risk is theirs, and I have great confidence in them. They're Swiss, actually, and may be in a position to supply a Swiss bank."

"How would they do that?" Alberto asked, honestly curious.

"They believe they can assassinate the bank's owner and put ah . . . an impostor in his place long enough for us to secure an account and bury it."

"Is this some kind of a joke?" Alberto asked, his curiosity fading.

"An impostor . . . ?" Leon added to Alberto's question.

Enrico realized that Rafael was losing his audience. He addressed Antonio, "How much do we have in the warehouse?"

"Just under forty billion, Enrico," Antonio replied without hesitation.

"If we pushed the Los Angeles cartel for a big sale, could we top it out at forty-five billion?" Enrico continued with Antonio.

"Perhaps. It depends on when you try. If they need the product, they'll get the money. We delivered a shipment three months ago. The market may not be ready yet."

"Saturation?" Enrico questioned.

"Exactly," Antonio confirmed.

"How long do we wait?"

"Three months," Antonio estimated, "if you want the market to be prime."

"What do they want?" Enrico asked of Rafael.

Before Rafael could respond, Alberto cut him off. "Am I the only one who thinks this sounds crazy?"

"Loco," Leon concurred with his brother-in-law's position.

"We only need one day. Less than that. Maybe one hour! All we really need is to get in, Enrico," Rafael argued. "Once we've got the account—once we're in—"

"Crazy," Alberto said shaking his head. "How long can they keep up a charade like that with the bank?"

"What happens when the death of the banker is discovered?" Leon probed, picking up Alberto's momentum.

"When the death of the banker is discovered, the ownership changes hands. But our account would already be buried, and beyond scrutiny. We could continue to use it," Rafael countered.

"What do they want?" Enrico repeated his question to Rafael. The table went silent as each man, in his own way, waited for Rafael's answer.

"Well . . ." he paused, and then rushed on, ". . . they want fifty million dollars, American. They want the money in cash; they don't trust banks."

"What?" Alberto asked, almost laughing.

"Loco." Leon replaced Alberto's question mark with a period.

"Are we stupid?" Enrico asked, looking from one stunned face to the next, "Are we?" When the silence lingered, he continued. "The American's think we're all poor itinerant farmers, led by uneducated psychopaths, interested only in drugs, sex, and money. What do you think, Alberto? Leon? Are you poor?" He paused to give them time to answer. They looked at each other and then back to him as he resumed his quest for answers with Rafael, "And you, Rafael. Are you a psychosexual? Or you, Antonio?" This time he didn't wait for an answer. "NO!" He slapped the table, and what was left of the silverware jingled in response. Then he repeated more quietly, "No. You're international businessmen taking your rightful place in the world of the twenty-first century." Again he paused for effect. His associates would need time for the rapture to settle in.

"We're not stupid, gentlemen. If we were, we wouldn't have collected forty billion dollars in just ten years. Think of it, gentlemen. We now compete with some of the largest corporations in North and South America. The profit from our product compares to that of the largest corporations in the world!"

Enrico had his group spellbound, and he knew it. Now was the time to clinch their support. He took a breath, relaxed, and smiled at his luncheon guests.

"We're not stupid, gentlemen. A few months ago, when Rafael first told me of this plan, I have to admit it seemed a little unstable. However, Antonio and I did a little research—"

"What do you mean, 'research'?" Alberto interrupted.

"What is the name of the bank, Antonio?" Enrico asked.

"Banque Nationale de Suisse," Antonio answered instantly.

"The *Banque Nationale de Suisse* is owned by an individual. What is his name, Antonio?"

"Wolfgang Metter." Antonio's robotic tone slipped easily into Enrico's trance-setting enthusiasm.

"In the event of his death, his board of directors would be in control for the time it would take to settle his estate. And that, gentlemen, could be quite some time.

"Antonio," Enrico pursued his associate, "how many members serve on the Board of Directors?"

"Seven, Enrico."

"And how many have we contacted?"

"Five."

"And, of those five, how many could be persuaded to uh . . . let a sleeping dog lie? Every man has his price."

"My best guess is all of them, Enrico."

Enrico looked at each man in turn, first Antonio, then Leon, then Alberto, and finally, Rafael. "Tell them thirty million, Rafael. We're not killing a president here." He turned to Antonio and smiled. Thirty million ought to be enough. Wouldn't you agree, Antonio?"

Antonio lifted his wine glass. "To Enrico Serva," he offered.

Leon and Alberto smiled at each other and pushed their glasses skyward. "Enrico Serva," they acknowledged.

Confused as to how he had lost their attention, Rafael was the last to reach for his glass. "Enrico Serva," he said more softly than the others, and a little late.

The sun calmly set sail into the Andean afternoon, and Enrico sat back to watch them sip their salute. He smiled confidently.

As Bernardo held the doors of Enrico's limousines for the others, Rafael hesitated by the front door of the estate. When he spoke to Enrico, his voice was low and guarded.

"There's something else, Enrico. One more thing the men in Switzerland want."

"What is it?" Enrico prodded patiently.

"They want us to uh . . . take care of an American woman for them."

"Take care of?" Enrico encouraged.

Rafael looked at Bernardo coming up the steps toward them and didn't continue.

To reassure Rafael, Enrico put his hand on Bernardo's shoulder. "Rafael has a problem, Bernardo."

Bernardo nodded and looked at Rafael.

Enrico continued, "It's okay, Rafael. Please go on. You want us to take care of an American woman. What do you mean, 'take care of'?" Even though Rafael had looked away, Enrico could see that his eyes were hurrying to keep up with his thoughts.

Rafael was uncomfortable with the change in focus from the Swiss to himself. "They want us to kill her, Enrico."

Enrico looked to Bernardo and smiled.

Bernardo nodded.

19

LOS ANGELES, CALIFORNIA
Summer, 2012

Like an old general, the sun rose above the Santa Monica Mountains and swung its feet down softly on Los Angeles. With an unhurried sigh, scouts of ultraviolet rays were dispatched to the west to find the sea.

Mulholland Drive, the snake of tar that stretches between the city and the valley, patiently accepted the troops of summer heat that started to crawl along its spine.

Slight breezes, like Santa Ana's spies, moved north toward the quiet Studio City house, tucked neatly into the hillside of the already warm, arid-green canyon. Brushing the lace curtains aside, they slipped over the windowsill and entered the bedroom. Silently, they observed the young woman as she moved into the morning.

Waking before the alarm, Jesse made her way to the bathroom with less dependence on her crutches than at any time before. Settling into her bath, she realized that she felt calm, surprisingly calm for the mission she faced. Giving up her crutches would be no easy task.

Her alarm clock radio came alive with its morning song, and she found herself humming along with the familiar tune. She was calm.

Holding the metal handrail that her father had installed for her, she leaned her back against the tub wall. She noticed, as she always did, the strange sensation created on her skin by the two extremes of the warm water and the cool porcelain. This sensation also reminded her that there was now a small, triangle-shaped pink scar at the base of her spine that didn't feel anything.

The cozy, fifties style bathroom, with its small window over the tub, was decorated in the pink and gray tile so popular when the house was built.

Without interruption from a disc-jockey, the radio played another song, and she closed her eyes to relax and reflect on the coming event. In a few hours, Coach would pick her up. He would not only expect her to throw away her crutches and proceed with a cane, but he would expect her to be excited about it . . . and fearless. Yes, he would expect her to be courageous.

Courage, however, was an area where she was having problems. The motivation—the desire—was definitely lacking. And, when she remembered the doctor's concern for what might happen if she reinjured herself, it was all she could do to hide her apprehension.

As she considered the possibilities of what the day might bring, she felt a twinge of nerves in her stomach. She forced herself to think of something else.

Her parents had insisted she give up her Mission Viejo apartment and take their guest room with bath. They had done everything they could to section off that area of the house for her privacy. Her father had gone on to install those things that would facilitate her recovery. After that, they had tried to leave her alone, because they knew she wanted it that way. But, like silent partners, they were surprisingly near when she needed support, and she was experiencing a closeness to them now that she hadn't felt in years.

The voice of the radio's morning man broke into her tenuous reverie as it called across the hardwood floor of her room. "Good morning all you happy campers! It's seven forty-one. The temperature is seventy-two degrees, and it looks like it's going to be another hot one in L.A. today. . . ."

She couldn't put herself in the "happy camper" category, but for the first time in months, she wasn't unhappy. She was calm. Whether that feeling was real or just a new version of an old emotional numbness, she wasn't sure. But she would settle for calm.

She dried and dressed, reclaimed her crutches, and went back to the bedroom. Seating herself at the vanity, she leaned the crutches against the wall next to the mirror in front of her.

She had almost finished the application of her make-up when her eyes drifted to the reflection of the sign hanging on the wall behind her own image. The fact that the letters were reversed by the mirror made no difference to her. It was a simple sign: two hand-written words. She had read it more times than she could count. It had been made to inspire her, and most of the time it did. "STAY TOUGH" it demanded, and most of the time, she had.

Her deep green eyes drifted from the encouraging words of the sign to the crutches leaning inertly against the wall. They wandered back to the sign again. Then back to the crutches. And then they froze somewhere in between, paralyzed.

It was the fear she had tried to repress earlier now surfacing in another way. It was the months of overwhelming pain and disappointment as she had endured the process of rehabilitation. And, it was the profound realization that she would never dive again. She didn't think in terms of walking; she thought in terms of diving.

With the ultra-thin eyebrow pencil poised a few inches from her fragile face, a single tear slowly edged its way over her lower lid and started a journey down toward the delicate curve of her full upper lip.

Like Dorothy being swept away to Oz, her unrestrained thoughts cast her mind into a dreamlike review of the wins and losses of the last six months.

The hospital room was filled with doctors, nurses, and family. Coach Braden leaned into one quiet corner next to a window.

The specialist stood at the end of the bed, frowning at the girl who was settling into her own self-pity.

"At the risk of being redundant," he said, attempting a professional smile, "let me repeat myself. You've been in a serious, serious accident. We've done everything we can do, and, let me remind you, these are the best services you can get. Still, I've reviewed your case very, very carefully. Judging by your x-rays, and all the other information this staff has provided, it is my prognosis that your wound is far too serious for me to believe that you should attempt to be ambulatory. The healing of your fracture is tentative at best, and I wouldn't want to be responsible for anything that might happen if you try to walk. Of course, we'll continue to review your case, but at present, we've done everything possible. I'm sorry."

When there was no reply, he started for the door. One of the nurses held it open for him and he left the room. The rest of the staff followed him out.

Jack Fortune forced a smile at his daughter and said, "I'll talk to him."

Ruth Fortune reached for Jesse's hand, but Jack urged, "Come on, Hon." She kissed Jesse gently on the forehead and said, "I'll be right back."

Not knowing what to say, Chris gripped her hand for a second and then followed his parents out of the room in silence.

The whole scene reminded Jesse of a funeral procession she had seen in an old movie.

"Bullshit!" Matthew Braden retorted to any doom-filled spirit that still lingered in the room. He continued to speak as he moved toward Jesse. "That doctor's never dived from a ten meter platform. He doesn't know what it means to be a champion. All we need is a plan. Wheelchair to crutches to walking. Elevation, execution, entry. You've done it before; you can do it again." He paused at the side of her bed and smiled. "You've already got a coach. I'll get us a gym and call you tomorrow." Then he strutted out of the room; a man on a mission.

She was making it difficult for him. More than difficult. She pushed her wheelchair hard into the mat-covered wall of the small Van Nuys gym, and locked the wheels. To him, it looked as if someone had stuck her to the wall. He yelled at her to turn around, but she stared straight ahead.

"How's the wall, Babe? Nice view?" he prodded.

She refused to respond.

"Whenever you're ready, we'll try again," he said softly, trying the gentle approach.

She gave no response.

"We've got a job to do, Jesse. It's time for you to be out of that wheelchair and onto these crutches." He pointed to the crutches leaning patiently against the wall near her. "If you're gonna sit on the 'pity pot'—I'm outta here. I'm too old for that kinda crap."

Still no response.

Turning on his heels, he went to the desk at the far side of the training room. Secretly, he hoped she might think he was leaving and turn around, but she didn't.

He picked up a large piece of cardboard and went around the desk opening drawers until he found a black marking pen. When he was finished scribbling, he looked up. She hadn't moved.

He fished around in the desk again until he found a roll of masking tape. Tearing off a strip about two inches long, he stuck it to the top of the cardboard, leaving an inch hanging.

On his way back to stand beside her, he thought about hunching down so he'd be at eye level with her, but decided against it. That would be babying her.

He couldn't think of anything to say, so he didn't say anything. He stared at her.

She stared at the wall.

They stayed that way for a few seconds.

And then he slapped the cardboard sign on the wall in front of her, leaning over her to do so. The free piece of tape came to rest on the wall, and he hit it hard to make it stick. The slap of his hand reverberated through the empty gym. It also startled her and the upper part of her body bobbed back in the wheelchair.

As it was unavoidable, she looked at the sign.

"STAY TOUGH" was its simple message.

She turned her head away so he wouldn't see her cry. She hadn't cried often in her life, and she hated every insipid teardrop, and the weakness it professed. "It's so strange . . ." she began, her words stuttering over a trembling lip, ". . . after all I've been through the last few months: the pain, the blackness, the loneliness; and the loss. I've lost everything, Coach. I lost him and I was too drunk and banged up to cry. I lost the use of my legs and I was too doped up to cry. I lost my diving and I was too numb to cry. Now that there's nothing to cry about. . . . Oh, go away. What's the point? Just go away! Leave me alone!" Still not facing him, she wound down with, "And take that stupid sign with you!"

"What do you mean 'stupid'? What the hell's wrong with my sign?" In the midst of her self-pity, he heard a glimmer of hope. Her casual arrogance toward his sign was the most human she had sounded since her return from Europe.

"It's stupid," she said still not looking at him, but her voice lost some of its tears.

"You're stupid," he said to the back of her head.

"So are you," she rebutted, trying not to smile. "And dumb too."

"How would you know? You're so stupid!"

"You're a dumb coach. You couldn't coach a puppy out of a paper bag."

"Hey! Let's not get personal!" He put his hand on the arm of her wheelchair and hunched down on his heels, hoping his effort would get her to turn and face him. For a moment, nothing happened. Then suddenly, she turned and put her arms around his neck. She squeezed hard and he heard her try to speak through new tears.

"Please don't give up on me. I can make it. I can stay tough. I know I can."

"Crutches," was his simple reply.

The telephone rang and she dropped her eyebrow pencil. She didn't start for the phone immediately, although it was across the room on her night stand and would take a minute to get. She took a tissue from the box and wiped the unpaired tear from her cheek. The phone rang several more times before she answered it.

"Hello?" she asked calmly.

"Jesse?" Coach barked.

"Yes, Matt, it's me."

166

"You sound just like your mother. Sometimes, when I call—oh well—it's *cane* day! I'll be there in fifteen minutes. Be ready."

20

LOS ANGELES, CALIFORNIA

He was young and dark and his shoulder-length, shiny black hair was combed back in a manner that reflected his juvenile, overzealous confidence. He was shorter than most of the other men who shared his walk down the long tunnel from the gate to the lobby area of Los Angeles International Airport. He didn't bother to look at the paintings, done by the second and third graders, which were framed on the yellow tile walls; just as he had ignored the posters of France and Switzerland that mingled with the final chance slot machines in the Las Vegas airport.

Juan Carlos Cepeda was impatient to make his contact. From behind a pair of ultra-dark sunglasses, his youthful eyes danced from face to face as he sauntered down the concourse toward the terminal, ignoring the sign directing him to the baggage claim area. He headed for the exit, trying his best to go slow and be cool.

A few small drops of sweat from his hairless brown chest seeped, like ink from a broken pen, through the white T-shirt under his pre-washed, pre-faded Levi jacket. He also wore matching Levi jeans, a thick black leather belt with an elaborate silver buckle, and expensive gray leather cowboy boots. He had soaked himself in American television so he would know what to wear, what the latest fashion was, what was hip.

When he entered the lobby, a stranger approached from his left and began walking with him, matching his steps. They didn't look at each other.

"Mister Cepeda?" the stranger ventured. He had no doubt that this was the right man.

Juan's head bobbed slightly as he tried to hide his surprise—he had never been called "Mister" before. He felt the sweat, like oil under his arms.

"*Si,*" he answered. He was immediately worried that his English wouldn't be good enough. He hoped the stranger would speak slowly. There was sweat on his back now, under his jacket.

"Do you have any luggage?" the stranger asked, still not looking at him.

"No." He wondered if it would have been hipper to have some luggage, but there wouldn't have been anything to put in it. "You're supposed to have what I need," he said, his thick accent apparent.

"I have what you need," the stranger said. For the first time, he looked at Juan and smiled. "I have exactly what you need."

Kelly spotted him the moment he came through the gate. As he passed the passenger service counter, Kelly compared him to the current picture that had come to his smart phone earlier that morning. He waited until Juan was a few yards down the concourse, then he took up pursuit. Calmly, he hit send on his phone and put it to his ear. His usually whispery voice was even softer as he spoke: "He's here. Get your motor running." Casually, he watched Juan connect with his L.A. contact, whose picture was also on the smart phone.

At the curb, he turned his back to the pair as they waited for a black Dodge Charger to maneuver through the habitually chaotic crowd of cars fighting for a piece of the No Parking Zone. Then he walked right past them to where Larry Anderson had made arrangements to be double-parked and ready.

They got into the back seat of the Dodge.

Kelly got into the passenger side of the waiting Ford.

The Dodge drove away.

The Ford followed at a safe distance.

"Let's see it." As he spoke, Juan bent forward and flicked off a cigarette butt that had stuck to his boot.

Sitting behind the driver, the stranger smiled at Juan and retrieved a silver, hard-shell briefcase from the front passenger seat. He handed it to Juan saying, "Just what the doctor ordered."

Unfamiliar with the phrase, Juan didn't respond or even look at the stranger. He opened the case. The parkerized, matte-black finish of the Uzi peered up at him from its snug resting place on the gray foam rubber.

"Perfecto," he said, smiling.

"One Uzi. One thirty round magazine. Nine mil." The stranger settled back in his seat with the confidence of a job well done.

"Only thirty rounds?" Juan asked, taking the weapon from its case. "No extra mags?"

"We were told it was a single hit," the stranger said, staring at the back of the driver's head. "You want it to look like a drive-by. Thirty rounds, one man. Sounds like pretty good odds to me."

The driver chuckled.

"If you're any good, that is," the stranger finished.

Juan put the gun back, closed the case and tried to relax. "It's a woman," he corrected the stranger, and instantly wished he hadn't.

The driver chuckled again.

"The odds just went up!" the stranger said, more to the driver than to Juan.

"In your favor," the driver added, finding his partner in the rearview mirror.

They both laughed.

Juan knew they were laughing at him. If he'd been able to bring his own gun, he would have found the time to kill them both before this job was over. He felt the wetness of sweat in his boots.

As they followed the Charger, Kelly was distracted with the memory of Hunt's brief phone call: "Enrico Serva will be in Las Vegas for several days—most likely to meet with his West Coast buyers. Whatever's going down, it must be big enough for Serva to leave Bogotá."

"Is this for real?" When there was no immediate reply, Kelly had regretted the question. It had been meant as a show of his astonishment and an encouragement to the conversation, but Hunt had taken it as a challenge to his intelligence gathering machine. "Serva never leaves Colombia," he had added quickly, attempting to smooth things down a bit.

"In point of fact, he has never been out of Bogotá," Hunt had expanded.

Kelly was relieved. Hunt was back to his old, officious self. "Do you want me to go to Vegas?"

"I have no choice but to be on stage for the majority of the time Serva will be there," Hunt had gone on. On stage meant Washington D.C. "I've made some calls and Las

Vegas SWAT has agreed to be our eyes on the ground. I want you to keep doing what you're doing. Stay on top of the L.A. family. Let's see who goes to meet with him. This may be a great opportunity for us, Agent Kelly. Let's not let it get away. I'll get back to you with further instructions." Hunt had not waited for an acknowledgement, and the call had ended with the familiar sound of silence.

Two days later, Hunt had called from Washington: Juan Carlos Cepeda, Serva's adopted son, had reserved a flight to Los Angeles. Hunt wanted him followed. He wanted a full report on Juan's activities.

This was a new development. Juan had never done anything on his own. Up to now, Juan had only been the gofer who tagged along with Serva's lieutenant, Bernardo.

The Dodge pulled to the curb and stopped. The driver turned off the ignition. On the way from the airport, Juan had been given all the information he needed to know, but as they waited, the stranger gave one last instruction. "We've gone to a lot of trouble to find your target." The stranger smiled. "Make it good."

Juan realized that the stranger had known all along that the target was a woman. Of course, he thought. They couldn't find her if they didn't know who she was. The stranger's earlier reference to a man had been figurative. It was the language barrier, he told himself to keep from feeling stupid.

He slammed the magazine into the Uzi and pulled back the bolt to its locked position. He pushed the safety off. "Just drive," he said with enough accent to be cool.

They both chuckled again.

Damn, he thought. They can't drive until the target shows. Fuck English, man! And fuck these jerks. I'll show them how to kill somebody.

Juan opened the window of the Dodge.

21

VAN NUYS, CALIFORNIA

"That doctor didn't know shit. Never walk again—hell, look at you—and with only a cane."

Strutting, Matthew Braden followed Jesse down the narrow hallway toward the heavy metal security door of the gym. The soft glow of the EXIT sign added a red aura to the dimly lit passageway. Being careful not to rush her, he added, "I always knew you were a champ."

She walked ahead of him, constantly adjusting her grip on the handle of her new cane. "It's been a long six months, Matt, but with your coaching . . . no more wheelchair, no more crutches."

"And maybe in a while," Braden motioned to the cane, "we'll wean you off of that, too."

Jesse was exhilarated.

Before the workout, Coach had given her the cane. She had thrown her crutches aside to accept it.

"I had it made for you," he had been unable to keep himself from saying.

It was actually an Irish shillelagh: forty-two inches of straight, strong, molasses-colored oak, crowned with a curving brushed-brass handle. Beautifully carved flowers grew toward the top and their stems wove downward into an elegantly tangled design. The pattern ended about halfway down, and the rest of the cane had a smooth, glassy finish.

Twisting it around in her hands, she had noticed the words, "Stay Tough" unobtrusively hand-worked into the polished wood.

The workout had gone even better than they had expected.

At the end of the hall, Coach reached ahead of her to push open the heavy door. She let him. She wanted to try opening the door with just the cane for support, but he was already doing it. There would be other doors, soon enough.

Stepping out into the brightness of the California afternoon, she had to squint and blink several times before her eyes could adjust to the sunlight.

Coach came out behind her. "You wait here, I'll get the car," he said indifferently, as he systematically slapped each pocket of his pants and shirt. Satisfied that he couldn't find what he was looking for, he said, "I must have left my keys in the office. I'll go get them."

A black Dodge Charger came to life and started to cruise, shark-like, toward them at about five miles an hour.

"No, let me get them," she insisted, showing her new found courage without crutches.

He opened the door for her.

Jesse stepped back into the hall. The door slammed thunderously behind her and she heard loud spits and taps, like hail knocking and beating, trying desperately to follow her in.

Thirty full metal jacket 9mm rounds hammered at the front of the building. The front window cracked, then shattered, then collapsed. Large pieces of glass fell on the sidewalk and broke into smaller pieces. There was a screeching groan of squealing tires, and then it was quiet again.

She turned and pushed herself against the industrial door. It resisted, but with a second effort, she opened it.

"Matt?" she called, desperately trying to focus on the place where he had been less than a minute ago. And then she saw him.

Matthew Braden lay in a twisted heap on the pavement, his blood already forming a sticky pool around him. It was oozing through his clothes and a small stream of it was inching its way to the patch of brown grass between the sidewalk and the street.

Jesse dropped her cane and fell down next to him. She put his head in her lap and cradled it. "Oh God, oh God, Matt! Help! Somebody help me!"

The door to the gym opened and two college-aged jocks in full sweats burst onto the sidewalk.

"Oh shit! I'll call the police," the younger of the two said. He turned and ran back into the gym.

"Oh God, Matt! Don't die. Please don't die!" Jesse begged and cried.

"Come on, Lady, there's nothing you can do for him." The older jock bent down to take her arm and help her up.

"Get away from me! Don't touch me!" she yelled and pulled her arm away. Then, as quietly as a mother singing her child to sleep, she said, "Hold on Matt, help's coming."

She couldn't look away from him, as if in doing so, she might lose his spirit. "Please, God . . . oh please . . ." she whispered. And then, even softer, she said, "Stay tough, Matt."

The sirens seemed to be almost on top of her before they stopped. When the ambulance attendants separated her from the man in her lap, she was soaked in so much blood they thought she'd been shot as well.

"Who?" Hunt yelled into the cell phone at Kelly's left ear. Even though Hunt's voice was blasting, Kelly put the index finger of his right hand into his right ear so he wouldn't miss anything Hunt might say.

"I didn't recognize him as anyone we know," Kelly responded.

Behind the wheel, Anderson grunted as he diligently pursued the Dodge, trying to keep up without being too obvious.

"I only got a quick look," Kelly continued, "but I'm sure it's not anyone in the L.A. cartel—"

"Give me a description, damn it!" Hunt interrupted.

"White male—late fifties, early sixties—short—stocky— red hair, looks like a high school football coach."

"Forget Juan," Hunt started, and then stopped himself. "Is he headed for the airport?"

"Affirmative!"

"Then forget him," Hunt continued. "We can get him anytime. Go back. Obviously, Kelly, there's a new player in the game. I want to know who he is. Find out!"

"Understood," Kelly said. He punched the End button on the phone and put it back in his jacket pocket. Turning to Anderson, he said, "We're going back."

Anderson grunted his disapproval of the new orders. He had been hoping for the command that would have led to a high-speed chase, and some real action for a change.

They parked across the street and down from the Van Nuys Gym and watched and waited for the ambulance attendants and uniformed officers to finish their business. When the last Black and White was out of sight, Kelly turned to Anderson. "You take the clientele; I'll talk to the management."

"The jocks and jockettes," he grunted, acknowledging the order. He was clearly disappointed that he wasn't in the midst of a roaring shoot-out.

As they entered the gym, they passed the stain of blood drying in the late afternoon air, and the broken glass from the window crunched under their shoes.

"Cream and sugar?" the nurse asked. "I guess I should have asked before I brought you the coffee." She smiled. It was a warm, pleasant smile that went beyond professional courtesy.

"Please," Jesse responded in a monotone, almost imperceptible voice.

"I'll be right back, Honey. You try to relax." She put the coffee on a plastic tray next to Jesse and left the room.

The steam from the Styrofoam cup mixed itself into the cooler examining room air of the Sherman Oaks Community Hospital.

Jesse stared at the closed white curtain that separated this part of the trauma unit emergency room from the space where Matthew Braden's body lay. She began to feel an overwhelming sense of loneliness.

Two orderlies, wearing surgical-green scrubs, strolled down the hall towards her, talking quietly to each other. They brought a gurney, and an antiseptic smell that annoyed her nostrils.

She watched them push back the curtain to expose the precious body of the man who had been her mentor, her coach, and most of all, her friend. She could do nothing but stare.

She wanted to scream, *Leave him alone!* as the two men put what was left of the man she had loved and respected, almost as much as her father, onto the gurney and began to wheel him away. *No!* she wanted to cry out, as a last ditch attempt to keep Matt from leaving her. She felt a hand on her shoulder.

"Are you okay, Jess?" Chris sat down next to her and put his arm around her.

"What did he ever do to deserve this?"

"I don't know, Jess. But there are a couple of cops that need to ask you some questions. Do you think you're up to it? I'll stay right here with you."

"Okay."

Two men approached her. They were both large, and gave the atmosphere a crowded feeling. They both wore slacks, white shirts with ties, and sports jackets.

"Miss Fortune, I'm Detective Taylor and this is Detective Morrison. We need to ask you some questions. Will you come with us please?"

Both Chris and Detective Taylor reached to help her, but she waved them away and took her cane as she got to her feet. She followed the detectives down the corridor to an empty office.

"Is this okay?" Taylor asked, indicating the room. "Please sit down."

"Fine," she answered, sitting down in the only chair in the room. Chris stood behind her.

Morrison leaned against the wall.

"Miss Fortune," Taylor began, "do you know the men who shot your friend?"

"No."

"Did you see them . . . could you identify them?"

"No. I had just stepped back inside."

"Do you know what kind of a car they were driving? Did you get a license number?"

"It all happened so fast. I was in the gym for most of it."

"What was Mr. Braden doing standing outside alone?"

"He was waiting for me to go back in and get his car keys."

"Did you always get his keys for him?"

179

"No, but today was my first day on the cane, and I wanted to show him . . . I could walk." She looked away from the detective.

"Miss Fortune," Morrison spoke for the first time, "this seems to be one of those senseless, drive-by shootings; you know, teenage gang kind of thing. That's what we figure, unless you know of someone who might want to hurt Mister Braden."

"Matt didn't have an enemy in the world. Everybody . . . loved him. . . ." She stared down at the unswept floor. She felt as if she were going to cry again. She didn't want to do that. The time for crying was over. She felt sick to her stomach.

"Are you all right, Miss Fortune?" Taylor asked, sounding truly concerned.

She nodded but didn't look up.

"There are just a few more questions," he said, still worried for her.

She nodded again.

Before he could proceed, another man appeared at the door. Morrison left the room.

After a minute, Morrison reentered and interrupted the questioning by motioning for Taylor to come with him. "Thank you, Miss Fortune. If you think of anything else, please call me." He handed her one of his cards.

The two detectives left the room. On the way out, they left the door open for a tall, well-conditioned man who had been standing out in the hall.

Jesse rose and started to leave.

"Miss Fortune, I'm Agent Thomas Kelly from the Drug Enforcement Administration," Kelly said, showing her his credentials. "I'm terribly sorry to hear about your friend."

"Thank you," she said and continued toward the door.

He didn't move out of her way.

She stopped and looked up into his calm blue eyes.

They stared at each other for a moment, and then Jesse broke the silence.

"Is there something I can do—"

"Miss Fortune, I know this is a difficult time for you so I'll try to make this brief. You're an athlete, is that correct?"

His voice was as calm as his eyes. It didn't seem to be any more than a whisper, but she heard every word clearly.

"Not quite. I was an athlete. But what's that got to do with anything?"

"And, up until a little while ago, you and your coach traveled extensively throughout America, Asia, and Europe . . . diving, I believe."

"Yes, that's right."

"And you had plenty of opportunity to meet the citizens of those foreign countries?"

"Yes," Jesse said tentatively, remembering Mikel.

"You often mingled with the locals. Is that correct?"

"Yes." Once again, she remembered the few moments with Mikel before she became his widow. "What's your point?"

"Did you ever compete in South America?"

"No. Why?"

"Do you know the men who tried to kill you?"

"She's already been over all that with the other cops," Chris interrupted.

"Thank you, sir, but I need to hear it from her," Kelly replied.

"No, I didn't know them. Just a minute, you said me . . . tried to kill *me.* They weren't *trying* to kill anybody. It was a drive—"

"Do you know a man named Juan Carlos Cepeda?" Kelly interrupted.

"Who?"

"Juan Carlos—"

"No. I don't know any Juan."

"Do you know Enrico Serva?"

"No."

"Well, for not knowing any of the players, you seem to be involved in a very dangerous drug game, Miss Fortune." Kelly was looking past the teary eyes and the runny nose of the distraught young woman. She was definitely beautiful, even with tears smearing her make-up, and trauma staining her persona. But there was something else about her that held his attention; something he knew better than to examine or even think about. Why was it always the beautiful ones who got mixed up in the drug scene?

"Drug game? Listen, Detective—"

"Agent . . . Agent Kelly," he softly interrupted.

"Listen, *Agent* Kelly, I've never taken a drug in my life. I don't know who you've got me mixed up with, but I'm not part of the 'game'."

She had spunk. He had to admit that. Maybe he was wrong about her involvement. Maybe she was telling the truth. Sure, Enrico Serva had nothing better to do than order random murders on people he didn't know. Right. Kelly wasn't going to let himself be suckered by some beautiful eyes and a pretty face. "Can you explain why Enrico Serva might want to kill you . . . or your coach?"

"I told you, I don't even know Enrico Serva."

"Well, he seems to know you. Do you think it's possible that Mister Braden was involved with the Serva drug cartel?"

"Impossible. Matt wasn't involved with *any* drug cartel. If there was anything like that going on I would have known about it."

"You were that close to him?"

"I was that close."

"Then you don't think he was the target of this shooting?"

"No."

"Then it could be you."

"What? Why would anyone want to kill me?"

"Maybe you double-crossed someone—took something that didn't belong to you. Drug dealers don't like that. They're very quick to take care of mules who try to rip them off."

"Mules? What are you talking about?"

"Yeah, what the hell are you talking about?" Chris interjected. "What's going on here?"

Kelly continued to stare at Jesse. "A mule is someone who transports drugs from one location to another . . ."

"And you think I did that?"

". . . usually across international borders."

"I'm not a mule."

"They're chosen because of their ability to travel easily from one country to another. You know, like corporate salesmen, entertainers, and sports figures."

"I'm not even going to respond to that, Agent Kelly." She held his eyes with her own.

"I think you're going a little too far, man," Chris added. "If you're finished, I'll take my sister home."

"I really am sorry for the loss of your friend. I'm going to give you my number on this card. If you think of anything you've forgotten to tell me, or you'd like to change any of the statements you've already made, I want you to call me, all right?"

She didn't answer him right away and her indignant eyes held his confident gaze. Finally, she relented and offered a soft and simple, "All right."

Kelly turned to leave the room. Halfway out the door, he turned back. "You've become part of an international investigation. A lot of tax dollars are being spent to investigate a man named Enrico Serva. Somehow you're involved. I may have to question you further. So, of course, don't make plans to go anywhere, internationally or otherwise, without checking with me first."

She watched the self-assured sway of his strong shoulders until he was out of sight.

Kelly spent the morning gathering the details of Matthew Braden's and Jesse Fortune's life.

At the gym the day before, the manager had talked easily about his old friend, Matt Braden. Braden had been a medal winner in the '80 Olympics. For many years, he had been working with Jesse Fortune. She had won a silver medal in the 2008 Olympics, and was the number one pick for the gold in London. Then she'd been in a car accident in Europe. Currently, Braden had been helping her recover. To the best of his knowledge, Braden had no enemies.

"Has he ever been known to use drugs?" Kelly had asked.

The manager had laughed, shaken his head in disbelief, and walked away. Kelly had taken that as a "no."

With that overview, Kelly had gone to the hospital.

A quick Google search of both their names only confirmed what the manager had told him. Beyond that, he was discovering, there was very little information on either of them. To make things worse, the Olympics had only been of passing interest to him, so he wasn't even familiar with them in that regard.

He linked his computer to the CIA and FBI servers, placed numerous telephone calls, both domestic and foreign, and made frequent requests of Mama to get more data. But nowhere in any of it could he find even the slightest hint of either one of them being involved in any crime, or having relationships with any South Americans.

Matthew Braden and Jesse Fortune were as clean as it got. There wasn't even an outstanding parking ticket between them.

He had learned more at the gym the day before.

He noticed that, by nine-thirty, he had stopped thinking of her as "Miss Fortune" and was calling her Jesse Fortune in his mind. Somewhere around ten, he dropped the Fortune. From then on, she was Jesse. When he thought about her, he smiled to himself. He didn't know why. Or did he? He liked her. It sounded crazy and kind of dumb when he heard himself say it, but what the hell, he liked her.

By eleven-ten, as he raked the papers together that represented what he knew of Jesse, he realized that he was hoping he would find information that would prove her innocence.

At five minutes to twelve, he called her.

The ring of the phone startled her. She'd been in a daze. She was still in bed, but she wasn't asleep. She hadn't slept all night.

At first, she'd tossed and turned, unable to stop the horrific visions of Coach's blood-drenched body from colliding like snapshots thrown into her head. Then, flat on her back, frozen like a corpse, she had stared unblinking at the ceiling until a single teardrop rolled its way into her soft ear.

Finally, she had started at the very beginning and reviewed everything she could remember about Matthew Braden. She had allowed the wonderful memories to fill her mind: a mentally cinematic tribute to the man who had enriched her life beyond measure.

The phone rang again and she reached for it. "Hello?
"Jess—ah, Miss Fortune?"

"Yes?"

"This is Agent Kelly."

"Yes?"

"I need to ask you some questions."

"Yes?"

"I thought, perhaps, you might join me for lunch."

"Is that one of the questions?"

"No," he chuckled, "that's an invitation, if you're up to it. I thought it would be nice . . . nicer than my office."

"You mean now?" She cleared her throat as she sat up in bed. Even over the phone, his voice had that same strange quality to it, like his words were riding on a slow summer wind.

"It *is* lunch time," he said gently.

She could hear a smile in his voice as well. It was a kind smile. He was not laughing at her. She would have heard it if he was.

"I'm not dressed, Agent Kelly. To tell you the truth, I haven't slept and wasn't planning on—"

"Vitello's. Do you know where that is? It's close to you, I think. How about thirty minutes? Will that give you enough time?"

It wasn't an order. He wasn't playing the tough DEA agent with her. It was friendly. If it had been an order, she would have found a way to refuse it.

"Yes, I know where it is. But, give me an hour . . . and, I've got some questions too," she said quietly but firmly. She was trying to match his vocal quality. She wasn't sure why.

"One hour. Do you need me to pick you up?" he asked with polite concern.

"No, I'm driving now," she said proudly.

"Okay."

"Okay."

The sound of silence was his goodbye. Apparently, when he'd heard the word, "Okay," he'd hung up.

"Damn," she said to the unhearing receiver. "What am I supposed to wear?" She hung up the phone.

It rang again. She picked it up.

"Something casual," he said, his voice floating like a cloud.

22

STUDIO CITY, CALIFORNIA

"You said, 'something casual.' Is this okay?" For reasons
she wasn't quite sure of, Jesse wanted to impress this tall,
soft-spoken DEA man who had pushed his way into her life.
She had chosen pre-washed jeans that hugged her hips and
stopped snugly half-way down her calves, her best high heels,
and a lacy, lavender camisole. Delicate cloisonné earrings,
lavender to match her top, leaned lazily against her soft skin,
and her golden hair fell over the upturned collar of a faded,
light blue cotton shirt, which she had left unbuttoned. A small
denim clutch finished the outfit. Although her cane had
attracted some attention when she had entered the restaurant,
she had felt the appreciative stares of the men linger on her,
and she had accepted that as a confirmation that she looked
good.

"What?" he asked, as he stood up to greet her. He heard
the question and was trying to ignore it. In fact, he thought
she looked terrific the moment he saw her. He was starting to
get emotionally involved with her and he didn't like it. It was
crazy, and he would fight it until the feeling went away. The
best way to fight it was to ignore anything about her that
didn't have to do with the case.

"My outfit, is it casual enough?" She smiled and leaned
back slightly to give him a better view. She had never begged

for compliments before, but for some reason, she wanted his approval.

"Fine," he said, glancing at her briefly and motioning for her to sit down. Then he returned to his seat.

Wow, I guess I'm having lunch with Agent Grump. Disappointed with his lack of interest in her appearance, she turned her attention to the design of the restaurant.

He offered her a menu. "Do you know what you want?"

"Yes," she said casually, not taking the menu, "I'll have a small salad with the house dressing."

"Is that all?" he asked, not looking at her.

"I'm a cheap date," she said, smiling again. "The government will be happy. They're paying for this, right?"

"Right," he lied. The procedure was that he could go to her residence or place of business to question her, or summon her to his office for interrogation. Taking her to lunch was definitely on the wrong end of policy. He would pay for this himself. "Would you like something to drink?" He put the menu down and looked at her. He ignored her smile.

"Iced tea."

"Fine," he said.

"Fine." Her eyes drifted to the wallpaper adorning their booth.

When she'd had a chance to think about it, she had decided that his phone call, inviting her to lunch, had an underlying feeling of being friendly. In the shower, she had thought about the sound of his voice on the phone and tried to remember the details of what he looked like. While dressing, she smiled at his calling back, as if he had read her mind. Had he intended to be . . . romantic? She had stopped short of pursuing that thought and decided that her mind was playing games so she wouldn't think about the tragedy of losing Matt.

"You said you had some questions," he said, and went back to playing with the corner of his menu.

"Yes." But, before she could continue, a waiter stepped up to their table and began reciting the specials of the day.

As Kelly ordered for both of them, she studied his features. They weren't bad really. Kind of nice in a way, but he wasn't her type: too clean-cut, too straight, too cop. That was it. He looked like a young, athletic policeman. He had that military look, like her father; short hair, combed back. He definitely didn't have the long-haired, jet-set appearance that had made Mikel so irresistible. Nice eyes, though. He could definitely be trusted. If she had met him under different circumstances she'd probably think he was boring. So why, she wondered, did she want him to think she was attractive?

"So . . ." he said, handing the menus to the departing waiter, ". . . back to your questions." Damn, she's good looking, he thought. Then he reprimanded himself for thinking of her that way.

"You don't look like a DEA agent," she said, looking at the open collar of his plaid shirt and the sport coat surrounding it.

"What?"

"You're not wearing one of those khaki T-shirts and those baggy pants."

"Baggy pants . . . ? You mean BDU's? No, that's military."

"Well, what about that all black stuff with the goggles?"

"Goggles . . . right." Kelly almost laughed. "That's L.A. SWAT, and it's a Lexan face shield."

"Well, okay, but what about those black jackets with the yellow DEA letters on them that I've seen on T.V. Aren't you supposed to be wearing one of those?"

Kelly's smile broadened a bit. "There's more than one level to the DEA. The administrators wear suits and spend a lot of time in Washington. We have agents who wear those jackets, but they're fighting the daily battle on the streets. I fall somewhere in between. I deal mostly with gathering information, foreign and domestic, and I can wear whatever I want within appropriate limits. But I don't think any of this is important, and it certainly can't be what's on your mind. So . . . ?"

"Okay. You said you knew who shot Matt, this Juan somebody. How did you find out so fast?"

"Juan Carlos Cepeda. We were following him. He works for the South American drug lord I told—"

"You were *what*?" she interrupted breathlessly. Her face began to gather in a look of shock.

"I was following him," he said, a little confused.

"You mean you were *there*? You were right there when it happened? And you didn't do anything to stop it?" Her eyes began to tear and her voice cracked. "You could have stopped him—you could have saved Matt! What kind of a DEA agent are you?"

"Whoa, wait a minute! Sure, I was there. But I had no idea what he was going to do. Not until he did it. It was as big a surprise to me as it was to anybody."

"Did you go after him?"

"Yeah, we went after him."

"Well, did you catch him?"

"No, we were told to turn around."

"Who told you that?"

"My boss, Special Agent in Charge Evans Hunt."

"Why did he tell you to do that?"

"Because he wanted to know why they shot your coach."

"So he's just going to get away with this?"

"No, we're giving him more of a leash here so we can find out what he and his boss are doing. Juan is under continual surveillance, but we have to know what the end game is. Picking him up now won't bring your coach back."

She turned her head away so he wouldn't see her cry. She had expected that she might get emotional if she was asked to recount the events of the tragedy, and she had come prepared. She reached into her purse and retrieved a pair of blue-rimmed sunglasses. She wiped her eyes with her index finger and put them on.

"Look, we're already investigating these guys big time. We know who they are and they will be brought to justice."

She stared down into her lap and said, "I'm sorry. I'm sure you did everything you could."

For the first time, he had a glimmer that she might be innocent. She was either very, very good at lying, or she was telling the truth and she knew nothing.

"I didn't do anything. We've been investigating Juan's boss, a man named Enrico Serva, for several years now. I lost a partner a while ago, same kind of thing, shot and killed. I understand your pain. I'm sorry, too."

The waiter brought their food. They both remained quiet and stared at the table as he placed their plates in front of them. If he noticed their mood, he made no indication of it. When he had finished, he asked, "Will there be anything else?"

Kelly simply shook his head, no, and the waiter disappeared.

"Can you think of any reason why these men would want to hurt you or Mister Braden?" Kelly didn't want to look at her, but he did. She was obviously in pain. He didn't like the thought of her being in pain.

"No," she answered quietly but firmly.

"There's no chance that Mister Braden was involved in something you didn't know about?"

"I've known Matt since I was seven years old. He was like a second father to me. I loved him . . . and he loved me. If there was anything evil—especially this evil—in his life, I would have known about it. He wouldn't have had to tell me, I'd have known." She cleared her throat and took off her sunglasses. She was recovering.

"Look, Miss Fortune, these guys—"

"You can call me Jesse," she interrupted. She looked across the table and smiled.

Her smile was warm and friendly. Life was coming back into her face and charm was beginning to fill her aura. She was charming, he thought. The word sounded strange in his mind. He had never thought of anyone as charming before. Damn, she was beautiful! He had to use every bit of concentration to remember what he was going to say.

"Look, Jesse, these guys are pros. They don't make mistakes very often. If they want someone dead, then that's the person who dies. There must be some connection, even a small one, between Matthew Braden and Enrico Serva." As he waited for her to respond, he realized he was not pursuing the possible connection between Enrico Serva and Jesse Fortune.

She stared directly at him as she searched through her memory of the coach. Only the movement of her eyes told him she was thinking. He enjoyed studying her face without her apparent awareness.

"Tom! It *is* you. I thought it was you." A voice came from out of nowhere and surprised them both. Jesse looked up as the owner of the voice approached. She was probably the most beautiful woman Jesse had ever seen.

"Lorraine," Kelly coughed, coming to his feet. He smiled, but he was surprised when Lorraine put her arms around his waist and hugged him.

Jesse watched, expressionless.

Lorraine leaned back and looked up into Kelly's face. "You missed a great ballet. I was terrific—a standing ovation! I think you would have enjoyed it." She let her arms drop back down to her sides and turned slightly to look down at Jesse. "Hi," she said smiling, "I'm Lorraine Harte." She held out her hand for Jesse to shake.

"Hi. Jesse Fortune. It's nice to meet you," Jesse responded. She returned Lorraine's smile.

They shook hands and Lorraine turned back to Kelly. "Isn't this a wonderful man?" She put her arm around Kelly's back and pulled him toward her. Their sides touched.

Kelly felt awkward and off balance. He wasn't sure if he should put his arm around her or not.

"Tom," Lorraine said, looking up at him and smiling, "if this is what's been keeping you by the phone, I'm not making you cookies anymore!"

Lorraine stared at him. Jesse stared at him. They both waited patiently for his reply. It seemed an eternity before he said, "Cookies . . . right. They were great, Lorraine. Thanks again."

"Well, I've got to go," Lorraine bubbled. She looked down at Jesse once more. "It was nice meeting you, Jesse."

"Same here, Lorraine."

Lorraine squeezed him one more time. "Be good, Tom," she said. She turned and walked toward the door as if every eye in the restaurant was on her. It was.

"She's beautiful," Jesse commented, encouraging an explanation.

"Yes, she is," Kelly agreed. He sat back down.

When he didn't continue, Jesse felt a faint twinge of jealousy, although she wasn't sure why she felt anything at all. He wasn't her type; she had already decided that. He was definitely good looking; she'd admit that much. And she had wanted his interest and approval earlier, but now she wanted information. She realized he was staring at her. "Where were we?" she asked, with as little interest in her voice as she could muster.

"I think we were trying to find a connection between Mister Braden and Mister Serva. And, if we can't find one, then we should start looking for a connection between Mister Serva and Miss Fortune."

She noticed he wasn't smiling. He's back to being Agent Grump again, she thought. "Why don't you tell me about this man Serva? I might be able to figure out some connection if I know something about him." Jesse smiled her best smile. She was getting an idea, but she needed to know more about the drug lord. Maybe there was something she could do to straighten out this obvious mistake.

As their lunch progressed, Kelly told her what he could of Enrico Serva. It crossed his mind more than once that he was ignoring the correct procedure. He should be asking the questions and she should be doing all the talking. But something about her made him want to talk. He felt comfortable with her. The nagging voice of routine seemed to evaporate in the space of the table between them, and he fell easily into a conversation of his own making. He was encouraged to continue by her bright-eyed aura and the genuine interest she displayed in even the small details of his account.

By the time she was driving home, a plan had formulated in Jesse's mind. If she was the target of a dangerous drug lord, as incomprehensible as that might be, then she knew what she was going to do.

She called Chris.

23

IN THE AIR ABOVE NORTH HOLLYWOOD,
CALIFORNIA

"You're a hooker?" Chris asked.

"That's right," Jesse smiled. The intensity of her concentration made her eyes shimmer.

"And I'm your pimp?"

"That's the plan. What do you think?"

The FASTEN SEAT BELT sign blinked out as the 727 lifted them through the brown-tinged cumulus clouds hovering above Bob Hope Airport.

"I don't know, Jess. Is that the best plan you can come up with?" From his aisle seat, Chris smiled at the pretty blonde flight attendant as she passed. He continued staring at the back of her long legs as she moved gracefully up the aisle. She slipped into the small galley at the front of the plane and disappeared.

"Serva likes women. Can you think of a better way to get to him fast?"

His attention returned to Jesse. "Maybe it's because you're my sister, but somehow I have trouble imagining you as a prostitute."

"I'm not going to sleep with him. I just need to get close enough to tell him he's pursuing the wrong person. It's obviously some kind of mistake. If I can just talk to him, I can get him to stop. It's worth a try anyway."

The flight attendant appeared again, tugging on a drink cart. Another flight attendant, a shorter brunette he had not seen before, was assisting the blonde. The brunette was pretty too.

"I think you ought to let the police handle it. Or the DEA or someone . . . you know . . . Agent Kelly."

"Look, Chris, I can't even explain this to myself, how can I make the police understand? As far as Kelly goes, he thinks I'm one of them. Anyway, he can't blow his cover for a small-timer like me. He wants Mr. Big. He wants Serva for himself."

"I don't know, Jess. Can you act like a hooker?" He watched the blonde stewardess as she leaned over one passenger to give a drink to another. He enjoyed the curve of her back and the thinness of her ankles.

"This guy's rich, Chris. I doubt that he sleeps with cheap whores. All I have to be is sexy enough to attract his attention. I brought my sexiest dress, the black one with the low cut back. You've seen it; you know the one. You think I can be sexy enough, don't you?"

"Of course," Chris smiled. "I keep telling you you're a great looking girl. But this sounds kinda risky. We don't really know what guys like this are like. It's not like TV, Babe. Anyway, how are you going to get to him? You can't just go knock on his door."

"That's where you come in. Kelly said that he's staying at The Palms. I booked us a Salon Suite. We can change and be in the restaurant at least an hour before most people have dinner. He's got to eat sometime, so we wait."

As the flight attendant backed toward him and filled a plastic cup with melting ice, Chris once again focused on the conversation with Jesse, "Unless he eats in his room."

"I'm hoping he's more flashy than that. Kelly said he doesn't travel much. This is one of the few times he's been here. I'm betting he wants to see it . . . you know, have a good time."

"Kelly said, Kelly said. Kelly told you a lot about this guy." Chris looked at her curiously.

"Whether he realizes it or not," she smiled.

From the air, the lights of Las Vegas looked like diamonds, spilled from a torn, leather-brown sack. They rolled and sparkled their way across the desert floor, finally scratching up against the late afternoon horizon.

From the ground, everything in Las Vegas flashed with neon excitement: the capacious high-rise hotels, and the taxis that delivered their guests; the indiscriminate casinos with their billboards and barkers; the theaters, motels, and wedding chapels, each one with its own matching marquee.

They checked into The Palms and went directly to their suite. Jesse went into the bathroom to dress. Chris donned his suit and tie.

When she emerged, Chris was struck by the dramatic change in his sister.

The skin-tight, see-through black slip dress hugged every curve of her taut and shapely form. Its background was flesh-colored, creating the illusion that she wore nothing except for those certain parts of her that were hidden behind long, finger-like swirls of black sequins. The sequins stroked her body when she moved. The sexy décolletage followed the contour of her breasts, exposing just enough to make men stare and want to see more. The split back of the dress framed the indention of her spine from the nape of her neck to the small of her back, and just covered the small, deep-pink pyramid shape of a scar. From there to the hemline, well above the knee, the dress closed in five small rhinestone buttons.

Underneath the dress, she wore only sheer-to-waist panty hose with a delicate, tiny black beaded bow behind each ankle. A pair of six inch platform heels, that her girlfriends teasingly called "come-fuck-me-pumps" adorned her feet. Her shoulder length blonde hair was combed in a soft, fluffy style reminiscent of Marilyn Monroe in the fifties. Hollywood Red lipstick and smoky dark eye make-up finished the look. "Well, what do you think?" she asked, clutching her black satin evening bag with both hands.

"Man, Jess, you look awesome," Chris said, truly impressed.

She ignored his compliment as her anxious eyes gave him the once-over.

"You don't look like a pimp," she said, adjusting his tie.

"Well, you don't look like a hooker," Chris retorted.

"Hey, baby . . ." Jesse smiled sexily, ". . . why don't you buy me a drink?" She winked and licked her upper lip slowly. Then she picked up her cane and moved to the door, trying her best to imitate a streetwalker.

"Yo!" Chris said, following her. "When you be fucking, I be fucking making halfa what you be fucking tonight. All dollah-fifty of it," he said as he passed her."

His brass language surprised them both.

"Is that an Italian pimp, or a Black pimp?" Jesse asked, finally laughing.

"I have no idea. Maybe I should lose the accent."

"Yeah, both of them." She opened the door for him.

"How about an Asian pimp, "You want get rucky tonight? You have girlfriend? Why you no have girlfriend? You want girlfriend? Rook, she rook just rike Malyrin Monloe." Chris was engulfed in his imitations, and continued to tease Jesse on their way down the hall. They were both laughing as the elevator doors opened.

Behind the doors, two dark, well-dressed South American men stared out at them curiously.

They froze and their laughter faded down the hotel corridor.

Chris recovered first. He slapped the chest part of his jacket twice and turned to Jesse. "Yeah, Honey, I've got my wallet. Now gimmie my cane and let's go." He grabbed the cane from her hand and started for the elevator, limping enough to draw attention to himself. "Hold the damn elevator!" he cursed, hoping to keep their eyes on him.

Jesse picked up his cue and fell in behind him. She kept Chris' body between her and the two men so they wouldn't notice her slight limp.

"Good evening, gentlemen," Chris smiled. "And how are we all doing tonight?"

Both South Americans returned his smile, but neither one said anything. One of them tried to get a better look at Jesse, and made no attempt to hide his effort. The other one lost his smile immediately and gazed impatiently at the lighted floor numbers on the selector panel.

"We're going up," Chris said, keeping his voice as calm as possible. As he pressed the button marked for the top floor restaurant, Alizé, his knees began to shake. He made a mental effort to make them stop.

Fuck, what are the chances! Chris had no idea if these men were Colombians, or if one of them was the man Jesse was here to see. He didn't know what the men Jesse sought looked like. He didn't think Jesse knew either. She hadn't mentioned it. On one hand, he didn't believe in coincidence. On the other hand, how many wealthy South American men would be staying at this hotel this week? He couldn't take the chance that it wasn't them.

Something else flashed into his mind. If these were the men, and they were truly trying to kill her, then they obviously knew what she looked like. Even if they had hired someone to do the actual killing, they had to have a description of her. So far, they hadn't gotten a good look at her, but time was on their side. Chris' legs began to shake again.

As the elevator doors opened, Chris wanted the South Americans to exit first. He stepped back a little and said, "After you, gentlemen."

Both South Americans paused to allow Jesse to exit first. One of them looked right into Chris' eyes, as if to say, "We may be foreigners, but we still have manners." Chris was sure he could also read, "Asshole!" at the end of the man's thoughts. The other one moved slightly to try to get a better look at Jesse. He was still smiling. He was definitely interested.

Chris was lost. He glanced out the elevator doors and wondered why, in a hotel this size, at a time when lots of people should be coming and going, there was no one waiting impatiently for them to exit. There was no bustling crowd to mingle with and get lost in. Beyond the elevator foyer, he could hear the soft sounds of The Palms' most elegant dining experience. Time was running out. He knew he had already stalled too long. And then, he felt Jesse touch his arm as she passed him.

She knew they were in trouble. The excitement of the adventure washed out of her and was replaced by a strange and irritating nervousness. Feeling the same way she had felt the first time she had walked to the edge of a ten meter platform, she took a deep breath and moved past Chris and through the elevator doors.

She stopped just beyond the doors, and keeping her back to the three men in the elevator, she struck her sexiest pose. She spread her legs slightly and her long, black stockings pressed against the delicately thin fabric of her dress. She leaned gently to her left, which hiked the dress up even more above her knees and emphasized the firm contour of her ass, and she placed her left hand on her hip. Her right hand, holding the black satin clutch bag, rested softly on the upper part of her right thigh. As a last thought, she turned her head slightly to the right, not enough to give them a complete view of her face, but as if she were looking for a waiting admirer to come and adore her. She held her pose, she held her breath, and she waited for Chris.

"I want her." Enrico adjusted the lead-heavy silverware of his place setting on the thick white tablecloth. The flickering candlelight cast shafts of shadow, as well as light, on the dark skin of his face. It also emphasized the clean white shine of his teeth and shirt collar.

"That may be her husband, Enrico. He may not appreciate our . . . interest." Bernardo glanced up from his menu and tried to send Enrico a psychic message to forget what he was thinking. "She looks like a problem to me. Besides, I've got a couple of Latinas lined up for tonight that know how to take care of business. She's married, Enrico, forget the bitch. Trust me."

It was a losing battle. Bernardo had seen this look on Enrico before. If Enrico wanted something, he wouldn't stop wanting it until he got it. And it was usually Bernardo who got it for him.

Bernardo also knew American women. He didn't like them. In fact, he despised them. They were usually strong and arrogant. They had entirely too much freedom and acted more like men than women. They were all bitches and he hated them.

"That's never stopped us before," Enrico continued undaunted. "Sometimes, married women are the best. They know what they're doing. You don't have to show them anything." Enrico looked at Bernardo and smiled.

Bernardo shrugged. Enrico was the boss. That was that. He'd never had a problem with that before, he wasn't about to start now. "I'll take care of it."

"I knew you would." Enrico smiled and turned his attention to his menu.

Once more before they ordered, they both glanced over to the table where the young blonde woman sat with her back to them; Enrico because he wanted to, Bernardo because he had to.

"They're interested, Jess, they're definitely interested. Of course, they'd have to be turtle fuckers—sorry, turtle dunkers from East Borneo not to be interested. The way you look— you really look great, Jess. But are you sure it's them? I mean, how do we know?" Chris put his menu aside and looked past Jesse's left shoulder to the table where the South Americans were seated. "If it's not them, we're wasting a lot of time."

When Chris was nervous, he talked more than he normally might. That was all right with her. When she was nervous, she got quiet and said as little as possible. "It's them, Chris. I can feel it."

"Another one of your 'feelings'?" he asked, looking at her again.

"Another one of my feelings," she confirmed, without taking her eyes from the beautiful view of the Las Vegas lights that the top floor of The Palms' Alizé offered them. "I don't believe in coincidence."

"The *Angelinos* want to know when you want to meet with them." Bernardo tried to get Enrico's attention off the blonde woman.

"They need to learn a little patience."

"I think maybe they're curious because you're talking such a big deal."

"They can afford it," Enrico said confidently. "No problem."

"Yeah, but that doesn't stop them from being curious . . . and cautious. They know that they're always under surveillance, and they're uncomfortable that they have to come to you, here."

"You know . . . this town was built with vice money. The more illegal it was, the more money there was to build it. Gambling and prostitution." He glanced at the blonde, and then brought his attention back to Bernardo. "Do you know what they did with the profits, after they finished building?" He gave Bernardo a chance to answer, but he knew he wouldn't. "They bought into legitimate businesses. Just like our friends in Medellin and Cali . . . and Los Angeles are doing. You only need two things. A plan and the money to make it happen. I'm not worried, and you shouldn't be either. You know the plan, no problem."

Bernardo tried to think of other current business. Maybe there was a subject that would distract Enrico until he lost interest in the American bitch. "Rafael says that our Swiss friend is pissed off that we haven't taken care of the girl yet."

Enrico smiled and adjusted the position of the candle on the table. "Juan's taking care of it."

"Juan's fucking it up," Bernardo grumbled, but he knew better than to speak too badly of Enrico's adopted son. Bernardo knew he could push Enrico. He was probably the only man in the world who could. But there was a limit. He watched for Enrico's reaction.

Enrico lost his smile. "Juan's young. He'll be all right. The death of this bitch is unimportant to me, and it should be to you too. Let Juan take care of it. Didn't you say she was crippled? How hard can it be?"

A waiter appeared and they ordered coffee.

Enrico glanced over to the table where the blonde woman sat. His smile returned.

"Discúlpen, mi nombre es Bernardo. ¿Hablan español?" Bernardo introduced himself and asked if they spoke Spanish. He knew they wouldn't.

"Sorry, Pal, I don't speak Spanish. Do you, Honey?" Chris looked across the table to Jesse.

Jesse shook her head. Even in the elegantly dim lighting of Alizé, the man had cast a shadow on their table as he had approached. Now, as he stood over them, Jesse didn't want to look up at him. She kept her eyes on the tablecloth.

"My name is Bernardo," he said, switching easily to English. "My employer wishes to meet you. He's having a . . . private party, shall we say, in his suite, later tonight. He would like to invite you. May I tell him you'll come?" Bernardo was smooth. He'd done this many times. He got better every time.

Chris didn't look to the table where the South Americans had been sitting. He knew the other man was gone. He had watched him leave.

"Who's your employer, *amigo*?" Chris asked, leaning back and looking up. He had added an edge of impatience to his voice that bordered on contempt. He was pushing it, and he knew it. He didn't need to see the man's reaction to know he wasn't liked. But he wanted to stay in character. Right now, he was a pimp.

Bernardo stared at the woman. There was something familiar about her. He couldn't place it. He decided it didn't matter. "Enrico Serva is my employer," he said as if it should mean something. In Colombia, it did. "Mister Serva wishes—"

"Look, pal," Chris interrupted, "let's cut the bullshit. I don't think Mister Serva wants both of us at his little party. Am I right?"

After a slight pause, Bernardo answered. "That's right, pal," he said, putting a slightly sarcastic edge to the word.

Bernardo was more comfortable now that he knew he was dealing with a prostitute. That made things so much simpler. Where had he seen this woman before? Nowhere. He was sure of that. It was as if she had been described to him.

"Ten thousand dollars," Chris said confidently.

"*¿Que?*" Bernardo asked, slightly surprised.

"Ten thousand American *pesos, amigo,* and the little lady dances at your party."

"That's a lot of money, *amigo.*" Bernardo could push too.

"If you ain't got it, get lost." Chris said, and looked at Jesse. She still had her eyes pinned to the table.

Bernardo had his eyes pinned on Chris. He didn't like the way this *gringo* was speaking to him. If he hadn't been acting on Enrico's behalf, he would have left immediately. Then, at the right time, he would have stuck his knife into the soft skin under this man's jaw, and pulled his tongue out through the new opening.

"Bring the bitch to Penthouse B . . . ten o'clock." Bernardo's eyes narrowed until his lids appeared to have been separated by a switchblade. "She better be good . . . *amigo.*" He turned to leave.

"She'll be as good as your money, *amigo,*" Chris called quietly to his back.

Bernardo did not turn around.

"You can't go through with this, Jess. You just can't. Did you see the look on his face? This is way over our heads, Babe. I don't mind telling you, I was scared shitless. Of course, don't repeat that. I'll never admit it. But these guys are strange, Jess. You can't mess with them." Even in the relative safety of their room, Chris was still bothered. He was talking too much again.

"I was scared too, Chris," Jesse said, and meant it. "But I've got to talk to this man. If Enrico Serva is trying to kill me, he's making a mistake. You know that. I'm scared, Chris. But I can't just let it go. That way, I'm dead for sure."

Jesse sat on the bed. Unconsciously, her hand stroked the wrinkles out of the bedspread.

Chris sat in the chair. He had taken off his tie and unbuttoned his collar. He still wore the jacket to his suit.

"Listen to us, Babe." We sound like we're crazy. We're sitting here talking about the fact that someone's trying to kill you, and we're as calm as if we were talking about a movie we saw, a bad movie at that. "No pressure, Babe," he continued, "but I think we're in deep shit!"

"What do you think I should do, Chris?" Jesse stopped ironing the bed and looked at him.

"Go home."

"I can't."

"Then call Kelly," he pleaded quietly.

"He can't help," she said hopelessly.

"Then call the cops."

"And tell them what?"

"I don't know . . . anything."

"What time is it, Chris?"

Chris looked at his watch. "It's time to shit or get off the pot."

She took a deep breath and steadied herself with the cane in her left hand. She glanced back to her right and smiled at Chris, who had taken up a position approximately twenty feet down the hall. He smiled back, then leaned against the wall between two of the hotel room doors. They had debated whether he should stay close or go and get the house detective. They had decided he should stay close.

She gazed at her right hand as if it were someone else's as she reached out to knock on the door.

At first, there was no response to her knock. But as she went to knock again, the door opened slightly and she heard the sound of a man's voice on the other side. She couldn't make out the words, but she didn't think they were directed at her.

She pushed the door open farther, switched her cane to her right hand, where it was more useful as a weapon, and stepped in. She did not even think of closing the door behind her.

Her eyes fell immediately on the back of a man walking away from her. He had showered recently. He was wearing only a white bathrobe. His shiny black hair was slicked back and wet. She could see his legs from the knees down. He wore nothing on his feet. His left hand pushed a cell phone into his left ear. Obviously, he was expecting her, and had not wanted to break away from his phone call to greet her.

"Si, Rafael . . .¿Cuál es el problema? Yo sé . . . yo sé . . ."

He spoke quick, restless Spanish into the phone. His voice seemed slightly agitated. Still ignoring her, and without turning around to face her, he waved her in with his right hand.

". . . los hombres en Suiza están impacientes . . . yo sé . . ."

She didn't need more than a glance to know that this was one of the most magnificent suites she had ever seen. The living room area was more than spacious and the ceilings were two stories high. The room ended in a wall of glass that delivered on a promise of a breathtaking view of the continually sparkling Las Vegas city lights. There was an overstocked wet bar on one side of the room. Contemporarily designed leather, chrome, and glass furniture rested elegantly on plush, steel-colored carpet and sleek black marble floors.

". . . la mujer no es importante. ¡No es importante!"

The only bedroom she could see was on the opposite side of the room from the bar. The door was open and the lights were on in that room. She could see enough to notice that he had thrown the comforter and covers off the bed, most likely in anticipation of their night together.

"Una pregunta, Rafael, ¿Cuál es el nombre del dueño del Banco? No quiero cometer ningún error.

Surprisingly, her fear left her and she stepped toward the edge of the foyer.

Because her cane was unusual, and lacked the typical rubber tip, it made a small tapping sound on the burnished-marble floor as she crossed the entry way. That small sound was enough to get his attention.

"Si . . . Wolfgang Metter . . . *voy a tratar de recordar."* He turned to face her. Most of the room was between them. He tried to study her from a distance. His glance went from her cane to her face and back to her cane again.

"Mister Serva," she started confidently, "I'm—"

"You're the bitch," he said, as if it were an epiphany.

"I'm Jesse—"

"You're the bitch," he repeated, only this time his voice carried the tone of an abusive parent, angered to the point where real punishment would be dealt out. Cruel punishment. Unjust punishment. Punishment beyond reason. Deadly punishment.

He threw the phone down. It bounced off the leather couch and slid across the floor until it was stopped by a wall. And then he went for her, taking giant steps across the room.

She held her ground. She took her cane in both hands, like a baseball bat, and prepared for the worst. She was not about to back down now. She had come too far; she had had enough. She had no idea what this madness was all about, but she was prepared to see it through until she found out. The adrenaline exploded inside her. Seeing this dark man coming at her, with the intent to hurt her written in every feature of his body, she felt the electric shock of fear burst into tremors in her shoulders, stomach and legs. Her feet were frozen to the floor.

"What the hell's wrong with you?" she asked him softly, unable to raise her voice to the scream she wanted. She had played enough baseball as a tomboy to know what to do. She raised the cane over her right shoulder. "Make it a home run, Babe," she told herself, still unable to speak more than a whisper.

He stopped just outside of her range. It was the fear of what the cane could do, of course. But it was also the fact that she had spoken softly, and not screamed as he had expected. That had surprised him. He was in a hurry to take care of her before she could make too much noise. When she didn't scream, he had a split second to re-organize his thoughts.

The cane was a formidable weapon. His pistol was in the bedroom and would make too much noise anyway. Bernardo was in his own room and would take too long to summon. He needed her to be quiet. But first, he needed to get that cane away from her.

"Bernardo tells me you're worth ten thousand dollars," he said, turning on his charming smile. "Come. Put the cane down. Let's talk."

His complete reversal of attitude confused her momentarily. She relaxed a bit. "Look, I'm Jess—"

That one moment was all he needed. He grabbed the bottom end of the cane and pulled.

Stunned, Jesse held on to the cane with every ounce of strength in her. They both struggled and tugged furiously.

Enrico dropped one hand free of the cane. With the power and agility of a tennis pro, he smashed the back of his hand across her face. His bare feet slipped on the marble floor and he went down, losing any grip he still had on the cane.

The force of the blow caused her to stumble backwards. She let her momentum carry her through the still open door of his suite, and she didn't stop until she slammed up against the door of the suite across the hall. She still held the cane.

Chris immediately moved to help her.

The door to the suite behind her opened, and the middle-aged occupant stared at her curiously.

Enrico came through the door like an angry bull. He stopped himself when he realized that he and Jesse were not alone in the corridor. He stared, first at Chris, then at the other hotel guest, and then at Jesse.

He turned to go back into his suite.

"You're dead, bitch. You're dead," he called back over his shoulder as he went to find the phone.

As they hurried down the hall, Chris whispered, "I knew this was a bad idea."

24

LOS ANGELES, CALIFORNIA

"Hey, Kelly, it's quitting time. What're you doing?" Anderson had come through the office door and put his bulky frame carefully into the chair across the desk from Kelly. He had put one leg up on the desk, exposing a light blue sock, and folded his fingers together in his lap. "You've had your ass in that chair all day. Don't you want to get out? Maybe go shoot somebody, or chase some dumb fuck down the Interstate at speeds in excess of sixty-five miles per hour? You know, the things we thought we'd be doing when we agreed to turn our underpaid talents over to this overworked organization?" Larry Anderson was making another attempt to get closer to Kelly, but he was finding it harder to replace Jason Fenny than he had anticipated.

Kelly looked up. "Larry, I think that's the most I've ever heard you say in one breath."

"Yeah," Anderson smiled, "Maybe we should write it down . . ." he pointed to the bottom of his shoe, ". . . and take a long walk." He looked at the chaos on Kelly's desk that had once been a neat, if not complete collection of the histories of Enrico Serva, Matthew Braden and Jesse Fortune. "You doing a little light reading?"

Kelly's eyes followed Anderson's to his desk top.

"So, how does it end?" Anderson nudged.

"She's been gone all day. At least, I can't reach her, and her phone's off," Kelly said, barely glancing in Anderson's direction. Slumping over his desk, he returned his attention to the pages of notes covering his blotter.

"The Fortune broad?"

"Yeah, the Fortune broad."

"Hell, take a break from that thing. She'll turn up. What's the big deal, anyway? So Serva's got himself another mule. So what? Give it a break."

"How long have we been working this guy, Larry?" Kelly asked.

"You've been working him two, maybe three years. I've only had him for a few months. Remember? You were working him before I got here."

"And have we ever come across the name Jesse Fortune or Matthew Braden?"

"No, but—"

"Look at this," Kelly pointed to the information on his desk. "They're clean, Larry. Nothing . . . zip."

"So what? That just means they ain't been caught before."

"Neither one of them has been to South America."

"That don't mean shit," Anderson said. "So they got recruited here. It wouldn't be the first time. You need a rest, Sonnyboy. You ain't thinking like an agent. What—you getting interested in this broad or something?"

"Maybe she's telling the truth, she knows nothing. Maybe they made a mistake and got the wrong person."

"I don't think a guy like Serva's gonna make that kind of mistake. I don't think you do either." Anderson settled back into the chair. "So . . . where could she be?"

"I don't know."

"Well, let's ask Mama. Maybe she can tell us something."

They went to the computer and Anderson's fingers sped over the keyboard, clicking their way into the hard drive of the Administration, and the personal and public comings and goings of the suspected.

"What makes you think we'll find anything here?" Kelly asked.

"I don't. But we might as well check it before we clock out for the day." After a pause to read the screen, Anderson continued. "Fortune, J. made a reservation for two on Southwest flight 1110 to Las Vegas, and booked a Salon Suite at The Palms."

"What?" Kelly asked, although he heard Anderson.

"Wait a minute," Anderson coached as he continued to attack the keypad. "Yup. They're on that flight. She used her Visa card to pay for the tickets. Now why would she be going to Las Vegas?"

"Serva's in Las Vegas," Kelly said, staring at the computer screen in disbelief.

Anderson turned to look at Kelly, as if to ask, "You think I don't know that?"

"Can I get on that flight?"

"You're too late. The flight departed thirty minutes ago. The next one's the late one: departs 10:54 p.m."

"Shit!" Kelly said.

"Do you want to get a chopper?"

"No. It'll take too long to get Hunt's approval. Who've we got in the Las Vegas office?"

"The Las Vegas office was shut down over a year ago. Remember? Budgets."

"Shit!" Kelly said again. "That's right." He turned and went for the door. "I guess that just leaves me with one alternative."

"What's that?" Anderson questioned, looking truly curious.

"Speeds in excess of sixty-five miles per hour."

"Throw in a gunfight and you've got yourself a partner."

"I've got this one. She'll probably never get to Serva anyway. You stay here in case I need you to talk to Mama for me."

"Speeds in excess of sixty-five miles per hour. Some guys have all the fun," Anderson called after him, but he was already gone.

As the minutes and miles ticked away into the California-Nevada night, Kelly was unable to move his mind away from Jesse Fortune. He was angry with her. But he thought of how beautiful she was, and remembered the way her sparkling eyes had searched his face. He was furious with her decision to go to Las Vegas. But he also thought of how graceful her movements seemed, and realized that he didn't think of her as someone who needed a cane. He was more than frustrated with the fact that she had disarmed him and obtained information from him that he never should have given her. And, he was unwilling to face another truth: she might actually be guilty. In the time he'd known her, she had filled his thoughts continually. The more he thought of her, the more genuine she seemed: an innocent woman caught in the web of a great mistake—where her life hung in the balance. What was her involvement? Could she really be a part of Serva's plans, his organization? And what was she hoping to accomplish by going to see Serva? Each time his mind went over it, a thousand images of what might happen to an innocent Jesse Fortune, in the hands of Enrico Serva, filled him with fear.

As he came up over the last hill, and raced down to the edge of the city, he realized that somehow, whether she intended it or not, she had opened a door in him, and had stepped in. She was a part of him now.

Before Kelly could get to the hotel, Anderson called him.

"Kellyboy." Anderson's voice barked out from the in-dash, com-system of the Tahoe.

"Go."

"Fortune, J. just bought two tickets to LAX. Flight departs in 30. She's at the airport."

"Copy that. I'm on my way. Thanks."

Master Sergeant Jerome Johnson took his muscular but tired arms off the Southwest Airlines counter, and brought his complete six-foot six-inch frame to attention.

"There you are, sir. You're on flight 1124 to San Diego, departing from Gate 6." The ticket agent took the boarding pass from the computer and stapled it to Johnson's ticket. Handing it back, she glanced straight ahead to where her customer had been; only now, she wasn't looking into his face, but into the second brass button from the top of his olive drab jacket.

Her eyes traveled upward, past an impressive array of medals, and over the light green of his shirt collar. She tried not to stare at his neck, which she judged to be approximately the size of her waist. His commanding stature made her feel as though she were standing in a doll house.

"You've been eating your Wheaties, Sergeant."

Sergeant Johnson wasn't in the mood for a joke, but he smiled good-naturedly and responded with a friendly but still military, "Yes, Ma'am."

Johnson was tired and wanted to get home to a hot shower and his own bed. His SRO lecture, "Action and Reaction to Ambush," given at a seminar at Fort Bragg, had been decidedly more successful than his journey home was turning out to be. Flying commercial, he'd taken the puddle-jumpers to save money. In his attempt to be economical,

Johnson had discovered the inevitable frustration of civilian airports. Charlotte, Nashville, Dallas, and now a night flight from Las Vegas, and he still hadn't reached his Oceanside apartment.

Fatigued, he was aware of, but uninterested in the other late-night travelers that were beginning to group around him: a blonde girl, standing next in line behind him, talking quietly with her young male companion, and two dark-haired South American men who had come to stand behind the girl.

It was already a bad night for Bernardo. Juan Carlos Cepeda was making it worse.

Bernardo had been with Enrico from the beginning. He was the number two man. But when Juan had come into the picture, Enrico had immediately accepted him as family—and had adopted him.

Enrico and Bernardo were as close as brothers. But they weren't brothers. They weren't related at all.

Bernardo wasn't family as Juan might be, but he was Enrico's right hand. When Enrico wanted something done, he called for Bernardo. When left alone, Bernardo got the job done. When he did it his way, it always came off clean. Whether it was cutting someone's throat in a Bogotá back alley, overseeing drops and deliveries, or finding the kind of woman that could go all night with Enrico, Bernardo was the right man, the lieutenant of lieutenants. As far as Bernardo was concerned, every general needed a man like him.

But Juan, that was another story. Juan had somehow become blood to Enrico. And that was the only reason why Bernardo hadn't blown the little asshole away already. Enrico had no children. He wasn't even married. But some obscure tie made Juan a member of the family. An unneeded member as far as Bernardo was concerned.

217

Before Juan had come along, Bernardo had been content with his position. If he ever had the chance to off the *pendejo* and get away with it, he could go back to being content again.

Enrico's phone call had come shortly before 11 p.m. The instructions had been clear and simple: find the girl, take her somewhere she'll never be found, and leave her there—dead. If the call had ended there, Bernardo would have slipped easily into his modus operandi and gone about his duties with unlimited confidence. But the call had not ended there. Before Bernardo could hang up, he had heard the dreaded phrase, "Take Juan with you."

Juan. *El pendejo.* It seemed each time Bernardo found him, Juan was sitting in front of the television, cleaning his gun and watching reruns of Miami Vice.

Somebody ought to send this kid back to Bogotá. He thinks America is only what he sees on TV.

But there was nothing Bernardo could do. He had tried mentioning his reservations of Juan, but Enrico was not willing to listen. Juan was family. That was that. No hints of incompetence, small or large, could change that fact.

After checking with the desk clerk at The Palms, Bernardo, with Juan trailing, had called for the limo and struck out for the airport. At that point, Bernardo's only problem had been getting to the girl before she went through security. Knowing there was nothing he could do about that, his mind started to play the now familiar game of trying to anticipate what Juan might do to blow the job. It was pointless, of course, because Juan was always surprising him with new levels of ineptness. But Bernardo's mind played the game anyway.

The girl was easy to spot. At this hour there were few travelers departing or arriving Las Vegas, and the tall blonde stuck out like a cherry red nipple on a big white breast.

Bernardo motioned to the driver, "Pull in by the curb." Keeping an eye on Jesse through the window, he continued, "Leave the engine running."

Sitting in the back of the limo, Juan drew his pistol.

"Put that gun away and follow me. Don't do anything. Don't say anything. Leave this one to me."

They exited the car and entered the terminal.

As they approached, Bernardo began preparing the lie he would use to get the bitch to come with him quietly. *Enrico Serva wants to talk to you. Just talk. He knows there's been some kind of mistake . . . he just wants to talk. . . .*

Juan was too calm. That should have been Bernardo's first clue. But it was one of those nights.

As they approached the girl, Bernardo hesitated to scan the area, briefly noticing the tall soldier standing in front of the girl, to her right.

Juan walked past Bernardo and stood behind the target.

It all fell apart so fast, Bernardo didn't even have time to curse Juan Carlos Cepeda—the *pendejo!* Before Bernardo could stop him, Juan took the semi-auto out from under his jacket and pushed it gently into Jesse's back. Juan was sure it would work. He'd seen it a hundred times on TV. Someone showed the victim a gun, and the victim did what she was told, easy, no problem. Juan didn't expect what he got.

From behind the counter where Jerome Johnson stood, the petite brunette ticket agent looked past the giant's right arm and directly into the glint of the large, nickel-plated Smith & Wesson semi-automatic pistol that Juan held.

"Oh my God!" she exclaimed, her voice louder than she expected, "He's got a gun!"

As the dark blue Tahoe rolled down the departure lane of McCarran airport, Kelly hoped he wouldn't see her, that she was already gone. That hope vanished when he looked beyond the black Lincoln limousine idling at the curb. Through the plate glass window, he saw the two Colombians. He only needed that one glance to know that Jesse Fortune was, once more, the center of attention.

Kelly pulled the Tahoe to the curb, blocking the limousine. He didn't waste time turning off the engine. Before his car came to a complete stop, he pushed his foot on the emergency brake, jammed the gearshift into park, opened the door and stepped out. He reached under his jacket for the Glock with his right hand while his left hand went for his pocket and found his badge. As he moved toward the terminal, he held his badge up to the on-duty security officer and yelled, "DEA. Follow me."

"That's a gun!" the ticket agent yelled again and dropped to the floor behind the counter. From the floor, she reached for the phone and brought it to her. She dialed 911. Only then did she remember the emergency code for Airport Security.

Sergeant Jerome Johnson looked to where the girl's eyes had been. His reactions were instinctive. Years of training young men for combat snapped him into instant action. Fear never entered his consciousness. He had put too many pistols in the hands of too many amateurs, not to know how to diffuse a potentially dangerous situation.

The young punk was close enough that Johnson calmly, but with incredible speed, reached his right hand out and grabbed the pistol. His massive hand not only covered the weapon, but the young Colombian's smaller hand as well. With his left hand, Johnson seized the Colombian's upper arm, almost lifting him off the ground. Johnson swiftly turned the pistol, still in the young punk's grasp, and pushed the muzzle into the Colombian's face. His large index finger pushed under the trigger guard and over the punk's own trigger finger.

"What you want with this, Boy?" Johnson asked sardonically.

Bernardo's instincts were not as sharp as the seasoned Johnson's. His confused and delayed reactions sent him in the wrong direction. He grabbed Jesse by the arm. Drawing his own gun from his belt, he put it to her head.

"Everybody calm down," Bernardo almost yelled. Then staring at the Army Sergeant he said more quietly, "Let him go, asshole. Back off!"

Bernardo heard the sound of another semi-auto being racked behind him. From out of nowhere, he felt the cold steel of a pistol muzzle touch his temple. More confused than ever, he allowed only his eyes to seek out this new adversary.

"Put the gun down. Let her go," Kelly said, his voice slow and raspy and whispery. And then loud enough that everyone would hear, he said, "DEA!"

Chris was frozen with fear. His knees began to shake. He stared at his sister and his eyes began to water.

Lifting the young Colombian higher off the ground, Johnson stared into what seemed like a crowd of guns. "What the hell's going on here?" His voice was still calm.

Having followed Kelly into the airport lobby, and seeing all the guns drawn, the airport security officer drew his own pistol and tried to determine who to cover. He made his decision quickly to back up the DEA agent and put his muzzle on the man the agent was dealing with, his left hand hitting the button on his portable two-way radio connecting him with dispatch. "SWAT needed, airport. Code Red."

Seeing the pistol muzzle held at Jesse's head, Kelly's anger exploded. "Sergeant, I'm DEA Agent Thomas Kelly. Do you have your situation under control?"

"Yes, Sir." The Sergeant responded.

Then, to the Colombian holding his gun to Jesse's head, he said, "Let her go."

The cold metal on his temple told Bernardo that this man was not bluffing. In his mind he screamed at Juan. *You pinche pendejo! Look what you've done!*

Although Johnson had never been in a situation as bizarre as this one, there was still not one ounce of his two hundred eighty pounds that lost control. His awareness covered the entire situation. What had seemed perhaps an unusual mugging had expanded into something out of his experience. His attention took the circle in quickly:

-One man, approximately twenty, scared shitless, no weapon

-One agent, approximately thirty, Glock semi-auto

-One terrorist type, maybe forty, Browning Hi-Power, semi-automatic pistol

-One young woman, cane, no weapon

-Second terrorist, approximately twenty, Smith & Wesson semi-automatic

His expert eyes did not miss any detail:

-One airport security officer, Glock 17

-Security arriving from the left, weapons drawn.

His swift calculations came to rest on one final thought: protect the woman if at all possible.

The sound of sirens screamed into the terminal building, as four police units screeched to a halt outside.

The hissing sound of the opening doors was completely obliterated by the tramping of a forceful blue tide of police rushing into the terminal. With more sirens sounding in the distance, the officers present formed a semi-circle around the volatile group. Orders were mandated, shotguns were pumped, and then, suddenly, everything was quiet again.

"All right, put the guns down! You're all under arrest," an officer said with authority.

"We've got a situation here, Captain," Johnson yelled over the head of his captive.

Obviously confused, the Captain recapitulated. "Drop the guns and get down on the floor, hands behind your heads. Now!"

Bernardo realized that, for the first time in his life, his hands were shaking. He thanked a god he had never believed in that someone else held Juan's gun. *That pinche pendejo would have us all dead by now.*

Three more vans hit the curb outside and four men from each van ran toward the terminal. This wave of black carried assault weapons and their vests carried the letters SWAT.

Just loud enough to be heard over this new group, Kelly spoke into the Colombian's ear. "It's gonna be a lot easier to make bail than to make it out of this terminal with the girl. You've lost, *José,* give it up."

Kelly's logic made all the sense in the world to Bernardo. *What the hell am I doing? I don't need this shit! This is Juan's problem, not mine. He'll have to answer to Enrico, not me.* With that thought, Bernardo's whole body relaxed and the beginning of a defiant smile appeared on his thin lips. He moved the muzzle of his Browning away from Jesse's head, and slowly pinched the hammer, guiding it carefully down to its "at rest" position.

Johnson watched the terrorist. "Hold your fire, Captain, we're diffusing the situation. We're standing down!"

"Drop your weapons and hit the ground!" was the Captain's response.

Kelly looked toward the sergeant and nodded.

With what seemed an effortless motion, Sergeant Johnson removed the pistol from the younger Colombian's hand and pulled him to the ground face down. Looking back up at the others he said, "You do what I do," and he placed the gun on the ground and slid it out of reach of the immediate circle.

Kelly and Bernardo followed orders, sliding their guns away.

"Hit the ground! Hands over your heads," the police captain yelled. He turned to his men, "Move in. Secure the area. Make sure you read them their rights!"

Sergeant Johnson was still on one knee, bending over the young Colombian's prostrate body, but the police moved in so quickly, no one else had time to get to the ground. They were surrounded, moved away from each other, and read their rights. The captain began taking their statements.

Two of the vans were assigned to collect prisoners.

"What the fuck are you arresting us for? We didn't do anything. We were just standing here when these two jerks put guns in our faces," Chris said. His fear was finally escaping. He wasn't hearing the officer's repeated response, "You're not under arrest. But we do need you for questioning. I'm sorry, but you'll have to come with me."

Kelly waited until he was asked, by a uniformed officer, to produce some identification. Then, he drew his badge from his pocket and asked to speak to the captain.

Bernardo and Juan were under arrest. As they were being loaded into the police van, Bernardo, hands cuffed behind his back, turned to look back at Jesse.

"It's not over yet," he said to her with a smile.

25

ON THE ROAD FROM LAS VEGAS, NEVADA

"What the hell were you trying to prove back there? You could have been killed!" Thomas Kelly's voice broke the crypt-like silence that Jesse had begun to feel safe in.

"But I wasn't," she replied, her voice cool.

"Hell, you could have gotten us all killed!"

"But she didn't," Chris defended from the Tahoe's rear seat.

With one swift movement, Kelly turned sharply, pointed his finger at Chris, and exploded. "I'm not talking to you!"

Chris turned his gaze to the dark landscape beyond the window. He pulled his jacket tighter around himself, more for comfort than cold, and tried to sleep.

"Don't talk to my brother like that," Jesse said quietly. "He was only trying to help me."

"Damn," Kelly mumbled more than spoke. "With all that fire power, he's lucky he's still around to talk."

"It all worked out okay," she said, not looking at him.

"Okay? You call this okay? Any hope of cover I might have needed in the future is blown. Hunt had to go to the wall to keep this operation from terminating right here. And those assholes made bail before the judge could get his robe on. Do you realize the jurisdiction problems you've created? Hell, we just left a Federal Judge arguing with half of Las Vegas Metro and the DEA over who's gonna get this case. And let's not forget the LAPD. They think you're theirs. They want the investigation. They don't appreciate the DEA coming around, messing with their case. Hell, I didn't feel it was safe enough to go back to the hotel and get your clothes."

"I didn't think you'd help me. I'm a mule, remember?"

"You didn't think, period."

"I thought if I could just talk to him, he'd realize he had the wrong person."

"They'll be coming for you now—as fast as they can!"

"But why? What do they want with me?"

"You tell me," he said, sounding more frustrated than angry. "It's hard to believe you don't know. But, if you and your brother can stop putting yourselves in front of known killers for a while, maybe I can find out."

"I thought if I saw him face to face . . . I could straighten out the mistake." She was beginning to sound as tired as she felt.

"Do you think this little incident is going to make him go away? Stop? Shit no! It's like sticking one of those spears in a bull in a bull fighting arena . . . it just makes him madder."

"But—"

"What the hell were you thinking?"

"I thought—"

"Guys like that have no conscience. They pull their triggers as easily as they pull up their zippers after a pee."

"I—"

"How had you planned to get yourself out, lady—a cane to the crotch? These guys are dangerous! This isn't a game they're playing."

"Forget it! Okay?" She was wasting her time. He was not in a frame of mind to listen to reason. She tuned him out and began to count the mile markers as the Tahoe's headlights illuminated them.

"I wish I could." He realized his words were falling on deaf ears and he went silent until they passed the state line. At Barstow, he stopped.

"I need gas. I don't know if we're being followed so we won't take time to stop and eat. Here, take some money and go to the Bun Boy over there and get us some hamburgers to go. Chris, you go with her."

With the gas pump in his hand, Kelly watched Jesse and Chris cross the deserted highway that rested in the moonlit shadows of Interstate 15. His stomach was soured with the feeling that he might have hurt Jesse with his fast temper and harsh words. She was brave and determined. As he watched her move across the road, he could see that she was making every effort to keep up so Chris wouldn't have to slow down. Brave . . . determined . . . she wasn't the kind who would follow someone blindly. But, if she believed in a man, Kelly was sure there wasn't anything she wouldn't do for him. He was starting to believe she was one hell of a woman. He was starting to admire her. And, he was falling in love with her. The thought of her being hurt made him sick to his stomach and angry. It had to come out somewhere, and he had taken it out on her. She was in real trouble. She wasn't going to need any more of his wrath; she was going to need his help. He didn't know the reason why she had been placed in the middle of this madness, but he knew that the stakes were as high as it gets. She was going to need everything he had. Even then, it might not be enough.

Once the pump was running, Kelly sat back in the driver's seat and punched the Key number on his phone.

"Go," Hunt barked.

"I have the packages. ETA L.A. 0700. What are your instructions?"

"Have them in my office in 48 hours. That will give me time to get back from D.C."

On the road again, Kelly allowed them time to eat but ignored the food they had gotten for him. "Hunt wants both of you in his office in 48 hours. Until then, I'm in charge of keeping you safe. We'll use my house as a safe house."

"I don't know, man, do you think we really need a safe house?" Chris resisted from the back seat.

"Yes, you do."

"I'm supposed to be taking care of my folks home while they're out of town. I'd rather stay there. Can we think about that?"

"Someone's trying to kill your sister, Chris. Can we think about that?"

In the near dawn hour, the sun began to paint fiery shades of scarlet and crimson across the ominous darkness of the night sky. Separately and silently, they each noticed the sunrise chasing them to Los Angeles.

As they made the highway changes, I-15 to I-10, and then I-210, Jesse gazed at the San Gabriel Mountains stretching off to the North. The hills, thick black silhouettes against the morning, looked to her like a sleeping debutante: dark velvet curves and mounds, showing off precious diamonds, rubies and emeralds. She had watched the dusty desert landscape gradually change to rows of pastel painted, one story and split level homes, lined up like watercolors in a tin paint box. The houses gave way to small shopping centers. Squeezed in between were the few tiny homes of the holdouts, who had not moved even when confronted with the snapping jaws of progress.

Off the interstate, the headlights of the early morning traffic had already started crawling over the cramped roadways like a never sleeping beast.

They exited the Ventura Freeway at Coldwater Canyon and turned right on Ventura Boulevard. Turning left on Valley Vista, they wound their way to Long Ridge Drive.

Pulling into the driveway of the Fortune residence, Kelly braked gently and put the Tahoe into park. He left the engine running.

"I really wish you'd reconsider, Chris."

"Hey, just one day, man." Chris yawned and stretched and got out of the car. "I'll call you tomorrow, first thing." Although he wasn't speaking loudly, he could hear his voice roll down the deserted street. "What clothes do you need, Jess? I'll get them for you."

"I'm telling you, man," Kelly began, trying one more time to convince Chris, "these guys aren't gonna just give up and go away. They're gonna come looking for your sister. They may start in Mission Viejo, but, by now, they've got this address, too. I'd feel a lot better if you came with us."

"I know this place like that back of my hand," Chris interrupted. "No one's getting in without my knowing. Besides, I'm supposed to be watching the house while Mom and Dad are scuba diving in Bonaire. I can't just desert it. Hey, I can always call you."

"There may not be time to call me," Kelly said, looking to Jesse for support.

She leaned close to Kelly and stared up at her brother. "He may be right, Chris."

"Hey, I'll be okay, trust me. At the first sign of trouble I'll get the hell out, okay? I'll desert the damn house, okay!? What do I look like, Rambo or something?"

"Here's my cell number," Kelly pushed a card out the window. "Use it at the first sign of trouble. Otherwise, twenty-four hours and I'm coming to get you."

Chris agreed.

"Get me some jeans, a shirt and a pair of sneakers," Jesse requested.

Jesse and Kelly waited in silence as Chris entered the house. A few minutes later, he emerged with a brown shopping bag and handed it to Jesse through the window.

Kelly leaned past Jesse, "It's been fun, pal. We should do this again, real soon."

The unexpected levity caught Chris by surprise. After a moment, Chris chuckled, "Yeah, Kelly, sure."

"Take care, Chris, and thanks," Jesse offered as she leaned out the window to give her brother a two-armed hug.

"You're gonna be okay now, right?" Chris asked, nodding toward Kelly and smiling.

Jesse turned to look at Kelly, and then back at Chris. "How can I be anything else as long as I have 'Mother' here with me?"

With a quick shift in tone, Chris added, "I mean it, Jess. Do what Kelly says." He turned and walked back up the path to the front door.

"You heard the orders; you do what I say," Kelly said.

"We'll see," she said under her breath as she watched Chris disappear into the house.

Kelly turned the Tahoe around and accelerated away. In the rear view mirror, the Fortune home was being washed in summer colors by the sun's morning rays.

North Hollywood was a sharp contrast to Studio City. Out of the canyons, the larger houses gave way to smaller, plainer, less expensive homes. Vast apartment complexes, some boasting swimming pools and underground parking garages, packed themselves onto the flatter valley streets.

When he had driven the Tahoe down his driveway and parked it in front of the detached garage, Kelly grabbed the bag of Jesse's clothes and came around to open the door for her and help her out. But, she had already climbed out by herself. He put a hand on her arm, to escort her up to the front door, but she moved ahead, ignoring it.

On the porch, he looked for his keys. She felt a little awkward and a little silly as she waited for him to open the door. They both heard the dog growl at the same time.

"That's only RoboDobe," he smiled confidently.

"Robo who?"

"My Doberman," he tried to explain, but it was already too late. The dog had come through the open door and was sniffing her furiously.

"Oh, he's beautiful!" she said, bending as close as her cane would permit. She stroked the dog's head. RoboDobe wagged his behind and accepted each of her pets gratefully.

"Get in the house, RoboDobe!" Kelly commanded.

RoboDobe turned to look up at him, but continued to bask in Jesse's attention.

"Now!" Kelly half whispered, half yelled.

The dog reluctantly obeyed.

"Most people are afraid of Dobermans," he said, smiling again.

"I love animals," she said. She didn't return his smile as she moved into the house.

"Nice wall treatments," she commented facetiously as she entered the living room and looked around.

"You mean those paintings leaning against the wall?"

"Yeah," she smiled.

"I haven't had time to hang those up yet."

"How long have you lived here?"

"Three years."

"You're right. You haven't had time."

"I make mean scrambled eggs. Want some?"

"Breakfast . . . sure."

"There's the couch," he said, pointing to it, "Kick off your shoes, relax." He went into the kitchen. As he put the eggs on the counter, he heard the tapping sound of her cane: first on the hardwood of the living room floor, and then on the linoleum as she followed him into the kitchen.

"You want some coffee?" he asked, not looking at her but smiling at the fact that she had not blindly followed his orders to sit demurely on the couch.

"No thanks, too much caffeine . . . after being up for twenty-four hours."

"Sorry, how about some tea?"

"Sure, give me something with caffeine in it," she said offhandedly as she investigated his kitchen. She opened the refrigerator door as if it were her own and retrieved a half gallon of milk.

As he stirred the eggs into a frying pan, he kept sight of her peripherally. "Are you finding what you need?"

"How could I miss? There's only two beers, a half package of stale, furry hot dog buns, and enough condiments to sink a ship. Glass?"

"In that cabinet over there," he indicated a cabinet above the counter.

She poured an inch of milk into the glass and handed it to him. "Here, you try it."

"Is it bad?"

"I don't know; that's why I'm giving it to you. It has last week as an expiration date. You try it first. If you survive, then I'll have some."

"I don't like milk."

"Then why did you buy it?"

"Just in case some ex-Olympian, dressed like a hooker, drops by for breakfast. Here, give me that," he said, taking the glass of milk. He drank it like a straight shot of whiskey and set the glass down hard on the counter. With his best

John Wayne accent, he slurred, "Ahhh! That's good. Bartender, let's have one for the little lady here." He pointed to her with his thumb.

She gave in to a small laugh. The sound of it sparkled off the kitchen walls and windows, and seemed to fill the room with magic. It was the first time he had heard her laugh, and he liked it. He handed her half of the scrambled eggs on a plate.

"Is this it . . . a clump of eggs on a naked plate? This is your 'mean scrambled eggs'? Where's the bacon and the hash browns? Or even a garnish?" Her laughter lingered in her eyes.

"I've got your garnish right here," he said, handing her a fork and napkin.

He escorted her three steps to the kitchen table and held the chair for her. "Your chair, Mademoiselle."

Still standing, Jesse looked for a place to put her plate down, but she couldn't find a part of the table that wasn't covered with newspapers and windowed envelopes for bills and receipts. "Uh, where do I put my plate?"

"I beg your pardon?"

"The clutter . . ."

"I paid good money for that clutter, but if you prefer something simpler, I'll take it away."

As he moved the papers from the table to the counter, an 8 by 10 glossy photo of Lorraine Harte fell from the stack and landed lightly on the floor. He picked it up and put it on the top of the pile.

They both began to eat in silence, not knowing what to say next. After a few minutes, and without looking up, Jesse asked, "So . . . is that your girlfriend?"

"Is what my girlfriend?"

"Lorraine."

"No. She's just a friend."

"A friend, that's nice." Jesse's voice held a hint of relief.

The phone rang.

"Make yourself at home in the bedroom while I get this," Kelly said. He didn't wait to see the surprised look on her face in reaction to his directive.

In the bedroom, Jesse tried to relax. She remained fully clothed on his double bed, not knowing whether he meant to join her or not. Surprisingly, she wasn't sure whether she was offended by the possibility, or intrigued by it. It wasn't long before the delirium of the last twenty-four hours washed over her, fatigue touched every muscle, her mind shut down, and her eyes closed. She was asleep.

The empty airport lobby stretches before her, endlessly. A chilling breeze blows the pages of yesterday's newspaper across the dirty floor. Muffled voices speak in foreign tongues of departure dates and arrival times.

"The white zone is for loading and unloading of passengers only. . . ."

Forgotten magazines occupy the vacant plastic seats of the waiting areas; their pages flutter in the wind, waving to her . . . speaking to her . . . clapping for the dive . . . applause . . . applause.

Signs. . . . Caution, no lifeguard on duty.

Mom and Dad are underwater: diving masks over their eyes, rubber mouth regulators in their mouths. Bubbles float to the surface of a South American sea.

Chris walks by, carrying a suitcase in each hand. "The big E, Babe, the big E. Monaco, Babe," he smiles.

She calls to him.

He doesn't answer . . . he gets in line.

Mikel gets in line behind Chris. He looks at her and smiles. There's someone behind him. "Someone I should know," she hears herself say.

"I know you! Yes, I know you. You're Wolfgang Metter!"
He holds a finger to his lips and shakes his head.

"Look, Mikel, it's Wolfgang," she whispers, but he doesn't hear her.

Kelly, dressed in a suit of armor, stands behind the counter, giving out tickets and asking for passports.

Voices . . . foreign, all of them . . . strange . . . heavy . . . masculine . . . growling . . . angry . . . evil!

Faces . . . too many faces . . . they fill the lobby. They push past the baggage areas. They hurry for the taxis and the buses.

Tall, dark men push past her. Now they're touching her, grabbing her, pushing her into line.

"The white zone is for loading of passengers only. . . ."

They're pushing her out of line.

"The white zone is for loading—"

One man, dark man, evil man—his face pushes towards her. Close—too close.

"Go away! Go away! I don't know you. You don't know me. What do you want? Go away!"

"The white zone is for unloading of passengers only—"

Too many people—too many people in the lobby—too many people in the empty airport—crowding—pushing—

Only one man, his face is too close to hers. What's that in his hand? It's a gun. IT'S A GUN! HE'S SO CLOSE!

"The white zone is for unloading—"

She feels the round, cold muzzle of the pistol touch her forehead. His cold black eyes speak to her of death. She hears the tiny click of the hammer—"

Her eyes flashed open. She could still feel the cold steel of the gun muzzle at her head. Her ears pounded out each adrenaline filled pulse of blood that pushed through her veins. She was covered with sweat. Her neck was stiff and she couldn't move her head. Her eyes leapt from side to side, back and forth, trying to find the one man, the man with the gun.

He wasn't there. No one was there. No one was where? Where was she? Kelly's place . . . she was alone in Agent Kelly's bedroom. She tried to calm down. It was only a dream. She tried to go back to sleep. She couldn't. Someone had tried to kill her. Someone had actually held a gun to her head.

At the airport, fear and anger, panic and defiance had collided in her mind and she had gone into shock. She realized that now. She had been in shock for at least twenty-four hours. Her sleep, if that's what she had done, had been unmerciful. Someone was still trying to kill her. She didn't know why; she couldn't imagine the reason for this waking nightmare.

She tried to sleep again, but couldn't. She tried different positions to get comfortable. She started out on her back, and then rolled over on her right side. She couldn't calm down. She rolled onto her stomach, but her heart beat just as hard in that position. She tried her left side.

As her emotions calmed, she looked around the room to orient herself. How long had she slept? Minutes . . . hours . . . she couldn't tell. It couldn't have been too long, she still felt tired. She wanted to sleep, but not to dream. Like a child afraid of the dark, she was afraid of the dream.

She looked through the open bedroom door. Kelly was asleep on the couch. He lay on his side and she could see his thick, chestnut hair resting on the overstuffed arm.

Without thinking about it, she moved off the bed and went into the living room. RoboDobe lifted his head, the constant sentry. She stood for a moment in front of Kelly, looking down into his tranquil face. She considered waking him. Stupid, she thought. What am I going to say? Wake up, Agent Kelly; I had a bad dream.

She sat down gently in the middle of the couch, being careful not to wake him. He didn't move. He was asleep. She took his left arm in her hands and lifted it gently. In one smooth motion, she lay down next to him and pulled his arm over her shoulder as if it were a blanket. "Thank you for saving my life," she whispered.

Kelly smiled to himself as he inhaled the fragrance of her hair and listened to her breathing become calmer.

You're welcome, he thought.

26

BOGOTA, COLOMBIA

"We're ready, gentlemen—we are ready!" Enrico smiled as he looked around the polished walnut table of his conference room.

The enthusiastic group returned his smile.

Turning to Rafael, he asked, "Are the men in Switzerland ready?"

"Yes, Enrico. Uh . . . they're ready and waiting for us."

"Get them on the phone, Rafael."

After Rafael dialed the telephone directly in front of him, Enrico pushed a button on his extension, and the echo of a long distance ring confirmed the fact that they were on the speaker phone.

"Yes?" Ahmed answered, more resolute than curious.

"Ahmed, it's Rafael Santos. May I speak with Amir please?"

"One moment, *Señor* Santos."

The group waited patiently.

"Rafael, my friend, it is good to hear from you. You bring me good news?"

"We're on the speaker phone, Amir. I'm calling you from the Serva estate. We're ready."

"Good," said the cautious voice from Switzerland.

"We need to know the time and the place you've chosen for the meeting."

"We will meet in Marseilles. Are you familiar with the *Porte Moderne?*"

Enrico looked to Antonio. Antonio nodded.

After glancing at Enrico and Antonio, Rafael spoke into the phone. "Yes, my friend, we're familiar with that port."

"Can you be there in ten days' time?" Amir asked.

Once more, Enrico looked to Antonio.

"The *ACÈMILA* is prepared to sail to Marseilles. If it leaves today, it can be there in ten days.

"Good," the speaker phone echoed the voice of the man from Switzerland. "I am making all the arrangements for your account. I will have the number. Perhaps it would be wise for us to plan the exchange. The money for the number."

"Do you mean you want us to deliver your payment on the dock?"

"Can you think of a better way? There is going to be an explosion, a terrible accident that will take the life of a Swiss banker. That accident will occur in ten days at the *Porte Moderne.* I believe that I will be in the area of your freighter at that time. It would be a comforting thought to know our business could be concluded then. All I need to know, of course, is who I will be dealing with. Will it be you, Rafael?"

Enrico pushed the privacy button on the telephone console, allowing him to hear but not be heard by the other party. "I'll go myself, Rafael. Tell him I'll be the one to deliver the payoff."

"Is that wise, Enrico," Alberto injected, "to be in the same city with the shipment?"

"It's a lot of money, Alberto. And the number is very important to us. I think it's important enough that I go myself."

"We can carry the cash on the *ACÈMILA,*" Antonio argued. "Customs is very lax in Marseilles, but someone *carrying* that much cash might be asking for problems. I would worry for you."

"That's a good idea, Antonio," Leon added.

"I'll fly in and you can bring me the money when you arrive, Antonio." Enrico had made his decision.

"Are you still there?" Amir's voice called into the restrained air of the conference room.

Enrico pushed the privacy button off and pointed to Rafael.

"Yes, Amir, we're here," Rafael responded. "We'll meet you in ten days. Enrico will be there personally to close the deal. Well," he concluded, "I guess that's it."

"What about the other matter," Amir questioned.

Leon, Alberto and Antonio were not familiar with "the other matter." Rafael and Enrico were all too familiar with "the other matter."

Enrico knew that Amir would not recognize his voice, as they had never spoken to each other. But he couldn't stop himself from testing. "If you want the girl dead, you'll have to do it yourself. There's nothing in it for us."

There was a prolonged silence on the long distance line.

There was a mixture of quiet confusion, impatience and anger in the conference room.

"No girl . . . no bank," the hard-edged voice whispered from the speaker phone.

A click stopped the static, and filled the room with silence.

"Antonio," Enrico's eyes slid toward the man, "have the *ALBARDA* ready to sail to L.A. in five days."

After his business partners had accepted their farewell handshakes, gone out the door to Enrico's waiting limousines, and had been driven away, Enrico went to find Juan.

Juan sat on the floor of his room with his back against the bed, an unlit cigarette between his lips and his pistol in his lap. A yellow cloth, stained with gun oil, lay across his left knee. An ashtray stuffed with cigarette butts rested on the carpet near his right hip. A syndicated episode of Miami Vice danced on the flat screen for his mesmerized eyes.

Enrico went directly to the television set and turned it off.

"Hey, what'd you do that for?" Juan complained, still staring at the darkened screen.

"We have to talk," Enrico began. "I need you to do your job. I want you to get that girl, Juan. And don't fuck-up this time. The *Angelinos* are doing everything they can to locate her for us. Get on the jet and get your ass to L.A. I want you there when they find her."

"Okay, Enrico, okay," he said, pushing past Enrico's leg and turning the television back on.

27

ZURICH, SWITZERLAND

Zürich slept the sleep of the old. The Institute was empty and the museum closed. The funicular railway cars, exhausted from their daily routine of multiple ascending and descending of the mountain slopes, lay spent in their chilly alpine lodgings. At this hour, there was no one on the fashionable Bahnhofstrasse or the quays lining the lake.

Wolfgang Metter slept the sleep of the wealthy. At thirty, he was the current end-link on the long golden chain of the Metter banking family. He could trace his lineage back to the time of Charlemagne's grandson, Louis the German, who had established the Benedictine abbey here in the ninth century. His father had died two years ago, and his mother had followed a year later. Although he missed them dearly, he had very little time to mourn them as he administered the business they had left him. Until he married and had children, he was the sole and final heir to the family name.

His bedroom sprawled leisurely across the third floor of his four story home, and gave him, when awake, an inspiring view of the left bank and the lake.

The gentle, silky light of the moon moved through the age-rippled glass of the twelve-foot-high, two-centuries-old French doors and brushed past the thick, silver and gray striped drapes to cast box-like patterns of shadows on the white ceiling and quiet white walls.

Vague light and determinate blackness fell in alternating strips, like paths to a dream world, across Wolfgang's goose down quilt and over his marble-topped nightstand, then angled up to make darker shadows around and behind the hand-carved, gilded frame that held the portrait of his mother.

Another shadow stood just inside the slightly open bedroom door . . . a darker shadow than the crisscross lines on the ceiling . . . a deeper shadow than the one between the picture frame and the wall. And this shadow could breathe. This shadow could move to the end of the bed and smile cynically. This shadow knew that it was Sunday night, the servants' night off, and Wolfgang Metter was alone in the house.

Mikel Rhen watched his friend sleeping. He smiled at the fact that there was a hint of a snore emanating from Wolfgang's parted lips.

Everything Mikel needed he carried in a small, black nylon duffle bag, which he placed quietly on the carpet by the left side of the bed, close to Wolfgang. Although it had a zipper, Mikel had intentionally left it undone—so there would be no sound when he retrieved the items Uncle had carefully packed for him.

Since the moment Uncle had learned of Jesse Fortune's miraculous survival, he had been more adamant than ever about detail. Each object had been padded and wrapped so there would be no noise when the bag was carried and no sound when the articles were extracted. Uncle had gone over every detail of the plan until Mikel was sure he could repeat it in his sleep.

Mikel removed a plastic bag and slowly unfolded it. He withdrew a cloth from the plastic and held it between his palm and two fingers as he refolded the bag. There was still a small pool of liquid in the plastic.

The cloth was soaked with insoflurane and a few drops fell on the carpet.

He laid the bag back on the duffle.

Holding the cloth with both hands, he turned to his slumbering friend. Bending over close to Wolfgang's face, he paused for one second to prepare.

In one swift motion, Mikel covered Wolfgang's face with the cloth and when he started to wake and move and fight against this living nightmare, Mikel sat down firmly on his chest, negating Wolfgang's effort to bring his arms up to rip the cloth from his eyes, nose and mouth.

It wasn't long before Wolfgang stopped struggling and the room was motionless again. Satisfied that Wolfgang was unconscious, Mikel left the cloth on his face while he got the plastic bag again. He replaced the cloth and re-folded the bag.

Next, he started to unpack everything in the duffle bag and place it on the carpeted floor. While he was doing this, he glanced up at Wolfgang to make sure he was sleeping soundly. His eyes caught a soft glint from Wolfgang's wire-rimmed glasses on the night table. The idea struck him immediately.

Mikel realized that Wolfgang had not seen his attacker. His eyes had been covered with the cloth. It was too interesting a thought to go ignored. He wondered what Wolfgang's reaction would be if he looked at the man who was going to kill him and saw his own face. He had to know. Besides, if his friend had to die, Mikel might as well give him one last thrill. He had to know.

When everything was out of the duffle bag and arranged neatly on the floor, Mikel drew back the covers to expose Wolfgang's naked body.

He sleeps naked, he thought. There's a detail Uncle didn't know. He took a breath to clear his head, and went to work.

He went to the closet and got Wolfgang's boating clothes, returned to the body, and dressed him.

Uncle's instructions rang in his head. Even though they didn't expect any part of Metter's body to ever be found, Uncle had planned every detail as if it might be. Mikel stuck to the plan.

He adjusted Wolfgang's body so it was straight and the legs were together. He got the roll of gauze and cut strips with a small pair of surgical scissors. He quietly retrieved the pre-cut, one inch wide strips of surgical tape and stuck half of a patch of tape to one end of each piece of gauze.

He went back to the body and wrapped each ankle separately. He repeated the maneuver with Wolfgang's knees and wrists.

He found the pre-cut, duct tape and secured Wolfgang's ankles and knees, being careful not to let the duct tape go off the gauze. He rolled him over and taped his hands behind his back. Then he rolled him face-up again.

This would serve two purposes. First, it would make Wolfgang easier to carry. Even tucked in the body bag, loose arms and legs would be an annoyance. Mikel had to carry him alone. Second, and most important, if, by some chance, a body part were found, Uncle did not want that part to show any residue of tape. The gauze would protect the skin and hair from being ripped away. Later, they would remove it carefully.

Mikel spread the body bag out on the bed and wrestled Wolfgang's moderate frame into it. The plan called for him to kill Metter immediately.

Earlier in the week, Mikel had taken a flight to Marseilles and gone to Wolfgang's boat, the *MARIE-CLAIRE*. The small maintenance crew had easily accepted him as Wolfgang. He was the owner; there was no problem with his being there.

He had gone to the lounge and waited until he was sure no one would notice. He had taken a small axe from his coat and chipped a three-inch piece of wood from the top of Wolfgang's desk.

This would be his weapon . . . his instrument of death . . . a simple piece of wood. This was the needle and he, himself, would be the syringe. He would inject it into Wolfgang's head, wrap and pack the wound to keep it from bleeding, close the bag, and leave with the body. Amir had thought of everything.

Making sure it was sharp at one end, he had replaced the desk blotter, left the boat, and had flown back to Zürich.

Mikel stared at the three-inch piece of wood in his hand. He looked over to the antique-framed glasses. He had to know. He looked at Wolfgang resting peacefully on the king-sized bed, oblivious to his presence. He had to know! He looked at his watch; there was time. He put the wooden sliver in his pants' pocket and sat down on the edge of the bed to wait. With his elbows on his knees and his head bowed, he repeated, "I've got to know" to himself to pass the time.

After thirty-two minutes had passed, he prepared more gauze and tape. He got the special rubber stopper Uncle had made expressly for this execution and made sure it was clean. He checked the suction snap. It worked correctly. He went back to waiting.

Three minutes later, he decided to give up and go ahead with the plan. Then he heard a change in Wolfgang's breathing. He was elated.

Almost too late, he realized that if Wolfgang woke all the way up, he might scream. Mikel couldn't tape his mouth; that would leave traces.

Wolfgang moaned.

Mikel panicked. He looked desperately at his collection of items on the floor. There was nothing there he could use. He grabbed the duct tape. What the hell. What was Uncle going to do? Spank him? He had to know! He could always remove the residue with acetone.

He turned to Wolfgang and covered his mouth with a large piece of tape.

Wolfgang opened his eyes. Shock filled him everywhere as he became horrifyingly aware that someone was standing over him. Someone was in his bedroom. Someone he knew instinctively meant him great harm. He realized that he couldn't speak. He tried to yell, to scream this phantom away. His mouth was stuck shut. With each second that passed, he discovered another part of his body was bound. Finally, on the verge of hysteria, he began to cry.

"Wait," Mikel whispered as he sat down on the bed close to Wolfgang. "Wait, don't cry. Look, it's me, Wolfgang. You're right here with you. There's no need to cry. Wolfgang will protect you." As Mikel spoke, he got the piece of wood from his pocket, and retrieved the rubber mallet from the floor. "Do you know who I am?" he asked quietly as he put the stopper close to the body bag where he could get it quickly. "I'm Wolfgang. Don't you know me? I'm you."

Wolfgang Metter was beyond knowing. He was too scared even to recognize Mikel's voice. He realized he was in some kind of bag. *A BODY BAG!* When he saw the mallet, he began to beg through his tears. His head swung violently back and forth and his eyes pleaded—no, No, NO!

"I know what it is," Mikel continued quietly, "you can't see me." He reached for Wolfgang's spectacles on the nightstand. "Now, let's put on our glasses so we can see who it is."

Wolfgang's head twisted and slammed in the bag.

"Come on now. That won't do. Don't you want to see Wolfgang? Here, I'll turn on the light."

Wolfgang's head stopped abruptly and he stared at the figure hovering above him.

"That's it," Mikel said as he put Wolfgang's glasses on him.

Even though he was far beyond anything remotely sane, Wolfgang saw, for the first time, who was in the room with him. For the briefest moment, they stared at each other.

For Mikel, the pleasure was so great he almost choked trying not to laugh. Sitting on the bed, his head began to bob up and down as he said, "That's right, it's Wolfgang . . . it's Wolfgang! You know . . . our secretary, Margreta, had the same reaction to us Friday night . . . just before we choked her to death. And now it's your turn."

For Wolfgang, the shock was so intense his eyes rocked back in his head and he passed out.

Removing Wolfgang's glasses, he opened his right eyelid and gently cupped the tiny spear of wood over his eye. Holding it with one hand, he reached for the mallet. He slammed the mallet down on the end of the three-inch spike, driving the shank through the soft tissue of the iris and retina, and into the brain. He tapped it again to sink it.

A small squirt of blood slapped onto Mikel's black turtleneck sweater. He quickly grabbed the rubber stopper and placed it over the eye socket. He pushed it down to get suction, and then snapped it in place. It held. The blood stopped, just as Uncle had said it would.

Mikel gathered his tools and put them back in the duffle bag. He undressed and put his clothing in the duffle bag as well. He went to Wolfgang's closet and put on one of his robes. Then he carried the body bag over his shoulder, and the duffle bag in his free hand, quietly down the back stairs and out the rear door.

Uncle was waiting for him in a small, refrigerated truck procured for the purpose of preserving the body.

"That took a long time, Mikki."

"Yes, Uncle." Mikel hid his smile as he loaded Wolfgang's body into the truck, and retrieved the hanging bag with the altered Brioni suit.

"Did you have any trouble?"

248

"No, Uncle."

"You know what to do tomorrow, Mikki. Stay in the bank only long enough to open the account."

"I know, Uncle," Mikel said impatiently, his bare feet feeling the cold of the alley stone.

"Tomorrow, have a secretary open a numbered account for you, get the number and leave. Don't forget to emphasize your cold and sore throat. Even though your imitation of Wolfgang is very good, we don't want anyone questioning your voice. Remember to tell her that you are going to spend a few days on the *MARIE-CLAIRE* recuperating."

"Yes, Uncle," Mikel said, distracted by the cool fog edging down the alley.

"Don't spend any more time in the bank than you absolutely have to. Then get to Marseilles as soon as you can."

"Yes, Uncle," he said obediently. He turned and went back into the Metter residence to go to bed.

Amir drove the truck through the pre-dawn mist of the city and took the road to Marseilles.

The next morning, Monday, 9:00 a.m., Wolfgang Metter entered the *Banque Nationale de Suisse*, and performed his presidential duties perfectly. At 9:39 he left the building. Driving away from the bank in his CLS550 Mercedes-Benz, Wolfgang gave one final false sneeze that sounded like the word "Ferrari": Mikel Rhen's laughter filled the car's interior, and visions of a new car filled his mind.

28

BURBANK, CALIFORNIA

A robin called from one of the higher branches of a tall, carefully cultivated pine tree. Its mate answered melodically. Both birds were oblivious to the significance of the hallowed ground beneath them.

This is all wrong. From behind a pair of black-rimmed sunglasses, Jesse's eyes wandered across the freshly mowed lawn as she waited for Kelly to come around the Tahoe and join her.

The thin line between spring and summer had evaporated like a drop of water on the late morning grass, and the day was already hot and sunny.

Why isn't it raining? This was the first funeral she had ever been to, and although she knew it wouldn't be like the movies, she needed to direct her anger at something. The beautiful California morning would do.

Wrong. All wrong. It should be dark. There should be rain. There shouldn't be anything happy about today.

Kelly handed her the single red rose, wrapped in green cellophane, that she had left in the Tahoe. He became aware of how vulnerable and fragile she looked wearing the simple black dress and plain black heels they had purchased on their way here.

As they moved across the manicured grass, Jesse noticed that a group was already gathered at the grave site. "We're late," she said, annoyed.

Kelly did not respond. He had advised her not to come. As far as he was concerned it was too dangerous, and they shouldn't be there. Seeing her reaction to his advice, and knowing he couldn't win, he had made her promise she would leave immediately after the ceremony, and not talk to anyone.

As they approached the burial plot, she realized there were more people in the gathering than it had appeared from the car. Among the mourners, she saw Cindy and her family, the manager of the gym and his wife, and the two jocks that had helped her. There were others, some she knew from Mission Viejo, and some she had never seen before. She managed a smile at Cindy.

"I didn't remember Matt had so many friends," she remarked to Kelly. "I guess I never stopped to count them all."

Kelly nodded, but his attention was somewhere else. His eyes hadn't stopped moving since they had begun their walk across the lawn. He picked up Anderson five hundred yards to the west and as he continued to scan, he saw the other agents Hunt had sent to protect them. He knew that Hunt had requisitioned a sniper and he also knew he would never be able to spot him.

Jesse moved through an opening in the group and stopped a few feet from the priest who was delivering the final prayer. She allowed herself to look beyond him.

A smooth, Florentine-gray casket with heavy brass handles sat on a bier, and astro-turf was appropriately placed to cover the mounds of dirt and the deep hole in the ground.

When the priest finished, everyone remained silent and unmoving.

Kelly waited as long as he could, and then he whispered, "I think we should leave."

"Don't rush me," she said with quiet anger.

As he looked down at her, he could see past the top of her sunglasses. Her eyes were red. A few tears snuck past the bottom of the glasses and were visible on her cheeks.

"I can't possibly protect you in the open like this," he said, sounding frustrated.

"Then don't. Just leave me alone." She moved forward and placed the rose she had brought with her on the casket. Silently, she blessed Matthew Braden for all he had been to her. Only then did she allow Kelly to escort her back to the car.

Cindy called after her. But, as she had promised, she ignored everyone and took her place in the passenger's seat of the Tahoe. Kelly got behind the wheel quickly and started the car.

As they drove away, Jesse saw a bewildered Cindy standing on the grass.

"They're here!" Chris almost yelled into his cell.

"Chris, is that you?" Kelly put the cup of coffee he had made for Jesse down in front of her on the kitchen table. He pushed his cell phone harder against his ear.

Jesse looked up at him.

"Yeah, Kelly, it's me. And like I said, they're here."

"Are you okay?" Kelly asked.

"What's the matter?" Jesse asked Kelly. "Is that Chris? Is he all right?"

Kelly motioned for her to be quiet.

"Yeah, I'm okay," Chris said. His voice was calmer now that he had connected with Kelly.

Jesse came to her feet. "Is he all right?"

Kelly nodded to her and continued to speak into the phone. "Tell me about it, kid."

"I couldn't sleep. I mean I was so tired I thought I'd sleep forever. But I couldn't. After all that shit at the airport, I was fried. My eyes just wouldn't close. I guess it was shock or something—"

"Hey, man, get to it. What did you mean, 'they're here'?"

"Right, I heard them coming up the street. It's pretty quiet on our street. You can hear the cars when someone's coming—"

"Listen to me, Chris," Kelly raised his whispery voice. "I need the short version. If they're there, we don't have much time. Tell me quickly, and then we'll figure out where you can go to be safe."

"Right," Chris replied, his voice steady. "There are three of them this time . . . one Mexican and two White guys. I don't mean Mex—I mean South Amer—"

"I know what you mean, Chris. Go on."

Jesse couldn't keep still any longer. "What's going on?"

Kelly had to remember to be patient with both of them. They weren't trained agents. They were totally unprepared for this kind of situation. As an answer to her question, he took her arm and gently guided her back to the chair she'd been sitting in. "Go on, Chris," he repeated into his cell.

"It's one of the guys that was at the airport. They were driving a new Dodge four door . . . black, I think. Yeah, black. I saw them coming and went out the back door. I made it through the backyard the same way I used to when I was sneaking out on my folks. They didn't see me, I'm sure of that. I came down here to Ventura Boulevard before I called you.

"How long ago, Chris?" Kelly had to strain to keep his patience.

"Five, six minutes. Seven tops."

"You got a friend you can stay with for a while?"

"Yeah, sure. But I want to help. Is there something I can do?

"Not now. Go to your friend's place. Call me when you're safe and I'll send agents to pick you up and bring you downtown. Kelly knew the best way to handle a non-professional was to leave hope and not argue. "Hang in there, Chris. Get back to me." He ended the call and turned to Jesse.

"They're on their way. They'll be here any minute. We've got to move fast."

"But I thought they didn't know where you live," she said, searching his eyes for some hope. "Isn't that why you brought me here?" She was starting to feel the fear again. And this time, she knew she wouldn't be able to lose herself in the comfortable oblivion of emotional shock.

"They know where I live. Don't kid yourself, they know. They made me in Vegas. By now, they probably know more about me than I do. And I brought you here so I could protect you."

"I blew it, didn't I? Going to Vegas I mean. I really blew it."

"I don't know why these guys want you, but if we're going to save your life, we've got to go now!"

Kelly got his wallet, gun and keys while Jesse waited. On the way to his Tahoe, Kelly criticized himself for not having sent some agents to cover Chris. It was a mistake that Kelly hoped he would not have to regret. Then, in the Tahoe, he worried that he might not get Jesse to safety in time. He was sure that even if the Colombian killers had picked up some local talent, they were not going to come into an armed and ready federal building. He just had to get her there. He went for his cell phone. He'd have to tell Hunt that he was bringing her in early for protection. He started dialing the Key number.

"Metter. Wolfgang Metter," she said, staring at the dashboard. She slowly turned her head to face him.

"What?" he asked.

"Wolfgang Metter! That's the name I heard Serva use on the phone." She waited for him to understand.

"So what?"

"I know him! At least I met him once."

"You what?" You know the man Serva was talking to?" He ended the call before Hunt could answer. He put the phone in his lap so he could keep both hands on the wheel.

"Maybe this is it. The connection you've been looking for."

"Who is this guy? What does he do? How do you know him?" He couldn't slow himself down. He wanted every bit of information he could get if it helped prove Jesse was innocent of drug involvement and murder. Hunt would have to be convinced.

"He's a banker . . . in Switzerland. His family owns the bank. They've had it for years. Actually, his parents are dead. So, I guess he owns the bank."

"Enrico Serva and a Swiss bank, that makes perfect sense. And it's owned by a Mister Wolfgang Metter. So how do you know this guy?"

"He was best man at my wedding," Jesse said, and tried to absorb Kelly's surprise.

"I guess that's a connection," Kelly said, not taking his eyes off the road. "That's a hell of a connection."

"That's a hell of a connection," Hunt coughed. He glanced at the curious group sitting on the other side of his desk. "Anderson, get me anything you can on Wolfgang Metter." He looked over to Jesse and addressed her next.

"What's the name of his bank?"

"I don't know. I don't think it was ever men—" She was interrupted by Hunt's next question, directed to Kelly.

"So, the New Man has found himself a bank. You think that lets this woman off the hook?" He turned his attention back to Jesse. "Excuse me for not jumping on your bandwagon, Miss Fortune, but seriously—you're trying to tell me that Enrico Serva is trying to kill you because your dead husband happened to bank at the same bank where he wants to launder his money? And you can't even remember the name of the bank!"

"I told you," Jesse began, her voice growing with frustration, "he was my husband's best friend. I know it's a long shot, but it's the only connection I can make. What else have we got to go on?"

Anderson was watching the others talk. He was stalling, hoping there might be something mentioned that would save him some research time.

"What are you waiting for, Agent Anderson? M-E-T-T-E-R, Wolfgang. Zürich, Switzerland. Google it or whatever it is you do!"

Hunt's words were like a slap in the face. Anderson turned and left the room.

"What *we* have to go on, Miss Fortune, it that *you* and your coach were trafficking drugs. You made a mistake, and they want you to pay for it."

"That's crazy," Jesse said, holding Hunt's eyes with her own.

"We've got nothing in the files to back that up, Sir," Kelly added. "Maybe there's something else in this deal: a factor we don't know about yet. This Metter connection—"

"Factors. Files. It's a lot simpler just to look at the facts." Hunt had never been impressed with theories, especially complicated ones.

"And what *are* the facts?" Jesse asked defiantly.

"The facts are, you're being hunted by a drug dealer," Hunt responded, matching Jesse's defiance. "That fact alone puts you on the wrong side of the game in my book."

"I need some coffee," Jesse said to Hunt's brick-wall stare. She got up and left the room.

With his elbows on his knees, Kelly sat staring at the floor. He could feel, as well as hear, the silence in the room. "I think she may have a point," he said without looking up. He added, "Sir" almost as an afterthought. He felt like he was asking his father for an allowance he hadn't earned yet.

"I think you may be getting involved with this woman, Agent Kelly."

"That's crazy," he lied.

"That would be a big mistake. You could lose your ability to make the right judgment. You could lose your edge, and you could lose your job."

"She's got a point, Sir. It's worth pursuing. A little investigating won't hurt us."

Anderson stepped through the door to interrupt. "I just saw Fortune leaving the building. Is that cool with you guys?" He put a piece of paper on Hunt's desk. It had the name of Wolfgang Metter's bank on it, and not much else.

Kelly's jaw dropped noticeably. He looked up, first at Anderson, then across at Hunt.

Hunt slumped back in his swivel chair and shook his head slowly.

Anderson took in the stunned, silent mood of the two men. "Was it something I said?" he asked, trying to make a joke.

Ignoring Anderson, Hunt looked over at Kelly. "Either she's going to ground, or she's going to Switzerland. I'm betting on the former." He leaned forward, putting his heavy elbows on the leather framed blotter on his desk. "I guess you better find out, Agent Kelly."

"48-B. This must be my seat."

Jesse heard the familiar, whispery voice as she was putting her bag under the seat in front of her. She looked up into his mischievous blue eyes. "What are you doing here? How did you find me?"

"You mean how did I know that you stayed with Chris at his girlfriend's house? And how did I know that this morning, you bought the clothes and that bag you've got there at The Broadway? And how did I know that you bought a plane ticket to Zürich? I'm a DEA agent; it's my job to know," Kelly said smugly, sitting down next to her. *And, if I was any good at it, I would have found you before you got on this plane.* He'd been a step behind her for the past twelve hours and out of his mind with worry for her. "So . . . Zürich huh?"

"I've got to find Metter, Thomas. He's the only lead I've got."

"Hunt wants me to bring you back."

"Hunt can kiss my ass!"

A smile broke over his face. "I've never heard you swear before."

"He's not trying to do anything to solve my problem. He thinks I'm guilty, and that's as far as he wants to think. I'm the one someone's trying to kill, not him. I need someone who's on my side for a change, someone who can help, someone who cares."

He slid his own small duffle bag carefully under the seat in front of him, remembering the hassle he'd gone through to get its contents past the airport security.

"Okay," he said slowly. "Here, I think you're gonna need this." He handed her one side of her seat belt.

29

ZURICH, SWITZERLAND

Because of her cane, the other departing passengers gave her more space and showed her more courtesy than they normally would, and she was two steps ahead of him as they immerged from the jet way and entered the Kloten Airport terminal. Her eyes searched out and found customs and she went in that direction.

During the flight, Kelly had called Hunt to advise him that Jesse Fortune had not gone to ground, but was on her way to Switzerland. He was going to need Hunt to call ahead to advise Swiss customs that he would be bringing in a firearm.

Kelly followed her, excusing himself when he couldn't avoid bumping into one of the other travelers. "Jesse," he said, finally grabbing her arm, "slow down."

"We've got to find Metter," she said over the agitated sounds of the crowded arrival area. She pulled out her smart phone and Googled Wolfgang Metter, Zürich, Switzerland.

Okay. But you're getting a little crazy. You're jet lagged. So am I. We need to rest for a few hours. I need to inform Hunt of what we're doing . . . as soon as I can figure out what we're doing. We may need his back-up at some point. Let's get a hotel."

"Metter, Wolfgang R. *Stadthausquai 54.*" She hit end on her cell phone. "Let's get a cab," she called back over her shoulder as she moved farther into the terminal.

"Damn," was the only response he could think of.

"I'm sorry; Herr Metter is not in residence at the moment."

"Can you tell me where he is?" Jesse asked the rigid but pleasant servant standing behind the solid oak door of the stone-brick mansion.

"He is out of town. Perhaps you could leave your card. I'll see that he gets it."

"This is police business," Kelly said, offering his DEA credentials.

"What my friend means is, it's very important that we find Herr Metter immediately."

The servant looked from Kelly to Jesse. He hesitated, confused.

"My name is Jesse Fortune Rhen. I think you knew my husband. He and Herr Metter were friends. Mikel Rhen?"

"Oh yes, of course. Herr Rhen was here many times." He paused to look closely at Jesse. He noticed the cane she had almost hidden behind her right leg. "A terrible tragedy, your accident. I am sorry about Herr Rhen. My deepest condolences. What can I do for you, Frau Rhen?"

"We must find Herr Metter today. It's very important. Can you tell us where he's gone?"

"Yes. He's in the south of France, on the *MARIE-CLAIRE,* recuperating from a troublesome flu. That's his yacht, of course. Let me get his itinerary. Please come in while you wait."

"We'll wait here," Kelly said impatiently.

After a few moments, the servant returned. "Herr Metter is in Marseilles until Tuesday, the *Vieux Port*."

"The *Vieux Port*, Frau Rhen," Kelly said under his breath as he turned to hail a cab. "Marseilles," he continued, shaking his head in frustration. "If he's got the flu, he'll still be there tomorrow. I'm not going anywhere until I get some food and rest."

Kelly held the phone closer to his left ear to dampen the hissing sound of running water coming from the bathroom where Jesse was taking a shower.

He was more tired than he wanted to be. The jet lag was doing its best to overtake him. He was losing his edge. He needed sleep. Jesse had wanted to continue on to find Metter, without sleep. Somehow, he had convinced her that they needed the rest.

He stared out the third floor window of the *Zum Storchen* hotel, but before his eyes could take in the urban alpine architecture, he heard the connecting click of the long distance call and the ring of the phone in the States.

"Hello?" Lorraine's voice echoed across the miles.

The sound of the shower stopped.

"Lorraine, it's me, Tom."

"Tom, where are you? You sound like you're a million miles away or something."

"I'm out of town unexpectedly and I need a favor."

"Sure, but if it's tickets to the ballet, you're out of luck. I got replaced."

"No, it's not tickets. I was hoping you could feed and walk RoboDobe for me. Just a couple of days, I think. Can you do that? You know where I keep the spare key."

"Sure, Cutie."

"I'm sorry to hear you got replaced. Are you okay?"

"Listen to you. You get whisked out of town, probably on some dangerous operation, and strange men in black cars come around looking for you, and you're worried about me. You're so cute."

"Tell me about the men in the car, Lorraine."

"It was yesterday, Tom. There were several of them. They drove down your driveway. That made RoboDobe bark. I heard him barking and looked out the window. He's such a good dog, and he never barks. That's why I went to the window."

"Did they try to get in?"

"No. One of them walked around the house while another walked up on the porch and rang the bell. RoboDobe barked like he does when strangers ring the bell. They didn't try to get in or anything. They waited for a while. Then they drove around the corner and waited some more."

"What time did they get there, Lorraine?"

"Gee, Tom, I think it was about twelve-thirty. Is that important?"

Behind his overly tired mind, new thoughts began to burst—first like tiny firecrackers, pestering his concentration, then loud explosions, shaking the foundation of his consciousness. Jesse's tormentors couldn't have missed them by more than a few hours. But worse, far worse, was the fact that they had driven down the driveway in broad daylight, and gotten out to examine the house when they could have been seen by any curious neighbor. They had to know that he was DEA and would be protected at the federal level. Their brazen attitude could only mean one of two things. Either they were overconfident and unconcerned with the amount of resistance they might encounter, or they were getting desperate, and needed to get the job done whatever the danger to themselves. He was sure it was the latter. He had hoped that allowing her to leave the country would throw off her pursuers. If they couldn't find her, they might give up; the danger might pass. But he was beginning to realize the folly of his wishful thinking. What did she have; what did she know; what had she done to cause a drug lord to want to kill her?

"Are you still there, Tom?" Lorraine's voice called from somewhere in the distance.

He heard the door to the bathroom open behind him, but he continued to stare out the hotel window. In order not to alarm Jesse, he spoke more quietly into the phone. "Thanks for the favor, Lorraine. But if they come back, don't go over there."

"Do you want me to bring RoboDobe over here so he's safe?"

Kelly felt Jesse moving behind him. He also thought he could feel her listening to his side of the call.

"No, he can take care of himself. I have to go now. I'll call you later. Thanks again."

"Take care of yourself, Tom."

After a pause he responded, "Yeah, you too."

"Who was that?" Jesse asked, drawing the terry cloth belt of the white, complimentary bathrobe tighter around her thin waist. She went to the nightstand and retrieved a comb from her bag.

"Lorraine," he answered. His voice had a distance to it.

"Oh?" Jesse felt a small spark of jealousy. She tried to deny the feeling. "Friends . . . that's nice."

"I needed someone to feed RoboDobe. I knew I could count on her."

"RoboDobe . . . oh, of course." Everything about her relaxed and she began combing her wet hair.

"She knows where I keep my spare key, so it'll be easy for her," he said, watching her closely.

"Really?" Her voice was light and inquisitive, but the comb stopped before it reached the end of the strand of hair it was gliding through.

"Jealous are we?" he asked as he lay down on the bed and put his arms behind his head.

"In your dreams," she retorted, but her eyes began to glisten as she moved across the room to look out the window. She started combing her hair again. "Did you book us a flight to Marseilles?"

"Yeah, I did that while you were in the shower."

"Before you called Lorraine?"

"Jealous. I thought so."

She turned to stare at him. "Why are you doing this?"

"Doing what?"

"This," she said, waving her arm at the room and everything beyond it.

"It's my job."

"Your job?"

"When I was thirteen my mother took me to the hospital because my appendix had burst. My father was a U.S. Marshall and had been called to assist in a major drug bust on the California border. There was a gunfight. He was wounded. They brought him to the hospital. I saw them wheel his gurney past my room. Mom was called out of my room to go to him. He didn't make it through the night. I couldn't even get out of bed to see him before he died."

"I'm sorry," she said softly. "I want you to take this the right way. If you're here because it's your job, and you're needed somewhere else—I'll be okay—"

Before she could finish, he came up off the bed, pulled her to him, and kissed her.

She pushed back and looked up at him.

The expression on her face was one he hadn't seen before and couldn't read. For a moment, he regretted having taken such a bold step. No matter how powerful his feelings were for her, no matter how much he wanted her or, in fact, loved her; there was no guarantee that she felt anything for him beyond a protector, and perhaps, a friend.

And then, she pushed herself into him and kissed him hard.

At first, he was surprised. But as her warm lips moved on his, and her eager tongue explored his mouth, and her anxious arms surrounded his shoulders; he wrapped his arms around her and guided her down on the bed.

He began by stroking her damp, golden hair as it lay across the side of her face. She went after his lips again, kissing them more gently but with no less passion.

He caressed her cheek and neck and pushed the collar of the robe off her soft shoulder. She took his face in both hands and kissed his eyes tenderly.

In his mind, Kelly had seen this moment many times. And just as many times he had fought to resist the fantasized image of Jesse's lithe body lying vulnerable and accepting, willing and waiting for his touch. Now he knew that nothing he could dream could meet the reality unfolding within the boundary of his arms.

As their bodies pressed against each other, Jesse felt warm and safe, excited and electrified, and most of all, completely alive. He had done more than save her life; he was giving her a new one. He was strong and honest and good. And, beyond everything else he might be, one simple fact was evident. He was in love with her. She could feel that in everything he did, the way he looked at her, and spoke to her, and protected her. He loved her. And now, she realized, she loved him.

He reached for the terry cloth belt. He pulled on it gently and it separated easily. She reached both hands up and began undoing the buttons of his shirt one by one, kissing his chest as it became visible.

He rose up slightly and reached to remove his shoes.

"Let me do that," she said softly.

As she sat up, the robe parted and he saw the beautiful contours of her exquisite body. Her stomach was flat and her breasts were larger than he had expected. The sensual white mounds ended with small round nipples, the color of dusty pink roses.

She took off his shoes and socks, then bent over him to un-tuck his shirt and finish unbuttoning it. She pulled the shirt gently toward her to indicate that she wanted him to rise up, and when he did, she took it off his shoulders and stared for a moment at his strong, thick-muscled chest. She unbuttoned his Levi's, and he helped her pull them past his hips. She drew them over his legs and dropped them off the side of the bed.

She reached out to touch his chest, but he stopped her by moving to take off her robe. When her arms were free, she wrapped them around his neck and kissed him again. They fell back on the bed.

She was on top of him, and she spread her legs to surround his.

He felt the wonderful softness of the inside of her thighs as they slipped over his skin. He took her head in his hands and lifted her face away from his. He wanted to gaze at her. He wanted to look at her green eyes and her soft pink lips.

She gazed back at him for a moment, and then she smiled and closed her eyes. She went to kiss him again but he held her head and wouldn't let her move. She opened her eyes and looked at him. "What is it?" she asked, concerned. She searched his face for the reason he was holding her away from his lips.

"I want to be inside you," he said without hesitation.

"Are you on the pill?" she asked with a slow smile.

"What?"

When she laughed, it was low and throaty and sexy, and he realized she had caught him in her tease.

He couldn't wait any longer. He rolled her over and looked down at her.

When she looked back at him, her expression held total acceptance. She needed no explanation. Whatever he was, whatever he did to her, she would make it a part of herself.

He moved over her, and their bodies collided in a pleasure so perfect it was painful, and a pain so perfect it was ecstasy.

She cried out, and he followed her with a cry of his own. And then, except for the sound of their breathing, the room was silent.

The afternoon slipped effortlessly past the hotel window. The clouds followed the sun across the Limmat River and cast their shadows reverently on the Lake of Zürich.

In the semi-darkness, he held her head on his chest and stared at the ceiling. His mind was filled with thoughts of the possible dangers she faced. He tried to calculate every consequence and plan a safe outcome. There were too many possibilities, and too many unknowns.

In tired frustration, he closed his eyes and came as close as he had ever come to praying. He promised God that he would die for her, if it came to that. He listened for an answer, but there was only the silence.

He looked down at her and whispered, "I love you."

Silence filled the room once more. She was asleep.

"The bitch is gone."

"What do you mean, 'gone,' Bernardo?"

"The best they can figure is she's on her way to Zürich."

"Zürich?"

"That's what the *Angelinos* are telling Juan."

"Did she go alone?"

"No. That fucking DEA agent is with her."

"All right, Bernardo. Tell Juan to get here to Marseilles as soon as he can. If she's in Zürich, she's looking for Metter. She'll be here soon. We can take care of her at this end."

As they walked to the rental car, Kelly asked her if they needed a phone book.

"What for?" Jesse asked.

"The address of Metter's boat," he replied.

"Smartass," Jesse said to his back.

"I heard that, Frau Rhen," he said smiling.

Inside, Kelly wasn't smiling. As they had exited the terminal, his trained eyes had caught a glimpse of two men in a parked car. The car was parked away from the loading area in a place that would not only be neglected by the searching eyes of the arriving passengers looking for friends and family, but would also be an easy place to leave, in the event the men wanted to follow someone from the airport. If Kelly was right, that was what these men wanted to do.

He had used the telephone book comment as an excuse for a second glance. He was right. It was the South Americans. Not wanting to alarm her until it was absolutely necessary; he had played it off as a joke.

He began a review of everything he could remember about Bernardo and Juan Carlos Cepeda. He didn't like what his mind was telling him.

The rented Peugeot sedan had more power than Kelly had expected and he was able to maneuver it almost gracefully away from the airport and into the cramped, angular streets of the ancient seaport city.

"Which way?" he asked, looking at her briefly and then putting his attention back on the *AutoRoute de Soleil.*

She studied the map she'd been given by the rental car agent. "It shouldn't be too awkward, Thomas," she said, turning the map sideways. "The A-55 takes us right to the harbor. From there, it's just a matter of following the *Digue du Fort Saint-Jean* to the *port.* We should be able to see the boat from the car.

He glanced at her again to confirm that she was wearing her seat belt. He debated telling her that they had been followed from the airport and decided against it for the moment. He knew she would ask the obvious question: How did they know we'd be here? Since he had no answer for that, he decided to wait.

Besides, he had questions of his own. So far, they had made no attempt to harm Jesse. They were just following along at a safe distance, almost casually. Could that mean that he and Jesse were heading into a trap? Could Serva have such control over Wolfgang Metter that he could draw him into a scheme to murder an American girl? Or, were the South Americans just waiting for the right opportunity to make the hit—a more secluded spot—a less traveled area?

As he made the left turn onto the *Quai de Port,* Kelly decided it was time to get some answers to his questions. He was just about to tell Jesse what he was going to do, when he saw something that stopped him.

Looking ahead to the larger, outer part of the harbor, he saw the design of Mutis Shipping on the stack of a freighter. He knew that stack. He knew that design. It had burned its way into his memory. It had crowded its way into a hundred nightmares over the year since the death of Jason Fenny. It had colored its way, like a blood stain on a carpet, into the fabric of his being. He was looking at the *ALBARDA!*

"There it is," Jesse cried with excitement, "The *MARIE-CLAIRE!* There it is!"

"Reach in the back and get my bag," Kelly said without turning to look in the direction she was indicating.

"What's the matter?"

"We've got company."

"What . . . how could that be?"

"Get the bag!"

She reached back and tugged the bag over her seat.

"Open it," he said. As she pulled on the zipper, he added, "Get the gun and give it to me." He glanced in the rear view mirror.

"What are you going to do?" Jesse did not like the feel of the pistol in her hand.

"I'm gonna coax these turtles out of their shell." He put a slight pressure on the accelerator.

"Maybe it's not them."

"Listen, Jesse," he said, taking the gun from her and putting it in his lap, "I haven't got time to teach you what to do. You've got to do exactly what I say. No questions asked. Just do it!"

Juan was frustrated.

Bernardo was calm.

Juan noticed it first. "He's pulling away. He's going faster. He's made us!"

"Okay, okay. Take it easy. Where can he go? Sooner or later he'll have to deal with us. Slow down, asshole, your driving makes me nervous!"

"He's getting away!"

"So what? We're gonna get them on our time. We don't need to do it quick, we need to do it quiet. Slow fucking down! You're gonna kill somebody."

"We're gonna lose him, man. We're gonna lose the fucker. Look, man, he's almost a block ahead!"

"Okay," Bernardo said, shaking his head. "Let's get it over with." He reached for the shotgun. "Get me close enough for a good shot."

"He's getting too far ahead, man!"

"Okay, Juan, take it easy."

"No way, man. He just made that turn. I can't see him anymore. We're losing him."

"How can we be losing him, you stupid asshole?" Bernardo barked in frustration. "There's only one way he can go. Every other way is into the ocean!"

"Get out," Kelly demanded, staring at her.

She stared back, uncomprehending. "What are—"

"Get out!" he yelled, and pushed her as he continued yelling. "There's no time to argue! Get out! Go to the *MARIE-CLAIRE*! Wait for me! I'll meet you there! Go!"

Jesse did as she was told, almost falling onto the narrow quai. Using her cane for support, she hurried off into the first shadow of a warehouse she could find. Then she turned back to see the South Americans go by in pursuit of Kelly.

He accelerated down the *Digue du Fort Saint-Jean* and made a hard left onto the dock entrance. He went halfway down the dock and stopped. He jammed the gearshift into reverse, took the Glock in his right hand, turned his right arm up on the seat back, and waited for their car to come around the corner. As it did, he put the accelerator to the floor. At the last second, he put his face down on his arm for protection.

He had figured that they would have to slow down to make the turn. He had also figured he'd be close enough that the collision wouldn't do much damage. He only needed a slight edge. A small surprise. And then, he would take it to them. He'd have it out with them here and now.

Finally, he had figured that their car, being a smaller Renault two door, would get the worst in a meeting.

The impact was far more violent than he expected, the damage much more severe. For a moment, he thought their car had blasted its way through his back seat and was going to

271

rip, tear, and crunch its way to his front bumper. Everything around him crumpled and folded in against him. Glass shattered, plastic and tin and cloth snapped and bent and tore. The smell of gasoline filled the inside of what was left of his car, and he felt the steering wheel push into the small of his back. Big mistake, he thought to himself, this was a big mistake.

Bernardo's head slammed into the windshield, his right shoulder and chest hit the dashboard, and then he slammed back into his seat. Stunned, almost to the point of unconsciousness, he let go of his hold on the shotgun and tried to get out of the car. The pain was everywhere. As his feet touched the street, his legs folded underneath him and he fell on his face. He couldn't get up. He gave an effort to pull his knees under him and crawl.

The crash had caused Kelly's door to fly open, but his seat had been pushed so far forward that he was pinned against the steering wheel. It was an effort to reach, and finally push, the seat belt release. When the belt snapped free, he was able to twist around, but only by snaking his way under the steering wheel was he able to get out of the car. He lay prone in the street for a moment before he looked up. He had not let go of his gun.

Without the seat belt to hold him, Juan met the steering wheel with his chest, breaking his ribs. Spikes of bone penetrated both lungs. His neck hyperextended, pulling several vertebrae beyond the critical point, before his head hit the incoming windshield, breaking his nose and shredding the skin on his face. Unaware that he couldn't breathe, he got out of the car and went for his gun. He tried his best to point it in the general direction of the DEA agent. There wasn't more than ten feet between them. He fired.

Kelly came to his knees when he saw Juan going for his gun. Leaning against the car, he squeezed the trigger of the

Glock. Something smacked the door of the car, above his head, and whizzed off behind him.

Juan felt the bullet hit his jumbled chest. There was no pain. He was beyond pain. He felt the bullet enter his body, and he was sure he felt it exit. It left a strange tingling inside him.

He was on his back. He didn't know how he got there, but he was staring at the sky. The sun was bright and warm, just like Bogotá, at noon, in the summer. But this wasn't Bogotá, and he was sure it was late afternoon. One enormous gray-white cloud seemed to want to cover everything. The last thought Juan Carlos Cepeda had was that the whole world looked like the snow on an early morning television screen, after the station had signed off.

After checking Juan's pulse, Kelly collected Juan's pistol and put it in the back pocket of his jeans. Then he went to the where Bernardo had fallen and was trying to crawl away. He put his foot on Bernardo's back and pushed him to the ground to stop his progress. "You got a gun, asshole?" He frisked Bernardo, and found nothing. He looked back into the Renault and saw the butt of a shotgun on the floorboard. "Stay down and don't move." He went to the car, got the shotgun and pumped out the live rounds. On his way back to Bernardo, he threw the shotgun as hard as he could off the dock and into the water. Then he took Juan's Smith & Wesson out of his back pocket, ejected the magazine, racked the slide for the round that was in the chamber and threw all of that after the shotgun.

Drawing his Glock, he bent down and put the muzzle close to Bernardo's head. He retrieved his cell phone, keyed Hunt, and waited for him to answer. "The *ALBARDA* is here, so is the *MARIE-CLAIRE*. Send me all the help you can."

Hunt's response was questioning, "What's the *MARIE-CLAIRE* got to do with this? The *ALBARDA* is in Los Angeles. We're running the sting now."

"I need back-up!" Kelly repeated, "The docks in Marseilles . . . The Old Port!" He ended his call.

The curious began to gather; a few fishermen and dockhands edged their way out of their waterfront hideouts.

He turned his attention back to the situation on the dock. He surveyed the area quickly to get his bearings. He had already decided to take Bernardo to the *ALBARDA's* loading area. He looked toward the ship and saw, for the first time, that it was the sister ship, the *ACÈMILA*. It made no difference to him. They were both under the control of the same man. The man he had pursued for more than three years. The man who had killed a friend of his. The man who was trying to kill the woman he loved. The name of the ship was unimportant. The name of the man was Enrico Serva.

He helped Bernardo to his feet. A huge bruise had begun to blister under the skin of Bernardo's forehead, and as Kelly led him away, he staggered like a drunk and would have fallen if Kelly hadn't kept him upright.

"I think it's time I met your boss," Kelly whispered into Bernardo's ear. "What do you think?"

Bernardo couldn't think. He had been blasted beyond his ability to think or comprehend the words of others. His right nostril began to show a line of blood. Stunned to a point beyond confusion, he followed the pressure of the tug on his right arm, and tried to fight the pain erupting in his head.

By the time they reached the warehouse, Bernardo was able to remember who he was. Everything else took more effort than he wanted to give.

Kelly stood Bernardo up against a ten foot high cargo container. Holding him up with one hand, he undid Bernardo's belt with the other and pulled it through the loops.

Two dockhands came toward them. One of them began speaking to Kelly. The other man noticed that Kelly was removing Bernardo's belt. He nudged his friend to silence him.

Still holding Bernardo with his left hand, Kelly turned to the workers and held up his right hand with the gun in it.

They stared at him.

"Okay," Kelly said loudly to the dockhands, "go! GO!"

They didn't need a translation. Both men turned immediately, ran through the large warehouse doors and disappeared.

Kelly spun Bernardo around and looped his hands through the belt and pulled it taut.

"You better kill me, fucker," Bernardo coughed over a tongue that was swollen from the blow to his head. "If you don't, I'm gonna kill you as slow as I can."

"Well, I guess you're coming around. You can talk. That's good. Because I want you to make a little 'telephono' call for me. How about it, Bernardo? Feel up to calling the boss?" He tugged on the belt to make sure Bernardo's hands were secured.

Enrico had spent the day alone in the bedroom of his suite. He had stretched out patiently on the bed, with his eyes closed, and waited for the telephone call that would summon him to the peer. The two oversized leather suitcases, with fifteen million American dollars in each one, leaned against the wall near the door. Hours had passed and he had grown restless. But there had been no call.

When the phone rang he ignored it; they had kept him waiting; now they could wait. When it rang again he turned to answer it. He felt the stiffness in his back from the reclining position he had held for so long.

"It's me, Enrico." Bernardo's voice was dull and lifeless.

It was not *el hombre de Suiza*—the man from Switzerland. His impatience was about to explode. "Yes, Bernardo, what is it?"

"I'm here on the loading dock. The DEA agent is with me. He wants to talk. Can you come now?"

Enrico wanted to scream into the phone: This is such a small problem. One girl. One little bitch. Crippled. The solution is so simple. Kill her. Kill the girl. Kill the little bitch. Kill the cripple. What's the fucking problem? Kill her! Kill her! KILL HER!"

He took a deep breath and tried to relax his shoulders. "Yes, Bernardo, I'll come now."

He called down to his driver and instructed him to come and get the suitcases and take him to Bernardo.

Enrico's limousine made its way slowly down the dock past the three Mercedes tractor trucks that he had hired to transport his forty-billion dollars to his new Swiss bank.

When it stopped, Kelly grabbed the collar at the back of Bernardo's jacket and pushed him toward the fading sunlight beyond the open warehouse doors. When they were outside, he checked the belt to make sure it was still tight around Bernardo's wrists. Then he pushed his knee into the back of Bernardo's leg, and Bernardo went down on his knees in front of Kelly. He put his gun to Bernardo's head.

The driver got out of the Mercedes slowly. He unbuttoned his jacket to reveal a Desert Eagle pistol resting comfortably in a shoulder holster. He opened the back door of the limousine.

Enrico got out of the limousine. He rolled his shoulders to adjust the fit of his black silk, designer jacket. His left hand delicately centered the knot of his white silk tie. He took a breath to relax himself, and smiled at Kelly.

That's one hell of a limo," Kelly started. "How do you get it through these tiny streets?" He didn't wait for an answer. "Tell your driver to throw his gun under the car and get back in."

Enrico spoke quietly in Spanish, and the driver did as Kelly instructed.

"Where's Juan?" Enrico asked Kelly.

"He's been in an accident. I guess he forgot to buckle up." Kelly did not take his eyes from Enrico Serva.

"He's dead, Enrico!" Bernardo called up from his knees. He coughed, and a bubble of blood popped out onto his lips. "The fucker shot him." He turned his head to look up at Kelly. His right eye was swollen shut. The lump on his forehead, above the eye, was blackening.

Kelly waited for Enrico to absorb the news of the death of his adopted son.

"You amaze me," Enrico said, his voice flat and distant.

"I do?" Kelly asked smugly.

"Not you, particularly, your bosses. Hell, all Americans. You fight like crazy bastards over petty things while the war goes on all around you, and you're losing. Your politicians give endless speeches on the righteousness of a drug free world and then go back to their hotel rooms and snort coke. Your courts roll over like dogs and give us every opportunity to maneuver around your laws. Your executives suck their profits up their noses. Your men and women go to work and give their children the money to buy from us."

Kelly tightened his grip on Bernardo. "How much of this shit am I going to have to listen to?"

"Think about it. With all the resources at your disposal, for all the time that you've had, you haven't even come close to winning the war. This is the real battle, the big one. Right here, right now. Not Los Angeles. And who do they send to fight it? One fucking agent. One fucking agent and a crippled girl."

Kelly's patience was running out. Hunt could deal with Los Angeles, Kelly had to protect Jesse. "Are you about done, jerkoff?" Kelly's whispery voice reached out to silence Enrico. "Cause if you're done, we can make ourselves a little deal. You remember how to deal, don't you, asshole?"

"You don't have anything I want, Agent . . . ah . . . ?"

"Kelly," he said without the whisper in his voice. He pushed the pistol into the back of Bernardo's head.

"Let him do it, Enrico!" Bernardo yelled. "Then you can blow this fucker away!" He hung his head and waited for the executioner's response.

"You've already lost one soldier today," Kelly offered, and the whisper had returned to his voice. "You want to go for two?"

"What's your offer?" Enrico asked a little faster than he wanted to. He took another deep breath and regained his smile.

"One 'cripple' for another." Kelly put as much sarcasm on the word as he had ever put on any word. "I want the girl. You want this piece of garbage. You tell me there's no more contract on Jesse Fortune, and I'll back out of here without pulling the trigger."

"Let him pull the trigger, Enrico," Bernardo said, his head still bowed.

"What makes you think you can trust me?" Enrico put his hands into the pockets of his jacket. "Maybe I won't keep my word."

"You'll keep your word," Kelly said confidently. "The girl can't mean shit to you. Whatever she's done doesn't come close to the price you've paid to take her out. Hell, I killed your boy, Enrico. I put a bullet through his fucking little heart. He died pissing and crying. You'll forget the girl because you've got other things on your mind now. You've got someone else to go after. And, when you come for me, I won't be a helpless girl. I'll stuff your fucking head up your dying ass. What about it, Enrico?"

Bernardo looked up to Enrico. "Kill him, Enrico. Kill him."

"You're right. The girl means nothing to me," Enrico said. "As far as I'm concerned, you can have the bitch. But it's not my contract. You'll have to talk to the man from Switzerland."

"What?" The word escaped before Kelly could stop it. Instantly, he was confused. He tried not to show it, but he was lost.

"The man from Switzerland, Agent Kelly." Enrico enjoyed repeating himself. He could easily read Kelly's confusion. He knows nothing, he thought.

"The man from Switzerland. . . ." Kelly was losing his edge. Enrico Serva was a step ahead of him. A giant step. A step he couldn't match.

"Metter. You know, Agent Kelly, *el hombre de Suiza*— the man from Switzerland—Metter!" Agent Kelly had a debt to pay. Enrico enjoyed signing his death warrant.

In an instant, Kelly's mind had gone from confusion to fear. If Wolfgang Metter had the contract out on Jesse Fortune, then Kelly hadn't pushed her away from danger, he had pushed her closer to it. There was no time to reason. There was no time for hesitation. There was no time. . . .

"I want you out of it," Kelly said. "You don't take the contract. Time's running out. Do we have a deal or not?"

"Deal." Enrico pushed the simple word across his lips. His smile was gone.

Kelly backed away from Bernardo, keeping the pistol trained at the back of Bernardo's head. He continued to back away until he could lose himself around the corner of the warehouse.

He started running, but not because he was afraid they would pursue him. He ran because Jesse was in trouble. Knowing her as he did now, he knew she would only wait so long for him to come.

279

Jesse waited on the *Promenade Louis Braquier,* across the street from where the *MARIE-CLAIRE* was docked. She watched for any sign of Kelly, but there was none. In desperation, she began listening for him, but all she heard were the sounds of the dock: the seagulls flapping and squawking and diving for one more hurried bite of fish before nightfall; the cries and crankings of the dockyard machines on another pier, somewhere beyond her vision; and the melancholy wail of a foghorn from a freighter whose destination lay somewhere beyond the Marseilles horizon.

More than once she whispered to herself, "Where are you, Thomas? Please get here." Then she watched in silence as the crew of the *MARIE-CLAIRE* began to disembark.

As they passed, she heard their *argot*—a broken, slang-filled French that she had trouble deciphering. But, as they straggled toward the *Quai du Port,* she pieced together enough to know that they had been dismissed for the evening. They wouldn't be needed until tomorrow.

Even though Kelly had instructed her to stay out of sight and wait for him, she couldn't pass up the opportunity to get on board without being noticed.

The setting sun fired the Marseilles sky with brilliant reds and oranges and cast them along the ropes and over the wooden stairs of the *MARIE-CLAIRE's* gangway.

She climbed aboard and found an empty cabin on the starboard side where she could watch the dock entrance and wait for Kelly's arrival.

By the time she heard the sound of the *MARIE-CLAIRE's* engines start, night had wrapped itself around the harbor. She couldn't wait for Kelly. Her only chance now was to find Metter immediately.

30

LE VIEUX PORT, MARSEILLES, FRANCE

Mikel Rhen cleared the stern line and hurried down the starboard side to lower and lock the gate. Then he disappeared up the stairs to join Uncle, before he could notice a hand come to rest on the gate rail where his hand had been.

On the bridge, Amir Hassasi turned on the outboard running lights and started the engines. He headed the thirty-five meter yacht away from the dock. As he moved it toward open water, he accelerated.

The wake left by the *MARIE-CLAIRE* moved off methodically to annoy the docked boats, forcing them to pull and tug on their spring lines.

After they were well away from the breakwater, Amir slowed the engines, set the automatic pilot, and sat back in the captain's chair. "In five minutes we will be far enough out to sea. I am going below to set the timer. Get Wolfgang's body from the freezer and bring it to the lounge. Leave it behind the desk. Then wait for me there and we will evacuate in the rubber dinghy."

Mikel tried not to laugh. He dearly wanted to. The vision of Uncle Amir's small, thin body, behind the captain's wheel, reminded Mikel of some corny cartoon figure he might have seen as a child.

"Have I said something amusing, Mikki?"

"No, Uncle. It's just that—"

"We don't have much time, Mikki. Shall we do as we have planned?"

"Yes, yes of course, Uncle. I'll go and get the body." He left the bridge before anymore could be said; he still had the smile on his face.

Amir went below. In the engine room, he strapped the explosives to a metal support with duct tape, and set the timer for fifteen minutes. As the boat's engines hummed, and the craft moved imperceptibly into the Mediterranean, he started back to the lounge.

Jesse made her way carefully down the interior corridor. The swaying of the boat made it more awkward than she wanted to admit. When she was in the dining room and close to the lounge, she heard the dull thud of something heavy being dropped, but the etched glass of the connecting door allowed her no detail of the next room.

Mikel sat down in Wolfgang's thick leather desk chair and poured himself a drink. With Wolfgang's body lying on the floor behind him, he wanted to enjoy these few minutes of opulence by helping himself to the aged sherry, which he released from a cut-crystal decanter. Ignoring the Plexiglas wall and the door to the sun deck behind him, he let his gaze drift over the rest of the room.

The cabin was designed in teak, which had a varnished red glow to it. There were storm doors to port and starboard to permit the captain or guests to enter from either side of the boat. Not being the socialite that Mikel was, Wolfgang had a sparse lounge that looked more like an office. In front of the desk, one other visitor's chair was strategically placed for a conversation with Wolfgang. There was another door, with etched glass filling its upper half, on the far wall, which led to the living quarters: the dining room, galley, staterooms and heads. Next to that door, an elegant bar had been built with the same red wood, and *MARIE-CLAIRE* was etched into the mirror behind the bar. Looking like afterthoughts, two small barstools were pushed up against the bar.

Taking another sip of sherry, he continued his survey by following the rose-colored wood back toward the desk. His eyes went back to the connecting door. Through the glass, he saw the silhouette. He knew at once that it was not Uncle.

Jesse pulled on the brass handle, opened the door, and went in. She closed the door and moved farther into the room, trying to get a better view of the man behind the desk. Before she could speak, he did.

"It is you, Jesse Fortune!" he said.

It was a simple greeting, filled with honest surprise, and delivered with a smile. But the words startled her, rocked her, and took her breath away. It wasn't the words—it was the voice. *His* voice.

"Mikel," she said, and the sound seemed far away, as if someone else had spoken. She tried to steady herself. The fingers of her right hand dug into the handle of her cane so hard that she thought she would break every fingernail.

She watched him rise and start to come around the desk toward her. She was sure her mouth was open, but she could neither close it, nor speak, except to repeat, "Mikel."

"Yes, Mikel," he said, smiling arrogantly, "And no, not Mikel. But that's another story. I don't think we have time for that since, in about oh . . . fifteen minutes, this boat is going to be blown to hell. Funny, isn't it? You're the one woman I really wanted, and the only one I never got. Oh well, no time for that now, is there? What a pity. You always seem to come into my life when there's no time." When he finished speaking, he was close enough to kiss her or kill her.

Returning from the engine room, Amir heard the voices in the lounge. Not wanting to expose himself in the glass door, he held his position in the adjoining dining area and listened to the quiet mumblings in an effort to determine who was sharing this conversation with Mikel. He debated opening the door that connected the two cabins.

Kelly had come on board as quietly as he could and ducked into the first shadowed area big enough to hide his large frame. He had waited nervously for one of the crew to discover him, but no one ventured past his hiding place.

When the engines had powered down, he had come out of hiding and gone in search of Jesse. He had climbed a starboard side ladder for a better vantage point of the deck below. He saw no one. He had looked through the bridge windshield. There was no one on the bridge, and no crew aboard. No crew was a plus. He needed all the pluses he could get. He went back down the ladder, silently.

Mikel Rhen reached out gently and touched Jesse's cheek. "Jesse Fortune, Jesse Fortune," he said calmly.

She felt sick to her stomach. The fact that Mikel might be alive—and that he was now Wolfgang Metter—was taking its time to filter through her mind and make sense. The confusion was causing her reactions to be far slower than she needed them to be. She realized that the closeness of his body made her cane almost useless as a weapon. And yet, if it really was Mikel, did she need a weapon at all? She felt his hand drift from her cheek to her throat. And then she felt him start to apply pressure.

His fingers gripped and tightened until he had complete control. "I wanted you," Mikel whispered into her face, "I really wanted you." He kissed her slack and confused lips.

She felt his breath on her cheek and could smell the sherry on it.

Kelly had hustled along the outside starboard corridor of the boat, crouching and peering into the portholes as he passed them. Finally, through the abundance of Plexiglas that wrapped around the stern lounge, he saw Jesse. He also saw a door at the back of the room and decided that entering there would give him the advantage of being behind Metter. He drew the Glock from its holster and went around the sun deck, opened the aft door and stepped in.

Jesse saw Kelly first. "Thomas, I'm so glad you're—"

"Step away from her," Kelly rasped at the man he thought was Metter.

Mikel turned around and smiled curiously at Kelly.

When Amir heard the new, masculine voice address his nephew, he drew his Walther PPK from his jacket pocket and entered the lounge.

"With pleasure," Mikel replied to Kelly's order.

As Mikel stepped back out of the way, Kelly saw the strange man framed in the etched glass door. He saw a spark of flame flash from the small object in the man's right hand. He heard the rude little snap of the Walther. He felt the stab of pain on his face, as if someone had stuck a burning hot poker through his jaw.

His reaction was automatic and instinctive; he squeezed the trigger of the Glock. He squeezed it again as he went down to his knees, and once more as he sat back on the floor. The sound of his pistol was enormous in the small lounge, but he was beyond hearing it as his world seemed to evaporate. He slumped forward, his legs went straight out in front of him, and when his body could go no further, he fell to his side and rolled over onto his chest. For a moment, he thought of how embarrassing it was to be lying with his face in the carpet in front of Jesse. He tried to get up, but couldn't. Then, he realized he was dying. His eyes filled with tiny specks and starry lines, and then his vision joined his hearing in a dark void.

Kelly's first bullet took Amir in the chest. It broke a rib and ripped through the fragile tissue of the lung. It also pushed him up against the door behind him. His head struck the etched glass and bounced back. The glass broke and small pieces of it stuck in his head and the back of his neck. The second bullet hit him in the chin and his lower jaw disintegrated into a spongy mess of blood, broken bone, and burned and torn flesh. A single tooth dropped from his mouth and stuck to his shirt. As the bullet exited the back of his head, taking with it part of his brain, scalp and hair, his head snapped back again. The upper half of his body went through the opening in the door the glass had left. With his body stuck half in and half out of the lounge, the third shot struck his leg just above the kneecap.

Amir Hassasi did not feel the third bullet from the Glock 19 slip unmercifully under the aging thigh muscle of his left leg. Hanging in the door frame like a forgotten puppet, he was already dead.

The cracking, hammer-like vibrations of the gunfire smashed off the walls and the stunned silence of disbelief filled the lounge. A thin silvery strand of smoke drifted across the room, carrying with it the acrid smell of spent gunpowder. Mikel could do nothing but stare at his uncle, hanging in the door. Jesse could do nothing but stare at Kelly, lying face down on the floor.

The crest of a swell caused the boat to lurch gently. That movement was enough to bring both Jesse and Mikel back to the moment.

"Oh fuck," he said, his voice still strangely calm. "We've only got a few min—" His words were cut off as Jesse's cane struck at the side of his head.

He caught her movement peripherally and tried to duck it, but the cane hit his right ear and bounced off his shoulder. The pain was intense. There was an immediate cold burning sensation in the ear and a sharp agonizing ache in the shoulder. With the most fury he'd ever felt, he struck out at Jesse with his fist.

The blow knocked her off her feet and she went down hard on the floor, close to Kelly. The aftershock echoed through her body and she felt herself getting weak, going under, and fading away. She tried to lift her head and drops of blood fell from her nose onto the carpet. She shook her head to clear it. That only made her feel worse. His voice seemed to be miles away.

"If I can't fuck you, then I might as well kill you."

In the dim light of the lounge, she could see that he was smiling. Even though it was Metter's face, it was the little boy smile that Mikel had used, and she had adored . . . once. Dazed, she pushed herself to a sitting position and looked up to see him start for the body of his dead uncle. He was going for the gun Amir had dropped.

She thrust the cane at him like a sword. It was all she could think to do. It seemed odd and silly and a useless effort against the inevitable.

The cane went between his legs and he tripped over it. The momentum of his body ripped the cane from her hand. It cracked up against the wall and rolled away under the desk. Her only hope of a weapon disappeared into the dark shadows.

"Bitch," he said, staring at her from his new position on the floor in front of the bar. They were only a body's length apart. "If I had the time, I'd rip you apart and fuck what was left. Then I'd kill you. As it is, I'm just going to kill you." As he spoke, his hand was searching for the Walther.

She wouldn't give up. It was not in her to give up. But she didn't know what to do. She had no weapon. He was out of reach of her hands and feet, and it would be impossible to get close enough for an effective punch before he got the gun. She couldn't take her eyes off him long enough to find Kelly's gun. She was sure that the moment she looked away, she would feel the cold hardness of a bullet penetrate her skull. She continued to stare at Mikel as if that were a weapon to hold him off. And then she saw his smile broaden as his fingers found the cruel metal of Uncle's pistol.

At first, it was only a pressure on the fingers of her left hand. She sensed it more than felt it. She looked down. It was Kelly's Glock. She looked past the gun and into Kelly's half open eyes. "You're alive," she whispered and started to cry. "Oh, God, you're alive. I love you."

The bullet ripped through the muscle of her shoulder and caused her upper body to spin around and face Mikel Rhen. The second bullet missed her as she was already falling backwards from the impact of the first assault.

Jesse Fortune came up with the Glock in both hands. With every ounce of strength in her, she pushed the gun toward Mikel's face and pulled the trigger. The kick of the gun slammed into the palm of her hand, causing it to fly upward. Her first thought was that the bullet had gone into the ceiling.

Mikel smiled back at her. Or was it Wolfgang's smile? She couldn't think. She couldn't move. There was no chance of getting the gun back on target. There was no chance of getting a second shot. There was no chance to do anything. She stared at the gun muzzle pointing directly at her face, then past it to the smiling lips of the man she had once loved, and then she waited for that same man, now with a different face, to take her life.

It was a single drop of blood. It fell on his upturned lip. Then a line of dark red followed it, flowing from somewhere above. She looked up into his eyes. They were still smiling, but that tiny red river was running down over one of them. She lifted her gaze. There was a small, dark hole just under the hairline of his forehead. The Glock hadn't missed. The bullet had cleared the muzzle before it could be altered by the recoil of the gun.

Mikel leaned his head against the bar, the hand holding his gun dropped to his lap, and still smiling that little boy smile, he died.

Jesse stared into his still-open eyes. It was as if he was speaking to her from somewhere beyond the living. In fifteen minutes this boat would be blown to hell. Less than that now, she thought. How many minutes had passed since he had said that? She wasn't about to waste time thinking about it. She had to get Kelly off the boat somehow and she had to do it now!

"Thomas!" she yelled at him. "Get up! We've got to get off the boat. There's a bomb. Thomas! We don't have much time. Can you hear me—Thomas!"

When he started to get up, she threw the gun down and reached to help him to his feet. An angry pain shot through her arm. She looked at her shoulder and saw the patch of a blood stain. She tried to ignore the pain as she turned back to Kelly. "Can you walk?"

"I think so," he tried to say, but it came out as an indecipherable mumble and the attempt sent a shock of pain up the side of his face. "The bullet must have hit my jawbone and knocked me out." He heard the words in his mind, but they came out of his mouth a jumbled mess. There was a burning sensation on his neck, under his ear. He put a hand up and touched it. The skin had been torn away by the fragmenting bullet. The stinging increased. When he pulled his hand away, there was blood on it.

Jesse went to retrieve her cane from under the desk and saw that it had rolled into an outstretched hand. Her eyes sped past the hand and up the arm to Wolfgang Metter's ghost-like, pale dead face staring back at her. There was no time for shock, concern, or even interest. She grabbed the cane from Wolfgang's lifeless hand and shoved it into Kelly's hand. "Here, use this!" When he tried to refuse it, she barked, "You need it more than I do! We've got to go! Now! There's got to be a dinghy. Come on, let's try the stern." She guided him through the aft cabin door and onto the sun deck."

Looking over the stern railing, she saw the black and yellow rubber dinghy tied to the swimmer's deck. An outboard motor clung securely to its stern.

"Can you climb down?" she ordered more than asked.

He nodded affirmatively.

She followed him down the ladder. "Hold the line," she directed as she untied the raft and pushed it off the stern. She took her cane from his hand. "I'll get in, then you jump in." She threw the cane into the raft, jumped in after it, and started crawling toward the motor at the back.

Kelly fell, more than jumped in behind her, and their small craft began to drift away from the yacht.

She pulled the starter cord and the motor came to life. Twisting the throttle to full open, she turned the tiller toward the harbor entrance.

The nose of the dinghy rose into the air as the churning propeller of the single engine pushed the back end down.

The thunderous explosion ripped through the night sky and rocked the dark blue water of the sea behind them. An ugly, billowing black cloud jetted into the air. Sharp fingers of flame grabbed and clutched at the cloud like the hand of an angry captain reaching for the back of a mutinous sailor.

A fierce, hot wind blasted past them, and Jesse lost her grip on the throttle as she fell toward Kelly.

He pulled her into his arms as fiery pieces of debris, charring wood, and smoldering, twisted metal rained down around them.

They held each other until a violent wave smashed against the back of the dinghy, rumbled under them, and rolled on toward the harbor.

Slowly, Jesse turned to watch the *MARIE-CLAIRE* put her bow into the Mediterranean. With flames engulfing her upper decks and an empty black hole on her port side, she slipped into the consuming depths.

Before they reached the shelter of the *Porte Moderne,* they could see that the dock was swarming with the familiar blue of the uniformed *gendarmes.*

Even though his mind seemed only semi-clear, Kelly's eyes found an object of interest on the Marseilles harbor skyline. He pointed toward the *Quai de la Joliette.*

Jesse stubbornly fought against the pain in her shoulder and the weakness and exhaustion that filled the rest of her. She looked in the direction Kelly was indicating.

A shiny black limousine rolled its way carefully down the old coast road, and away from the waterfront.

Behind the driver, Enrico Serva and Bernardo sat in silence. Each man left the other to his own thoughts.

Bernardo thought about the human storm behind them. They weren't being followed. He had checked that twice. That was good. They weren't being followed. That was that.

Enrico had seen the explosion. Out beyond the harbor, there had been a flash of lightning and a darkening on the horizon. That would be the *MARIE-CLAIRE*, he thought, just as planned. The men from Switzerland would be on their way back to the dock to meet him. They would want their money. That was unimportant.

What was important was that Agent Kelly was on that boat. He wanted to pull the trigger himself. He wanted to see it happen. But he would settle for the fact that it had happened. The agent was dead. The debt was paid.

He knew the *ACÉMILA's* engines were being started for the voyage to take his money back to Colombia. That was unimportant.

He did not think about the girl, the bitch, the cripple. He did not think of Jesse Fortune.

31

LOS ANGELES, CALIFORNIA

"That was one of the biggest and most expensive operations I've put on in years and it looks like we're the ones who got busted: thirty-seven agents in half as many vehicles, three gun-ship helicopters, L.A. SWAT as back-up—hell!—I think I even saw someone from Homeland Security. And, the *ALBARDA* was clean! We didn't find an ounce of cocaine on board." Hunt sat back in a chair which was as worn as he was frustrated, and surveyed the two other men in his office.

Kelly and Anderson took turns glancing at each other, then Kelly decided to be the first to respond. "So, the *ALBARDA* was a decoy?" he slurred, fighting back the pain in his jaw. His neck was heavily bandaged.

"Hell yes it was a decoy!" Hunt responded, leaning forward again and putting his thick forearms on his desk. "The whole thing was a damn decoy: his farming and storing of tons of cocaine so he could prove he had product; his calls to the L.A. family to negotiate sales; his trip to Las Vegas to meet with the L.A. bosses that he never actually met with—hell—the whole damn enchilada!"

"We stopped him from getting the bank," Anderson offered, looking over to the note he had left on Hunt's desk with the name of Wolfgang Metter's bank scribbled on it.

"And that's the good news, isn't it," Hunt said with a distracted sigh. "That's what this was all about. That's all he ever wanted in the first place. He didn't get it, thanks to you two."

"And Jesse Fortune," Kelly added.

"Yeah. . . ." Hunt reluctantly agreed.

"What's his status now?" Kelly asked.

"He's back in Colombia and sitting on, what we estimate to be, somewhere around forty billion dollars. The other cartels are keeping him from a place to put it. But, knowing him the way we've come to know him, it won't be long before he does some real damage with it."

"What do you want us to do now, Sir?" Kelly asked.

Silence filled the room. Kelly and Anderson stared at Hunt and waited patiently. To Kelly, it seemed as if the whole world was on pause.

"I want you both to go home and get some rest. Hell, get drunk if you want. Be here tomorrow morning, 0700, and let's get started on a new plan that will bring Enrico Serva down. He's fooled me once, I'll give him that, but not one ounce more. He'll never do that to me again." Hunt finished with, "Never."

As Kelly walked out into the bright Los Angeles afternoon, he knew what he wasn't going to do. He wasn't going to go home and he wasn't going to get drunk. He also knew what he was going to do. . . .

EPILOGUE

HANA, MAUI, HAWAII
Fall 2012

He stood on the beach, his bare feet in the sand, his hands in his pockets, staring across the ocean to the horizon, not really seeing it. His mind was adrift and lost in the vision of a world he didn't understand: a world where evil too often triumphed and good was too soon forgotten; a world where greed was worshipped and charity was unappreciated; a world where dangerously powerful men could too easily rob the less dominant of their faith, and the weak of their lives.

"Agent Thomas Kelly?" The beautifully soft tones of a woman's voice reached him, but he didn't answer her. Then two smooth, tanned arms slipped under his and hugged his waist. He took his hands out of his pockets and covered her arms with his.

"You're a great-looking man," she said in a whisper. "Are you married?"

"Yes," he said, his whisper matching hers. "I'm on my honeymoon." He felt her head come to rest on his back.

"Really? What's her name?"

"Jesse."

"Do you love her?"

He felt her question vibrate into him until it reached his heart. "I couldn't love anyone more," he said, finally turning to face her.

"Will you love her forever?"

"Probably," he replied with the hint of a tease.

She smiled. "You will. I have feelings about things in the future, and they're always right." She looked up into his eyes. "Always," she repeated.

His world disappeared and he allowed himself to be swept into hers.